The Hardest Words to Say

Kaye Scott

Cover design by Kaye Scott, using AI-generated imagery created through OpenAI's DALL·E platform with commercial-use rights.

First Edition: March 2025

ISBN: 979-8-218-65181-7

For more information, contact:

kayescottbooks@gmail.com

Dedication

Dedicated to Michaela, who has been reading my words and encouraging me since we were 14, and to Emilio, for his unwavering friendship through all the ups and downs.

Table of Contents

CHAPTER 1

October 2011

"I can't do this anymore," her boyfriend whispered from the overstuffed green couch. His voice was hollow, and he wouldn't look at her, his gaze fixed instead on his tanned hands resting in his lap.

"What… what are you saying?" Elena asked as the air in the room seemed to thicken, pressing on her chest and churning her stomach. Her petite 5'4" frame suddenly felt crushed under the weight of his words. Just moments ago, she had felt pleased with how she looked: the skinny jeans and olive-green sweater complimented her slender, toned body, a result of the exercise routine she'd picked up to manage her stress.

But now, she felt as though she were wearing a heavy, scratchy burlap sack. Her shoulder-length brown hair began to stick to the back of her neck as beads of sweat formed, and the heat radiated from her neck to her head, where a dull ache started building from the tension. Thankfully, she had worn minimal makeup on her pale skin this morning, as tears were already welling up in her bright green eyes.

Alex stood up and took a few steps toward her, glancing up only briefly, never quite meeting her eyes. "This—us," he gestured between them, "only seeing each other over video calls or in person every three months, flying and driving back and forth. I can't do it anymore. I love you, but this…this is too hard. Every time I see you, my heart breaks because I know I'll have to say goodbye again in just a few days." Unspoken tears filled his eyes, and she wished he would look directly at her, wishing to see the familiar yellow flecks that lightened his brown eyes. With a heavy sigh, he ran his fingers through his curly brown hair. "I love you, but this is too painful."

Disbelief washed over her face. He had a plane ticket to visit her for her birthday in a month, and she'd flown him out for the weekend so he could finally meet her new friends from school. They had even been making plans for him to move from New Mexico, where they both grew up, to California, so they wouldn't have to be apart anymore.

She had chosen graduate schools near cities he'd said he was willing to move to. She was here, in large part, because of him. Reaching forward, Elena lifted his chin, searching his eyes for a sign that this was one of his stupid jokes, not her worst fears coming true. But she found only sparkling tears and sadness staring back at her. 'Fuck,' she thought, 'he's serious. I bought the fucking plane ticket he used to break up with me.'

"So, you're giving up after five years together?" Her words sounded distant, muffled, as if they were bubbling up from underwater, barely moving through the thick air filling the room.

"I'm not giving up. I've tried to do this long-distance thing for the past year, but I can't do it anymore. It hurts too damn much."

"What if I quit school and moved back home?" She could hardly believe the words coming out of her mouth. Giving up her degree for a man was something she swore she'd never do, but she said it anyway. Would she give up her future career for the mere chance of a future with someone so afraid? In this moment, she didn't know.

"NO! Promise me that no matter what, you'll finish school! You can't give this up for me."

A part of her was relieved. She didn't want to give up school. Being a psychologist had been her dream since she was nine years old. But he was the love of her life—the one she hadn't been looking for when they met, the one she'd fought so hard not to fall in love with. She had tried to keep her guard up, but he'd stayed, breaking through every barrier she put up. She'd let herself believe in him, trust him not to leave her. They'd talked about getting married, having babies, and making a difference in the world. And now? It was over? Just like that—no warning? How could this be happening? "Okay. I promise," she whispered, struggling to push the words past the painful lump in her throat.

"Good. Look, I'm going to go. I'll stay in a hotel until my flight tomorrow. I'm sorry." He turned, grabbing his green duffel bag. Moving to the door, he paused for a brief second, then turned back to her. "I love you," he murmured, before leaning down to kiss her, the barest brush of his lips against hers. His mouth tasted like salt from unshed tears.

And then, with that featherlight kiss, he walked out the door and out of her life.

Her tears came freely now, and she struggled to catch her breath. Her chest ached, the pain feeling as real and physical as if her heart were truly breaking. It was a familiar ache—one she had chosen to risk because she'd let herself love again. She had taken the chance, knowing the potential hurt. She had lost people before, but they hadn't chosen to leave her; they would have stayed if they could. Did this hurt more or less than losing someone to death? She couldn't tell. Maybe it didn't matter—both hurt. Love was stupid, cruel, a risk too heavy to bear. She pulled her hair back into a ponytail, lifting the damp strands off her skin. Crawling into bed, she cried herself to sleep, his scent lingering on her pillow as a constant reminder of his absence.

CHAPTER 2

November 2011

Elena had no idea how she managed to get through the first month after her breakup. Somehow, she was still keeping up with graduate school, though nothing she read seemed to stick in her mind. Her papers were getting done, but they barely met the word count requirements, and whenever her professors spoke, their voices sounded like the incomprehensible "wah wah wah" of adults in Charlie Brown cartoons. Her friends and family were trying their best to support her, spending time with her, calling, and texting. But as the weeks went by, their sympathy began to fade. She didn't blame them, of course; it wasn't their fault. She understood that there was only so much others could do to pull someone out of depression.

Elena couldn't listen to music anymore; every song seemed to take on a new and painful meaning. There had never been a time in her life when music wasn't an essential part of her world. She and her dad had shared a deep love for music, and she'd never once imagined avoiding it—not even after he passed away. Now, though, the silence was starting to gnaw at her.

As a future psychologist, she knew some basic coping techniques, and she was trying to pull herself out of this heavy fog. When she couldn't bring herself to do anything else, she made sure to cover the essentials: eating something, resting when she couldn't sleep, drinking enough water, and making at least one social connection each day. It was a slow, painful process—a process she had to keep trudging through, even though she wished it would be over already. What she missed most was laughter, and her friends tried to bring it back, but the pity in their eyes made their jokes fall flat.

One evening, she was mindlessly scrolling through social media, trying to distract herself from thoughts of her ex, when she stumbled across an old friend's profile. It had been years since she'd spoken with Rodrigo, yet he'd once been one of her closest friends. They'd known each other since middle school, back when they were twelve, and had stayed in touch off and on since high school. But it had been three years since they'd last spoken.

"Hello?"

Elena hadn't expected him to answer, especially since it was midnight on a Wednesday, but she was glad he had. "Hey, Rodrigo, it's Elena."

"Hey, what's up?"

"Why are boys such idiots?" she asked, cutting straight to the point. After the fight with her boyfriend, she didn't feel like beating around the bush.

"What did I do now?" he replied with a chuckle.

She rolled her eyes at her empty bedroom. "Obviously, I'm not mad at you right now, but good to know you understand what I'm talking about. Alex is being a jerk, and I just needed someone to vent to."

Rodrigo let out a full-throated laugh. "So, you're just using me for my man brain?"

"Wait, you have a brain?"

"Women are mean. This is why I don't stick around any of you for long."

"Oh, really? You've kept me around for years!"

"I'm just waiting for you to become a rich doctor so you can buy me pretty things."

They had definitely veered off track from her original reason for calling, but the distraction was a welcome relief. "Anyway," she said, regaining her focus, "I do actually need to use your walnut-sized man brain. I was talking about the future with Alex. I want to go to grad school out of state in a couple of years, and I want him to come with me. Is that so crazy?"

"Well," he paused, as if weighing his answer, "how long have you guys been together?"

"Three years."

After a brief silence, he replied, "No, that's not crazy at all. Have you two talked about the future before?"

Elena began pacing around her small room, feeling her anger at her boyfriend rekindling. "Yeah, we both want more than just a Bachelor's degree, and we've talked about getting married and having kids someday. I thought we were both on the same page about our plans."

"Gross," Rodrigo teased. "Marriage? Kids? No thanks. I'd rather travel the world than settle down. Besides, kids are sticky."

"That's great, but we're kind of talking about me right now."

"A little self-centered, aren't we?"

Elena stopped pacing, feeling a small pang of guilt. "Ugh, you're right, Rodrigo. I'm sorry. I didn't even ask how you're doing. It's been months since we've talked."

"Eh, that's what happens when people get into relationships. Especially when things start getting serious." His tone softened. "Look, he's probably just freaking out because the future feels so close now. Maybe he hadn't factored in a possible move. Give him some time to let it all sink in, and if things don't improve, tell me. I'll go kick his ass for trying to mess things up with you."

Elena laughed. "How is it that you always know how to make me feel better?"

In a playful southern twang, he replied, "I'm your Huckleberry." It was a phrase he'd been saying to her since high school, and it left a smile on her face long after they hung up.

Remembering how he always helped her feel better, even on her worst days, she decided to message him.

I know that it's been a long time, and I'm sorry. I guess I'm not great at being a friend while I'm in a relationship. I know it seems like I only reach out to you when things are tough, but you always know how to make me smile. Things are kind of rough for me right now. Her hands shook, and she began to sweat despite the cool temperature as she typed. She hesitated for a moment before hitting send. Sighing, she finally clicked send and hoped he would respond.

Rodrigo rarely checked his social media accounts. The profile picture he had wasn't even of him. Instead, it was a picture of Pinky and the Brain, the two mice who tried to take over the world in the 90s cartoon. This choice in profile image did not reflect his appearance at all. He was an inch shy of six feet tall, with tanned skin, dark brown eyes, and shoulder-length deep brown hair. A five o'clock shadow adorned his face, which he thought made him look somewhat gruff, even though he was far from gruff. His workouts were starting to add muscle to his previously thin frame. He sighed to himself, thinking, "There is never anything interesting on here," which is why he tended to avoid it. It seemed to him that social media was just filled with people posting pictures of themselves with their pets, babies, friends, or at their weddings. He felt that people used social media to broadcast, "Look, my life is amazing, and everything is perfect. I'm not completely terrified that I'm wasting my life. Don't you see how happy I am buying organic produce at the farmer's market? Please don't notice that I only post about my 'adventures' every few months while the rest of the time, I'm sitting at home, lonely, studying, working, wishing I was somewhere else, or binge-watching TV shows." Maybe he was projecting—minus the posting part. Still, every once in a while, he checked in, partly to connect with some family and friends and partly because he was bored and avoiding homework. Sometimes, he found good travel ideas to add to his bucket list. He was surprised to see a message waiting in his inbox when he logged in that November afternoon, as December rushed toward him.

'Who is bothering to message me on here? Everyone who talks to me knows I never check this thing. Which means it's either a scam or an auntie,' he thought to himself. But when he clicked on his inbox, he saw it was someone from his past: Elena. He tried to remember the last time he had seen her. It was probably around five years ago, about nine months after they had graduated high school.

They were at his studio apartment in the city, lying on the old futon that doubled as his bed. There were tacos to eat and beer to drink while they half-watched a movie and talked. They made an excellent multitasking team.

"So that jerk cheated on you?" Rodrigo asked Elena, feeling a surge of anger that wasn't soothed by the delicious taco as it usually would be. He hated it when his friends were hurting.

"Yeah, three months was all he could last without his dick getting bored. Just another chapter in the story of my life," she said, sounding equal parts angry and hurt. His own body felt heated, and his hands clenched into fists of their

own volition. He was relieved that his relationships never lasted more than a week or two. He hated the look of sadness on her face, and it was better to focus on the rising anger on her behalf instead.

"You know where he lives, right?" He started getting up from the futon and reached for his keys.

Elena reached over and grabbed his arm, halting his progress toward the door. "As much as I would love to see you kick his ass, I don't think it's a good idea. He lives in a frat house and would have easy access to a lot of backup. I don't want you getting your ass beat by twenty frat guys over this."

"If Eddie wasn't sick, we would go over there and take care of him for you, twenty frat douches or not." Eddie was one of their best friends from school. He was tall and muscular from playing football and wrestling throughout middle and high school. Most of the girls who knew Eddie had a crush on him, not only for his good looks but also for his humor and kindness. Elena had been one of those girls. Rodrigo and Eddie had been friends since kindergarten. Unfortunately, Eddie had developed cancer at the end of

their senior year. He was a fighter, though, so Rodrigo remained hopeful.

"Yeah, but Eddie is sick." Elena said it gently, and that was enough to coax him back to the futon. She looked worried, reminding him of the other losses she had experienced. Three months with someone wasn't enough to keep her down for very long.

Rodrigo placed his hand over one of hers. "Okay, but if you ever change your mind, you know I've got your back."

She smiled at him. "Obviously."

The thought of Eddie reminded Rodrigo that he had seen Elena four years ago, not five. He pushed the memory aside, taking a steady breath and shaking off the vision of that cold, rainy day in January. They had spoken a few times since then, but she'd been dating some guy—his name escaped Rodrigo. As she and the "no-name guy" grew more serious, she and Rodrigo naturally drifted apart. Still, the fact that she'd messaged him today told him a lot; Elena rarely reached out for help. I guess things with 'no-name' aren't that serious anymore. He felt reassured in his decision to avoid love. Getting close, risking heartbreak, losing someone—it wasn't worth it.

Looking at her profile picture, he noticed that she looked much the same as he remembered—though her hair was now brown, whereas the last color he'd seen her with was red. Personally, he thought the red suited her better, especially with her sparkling emerald eyes. The smile in the picture captured her personality well, with that familiar hint of mischief, laughing both with and at the person behind the camera. But he doubted this picture showed how she was feeling right now. He wondered how long ago it had been taken, and he hesitated, staring into her eyes on the screen. Should he reply?

To buy himself some time, he decided to indulge in his usual vices. He poured a small glass of whiskey, grabbed one of his pre-rolled joints, and headed out to the porch. From there, he could watch the sun sink lower in the sky while he considered whether or not to reply to her. They'd known each other a long time, after all. His oldest memory of her went all the way back to middle school—Elena in her khaki pants and the blue polo shirt they all had to wear. He chuckled to himself. *We were twelve years old.* If he didn't count Eddie, she was his oldest friend. There had been others in their circle over the years, but aside from Eddie, she was the one he'd been closest to. Closing his eyes, he thought back to their younger days and recalled one of the times they'd spent together, just the two of them.

"Okay, you pick the music," Elena encouraged, as she steered her two-toned brown Sports Wagon—affectionately called The Boat—through town. They'd grown up in a rural spot in the middle of New Mexico, a place with only two stoplights, two restaurants, and one grocery store. By the time they reached high school, the town had started to grow, adding more stoplights, a second grocery store, a few gas stations, a movie theater, and a handful of new restaurants. The roads were still mostly dirt, but the town was slowly transforming. Still, it rarely kept their interest for long. Today was no exception. They were headed about thirty miles north, into the city.

"I don't know why you're having me pick the music," Rodrigo laughed, flipping through her giant binder of CDs, each one perfectly alphabetized by artist. His dark hair was still cropped short to keep cool in the lingering summer heat.

"What's that supposed to mean?" She feigned indignation, tucking her long red hair behind her ear.

Rodrigo paused, rolling his eyes at her. "I'll pick something, we'll listen to maybe one or two songs, and then you'll ask me to look for something else. You never actually give up control of the music." This tendency annoyed him when others did it, but he always found it endearing when she did.

"Really? I never noticed." She paused, then added, "Okay, I'll give you complete control over the music, I promise." She genuinely seemed surprised by his comment. While she might have felt a bit embarrassed by the revelation, it wasn't enough to make her blush—which would have been easy to spot on her pale skin.

He laughed. "I bet you won't make it fifteen minutes."

"Fifteen minutes? That's nothing—I could do that in my sleep!"

"You'd have to be asleep to make it that long!" he teased. "That's about five songs, give or take. You've never made it past two songs without asking for a change, not since I've

been riding in your car, anyway."

"I can totally make it for fifteen minutes!"

"Like, totally?" he said, mocking her in a Valley Girl accent.

"Uh, shut up!" She laughed, giving him a playful punch on the leg. "I bet you I can go fifteen minutes without changing the music you pick."

"Okay, what are we betting?"

"Hmm... let me think about that for a second." She kept her eyes on the road, pretending to be deep in thought. After a moment, she added, "And I'm not flashing you, so don't even think about it. Nothing dirty!" she warned before he could say a word.

He put on his best innocent face. "Would I do something like that?"

"You're a seventeen-year-old guy..."

"Of course you would," they finished in unison.

"Jinx!" he called out quickly. "Now you owe me a coke, too! I'll let you talk since we're in the middle of a bet, but you still owe me."

"I hate you," she teased. "And just for that, I'm going to win this bet."

"If you say so. When I win, you have to do my math homework that's due Monday—and buy me a coke."

She didn't seem surprised by his choice; he always tried to get her to do his math homework. She always refused, or worse, told him she'd do it for twenty bucks, which he never had. "Fine. And if I win?"

"What do you want?"

She thought for a second, then shrugged. "I don't know. You don't have anything I want."

"Hey! I have stuff!"

"Good stuff?" she asked, feigning disbelief. After another pause, she smirked. "Okay, when I win, you can buy me that new CD I want—the one that comes out next month."

"Deal." They shook on it. "Alright, as soon as I put this CD in, the timer starts." He took a disc from his backpack and slid it into the CD player.

He couldn't remember who had won the bet. Most likely, it was her; she could be relentless when she had a goal in mind. He considered replying to her message and, finding no reason not to, went back inside to his computer. Sitting down, he typed out a simple, sincere reply.

I'm sorry things are rough right now. Call me or text me anytime.

He added his number at the end and hit send, then sat back and waited, wondering just how long it might take for her to call.

CHAPTER 3

December 2011

Elena was watching television, barely paying attention, when her phone buzzed unexpectedly. She thought about ignoring it, assuming it was her mother checking in again. This thought triggered a wave of guilt; of course, it was natural for her mom to worry, but the repeated reassurances that she was better off without her ex weren't bringing her the comfort her mother hoped they would. With a sigh, Elena checked her phone, relieved to see a social media notification instead of another text. Seeing that it was a message from Rodrigo brought a small, involuntary smile to her face.

She started to dial his number, but hesitation froze her fingers. It had been so long since they'd last spoken—much longer since they'd seen each other in person. Could they pick up their friendship where they left off, or would it be as if they were starting over? And what if things felt awkward between them after all this time? That kind of tension was the last thing she needed right now.

"Ugh," she groaned, breaking the silence of her empty bedroom. "Stop being such a chicken. Just call him! He's one of your oldest friends." She stared down at her phone, finger hovering over the call button, hesitating yet again. "And stop talking to yourself out loud," she added, laughing nervously as her anxiety mounted. Finally, she pressed the button and made the call.

One ring. What if he doesn't answer? Two rings. What if he does? Three rings. What if we only end up making awkward small talk? Four rings. Ugh, this was such a bad idea. Five rings. Voicemail. "Umm… hey, Rodrigo, it's Elena. You gave me your number, so… umm… now you have mine too… umm… tag, I guess?" Her face flamed with embarrassment as she stumbled through her message. Damn, I sound so stupid. She ended the call and dropped her phone onto the floor, feeling her cheeks still burning.

The unfamiliar number flashed on his phone screen, and he hesitated before deciding not to answer. 'Maybe it's Elena,' he thought, but quickly dismissed the idea. If it was important, she'd leave a message, and he could always call her back later. The call went to voicemail, and a notification popped up. Someone had left a message, but he was too stoned to bother with it now. Whoever it was could wait until morning.

A full week passed before he remembered to check his voicemail. Instantly, he felt like a jerk—it had been Elena. She'd needed someone to talk to, and he hadn't even bothered to check in. Texting her felt like the safer route; texts were less confrontational, plus he could lie to her more easily without her hearing his voice.

Hey, sorry for the delay getting back to you. My phone's been acting up. How's life?

Her reply comes in less than a minute. **Well, life could be better. My boyfriend of five years just broke up with me, I'm in California surrounded by people I barely know, and next week, I have to take my finals. How's life treating you?**

Wait, when did she move to California? He hadn't realized she'd relocated to the West Coast. He could've found out easily enough from her social media, but he'd barely checked beyond her profile picture. **Damn, that sucks. I'm really sorry. Where in California are you?**

She notices he hasn't actually answered her question, but she lets it slide. **I'm in San Francisco. Well, technically, the Bay Area. I can't afford to live in San Francisco.**

That's cool. I didn't even realize you'd moved out there. He adds after a moment, Psychology?

You remembered. A tiny warmth spreads through her chest, comforting her in a way she hadn't expected. **Yeah, I'm working on my doctorate.** It feels good, knowing he'd remembered something so important to her after all these years apart.

That's awesome, Doctor Elena. Ambitious was the perfect word to describe her. Even back in middle school, she'd been talking about becoming a psychologist while he hadn't even known what a psychologist was, let alone what he wanted to do with his life at twelve. And brave, too— she hadn't known a soul in California before moving out there. A strong urge to hunt down her ex and teach him a lesson almost overcomes him. His protective instincts are coming back faster than he'd expected.

What about you? What have you been up to?

I'm still in NM, working on my bachelor's. I know, I'm slow. It took me a while to figure out what I wanted to do with my life. He feels a need to explain why he hasn't finished his undergrad yet, especially since she's already on her way to becoming a doctor.

That's cool that you took your time, she reassures him. **It's better than randomly picking something and just hoping it'll work out. Most people don't know what they want to do at nine. I'm the weirdo, lol.** Even through text, she senses this is a touchy subject for him.

He appreciates her humor, especially since she's the one who needs support right now. She hasn't changed, he thinks, remembering how she was always putting others' feelings first, even at her own expense. **So, you want me to go and teach this guy a lesson for you? Just give me an address.**

Lol, no. That wouldn't make me feel any better.

He holds back from saying it would actually make him feel better. **What would help you feel better?**

Tell me a story. Something funny.

What story could he tell her that might make her laugh? He remembered a moment from high school that she might find funny.

He dialed her number, and she picked up after a single ring.

In a small town, there wasn't much to do, especially after 9 p.m. However, there was one particular superstore that stayed open twenty-four hours a day. That night, it was their usual group of six friends. First, there was Elena, whose hair was long and currently a deep shade of brown. Then there was Rodrigo, whose hair was cut short but starting to grow out as the air turned colder. Eddie, taller than Rodrigo and slightly darker thanks to his summer football practices, had hair that was a bit longer on top but still short on the sides. Finally, there were the other three girls who rounded out their group.

Among them was Lily, a strikingly beautiful girl who was about the same height as Elena. She had long, flowing brown hair and warm brown eyes. Thanks to her mom's Latina heritage, she tanned easily during the summer months, but in the winter, her skin usually turned as pale as

Elena's. Lily and Elena had been best friends since kindergarten, much like Eddie and Rodrigo. Lily was a wellspring of information about people. If you wanted to know something about anyone in town, she was the one to ask. Importantly, she never gathered information in a malicious way. Instead, she was genuinely interested in the lives of others and loved sharing their stories. Additionally, she often warned her friends about people who might be bad news. While she sometimes sounded gossipy, she didn't care; Lily simply enjoyed knowing things.

Mary had stunning curly black hair that framed her face beautifully and light mocha skin that glowed. Being one of the few African Americans in their small town, she often straightened her hair so as not to stand out too much. She was a few inches taller than both Elena and Lily, yet shorter than the two guys. Mary played the role of the mother hen in the group. She always ensured that everyone was eating well, made certain that no one was overdoing it with the alcohol, and took care of her friends when they did overindulge. Additionally, she had some of the best advice available when someone was having a rough time.

Lastly, there was April. She sported shoulder-length black hair that complemented her features. April was of the same height and size as Elena, which meant they often shared clothes. Her olive skin was beautifully tanned because she had spent quite a bit of time outdoors, working on a vibrant mural on the side of her family's shed. April always found herself in competition with Elena. While this rivalry was mostly friendly, it intensified when it came to capturing the attention of boys; at those times, April could be a bit more aggressive. Despite this competitive streak, April and Elena were very close friends. Both girls shared a passion for science and theater and often discussed their dreams of attending college together. They were always seeking out new adventures.

Tonight, their adventure included the rest of their group and featured an epic game of hide and seek in the expansive superstore. The clerks didn't seem to mind their presence since they were not disturbing any merchandise, and no other customers were around to complain. A few of the clerks even lent a hand to the seeker from time to time. This exciting game lasted for about three hours until the best hiding spots had been used multiple times and were no longer viable options. Once they were all reunited, they began to wander leisurely through the aisles.

"Ooh, ponies!" Eddie exclaimed, as he and Rodrigo each grabbed a stick horse and proceeded to gallop around the girls.

Lily laughed heartily and said, "I have always liked cowboys."

"Well, hop on, pretty lady," Eddie said cheerfully as he galloped up next to her. She gracefully "sat" side saddle and held tightly onto Eddie's waist as they continued to gallop down the aisle.

Rodrigo sidled up to Elena with a charming grin and asked, "Care for a lift, miss?"

Elena laughed at him and replied, "Why, thank you, kind sir." She also "sat" side saddle, and together they followed after Eddie.

"I'm your Huckleberry," Rodrigo said with a playful twinkle in his eye, in his country boy accent.

"Wait for us!" April called out, following behind on her own stick horse.

Mary followed closely behind, shaking her head with amusement as she laughed at her friends. It was hard to believe that they would actually graduate from high school in just a few short months.

The group continued to gallop excitedly down the aisles until they stumbled upon the "granny panty" aisle. April suddenly stopped and enthusiastically shoved her stick pony into Mary's hands. "These are absolutely hilarious!" she exclaimed as she proceeded to slip the biggest and ugliest pair of panties on over her jeans. Hunching over dramatically, she pretended to use an imaginary cane and then pulled her lips back over her teeth, acting as though she had lost all her teeth. With a theatrical shake of her fist, she told the others to "get off my lawn." They all burst into laughter at how utterly ridiculous she looked. As their laughter filled the aisle, April carefully removed the panties and placed them back on the hanger with a sense of pride. Suddenly, a group of clerks clad in blue vests surrounded them, their expressions stern and serious.

"We'll have to ask you kids to leave now," the older man said firmly. "We can't have kids taking off their pants in the middle of the store."

"Who took off their pants?" Lily asked, her nerves making her voice tremble slightly.

"Yeah, I just tried on the underwear over my jeans," April admitted sheepishly.

The clerks exchanged uneasy glances, and the older man spoke up again, "It doesn't matter; it looked like you took your pants off, so you need to leave. You've been running around here for hours. It's time for you to go home. And don't even think about coming back for a few days."

 April reached behind her and quickly grabbed the granny panties she had just played with, slipping them into the pocket of her hooded sweatshirt when the clerks weren't looking.

Rodrigo noticed what she was doing and decided to provide a distraction. "If you just pull up the security footage, you'll see that we are telling the truth. You don't really have the right to kick us out. We haven't done anything illegal," he insisted. He had no idea if they would consider the three-hour game of hide-and-seek to be loitering, which technically could be seen as illegal. Fortunately, their town didn't have curfew laws, allowing them some freedom.

Eddie gathered up the stick ponies from the others and handed them to the leader of the store clerks. "I guess we won't be buying these after all," he said with a hint of sarcasm.

"Yeah! We'll buy our horses somewhere else!" Lily chimed in sassy and confident, now that she was certain they wouldn't get into any real trouble, fully aware that they had never intended to buy anything that night.

Elena rolled her eyes and said, "Come on, guys, let's just go."

The group made their way to the front of the store, closely followed by ten clerks. In fact, every clerk working the night shift accompanied them as they exited. The clerks lingered outside, patiently waiting until the six kids climbed into Elena's large brown car and drove away. Once they were out of the parking lot, April seized the moment to unveil the stolen granny panties to the rest of the group.

She held them triumphantly above her head and shouted, "The spoils of war!" Elena had to pull over to the side of the road because they were all laughing too hard.

Elena laughed heartily as Rodrigo concluded his story. Later on, April creatively decided to use the underwear for an art project. "Thanks, Rodrigo! That's the first time I've laughed in the past few weeks. It feels really good."

"Anytime! After all," he said, slipping into his country accent, "I'm your Huckleberry."

She laughed again, responding, "Yeah, you are. I need to try and get some sleep; school is tomorrow." She didn't want to end the call, but she knew it was best for her to get some rest.

"Alright, text me tomorrow! Goodnight."

"Yeah, night." She hung up, feeling as though she might finally be able to get some sleep.

Rodrigo hung up, a smile spreading across his face. It felt wonderful to talk to his friend again.

CHAPTER 4

It was Christmas break, and she found herself back in New Mexico. During this time, she focused on spending quality moments with her family, all while trying to push thoughts of her ex out of her mind, including what they might be doing together if their relationship had continued. The conversations she shared with her grandmother, along with the nearly daily texts from Rodrigo, provided her with some distraction. Christmas came and went, leaving her with a few tears shed in the company of her grandmother, as she felt exhausted from the pitying glances of everyone else.

"I know you believe he is the one for you, but if that were true, you would still be together. God has a plan for you, and he is not part of it. Right now, school should be your main focus." Her grandmother said gently. She was the only person Elena permitted to use the phrase 'God's plan' without prompting an eye roll. Elena had no room for a deity in her life. However, when her grandmother spoke those words, Elena felt a sense of comfort and care enveloping her. It was as if her grandmother genuinely believed what she said and wasn't merely using a cliché to fill an uncomfortable silence.

Her grandmother had been spending increasingly more time in bed, yet she poured the strength she had into supporting Elena. A significant part of that Christmas was spent with them sitting side by side in her grandmother's bed, where Elena allowed her tears to flow freely without holding back.

Rodrigo was also spending Christmas with his family. The atmosphere was chaotic. Everyone was present: his older brother, his older sister—the middle child—and her three kids, all under the age of five. His parents were primarily focused on the older children. Rodrigo's brother had brought his pregnant girlfriend from California to meet the family for the very first time, prompting the inevitable round of questions about her from the family. Meanwhile, the three little ones demanded a great deal of attention. He found himself spending most of his time with the kids. True, they tended to be sticky, but their simplicity made them less complicated than the adult relationships, especially when his mother finally shifted her focus to him, interrogating him about his lack of a girlfriend.

"M'hijo," his mother said, her hands skillfully rolling out dough for tortillas on the kitchen counter, "when are you going to bring a woman home? I want grandchildren."

"Ma, you already have grandchildren," he replied, feeling a mix of irritation and affection.

"Not from you!"

He leaned down to give his mom a quick kiss on the cheek and stealthily stole a still-cooling cookie from the rack. "I love you, Mom, but first school, then girls."

"You can have both, mi amor," she said, her tone teasing, as he retreated from the kitchen to check his phone. Speaking of girls, he should remember to say 'Merry Christmas' to Elena.

Merry Christmas! he wrote, hitting send without a moment's hesitation. They had been texting almost every day since reconnecting, and it hadn't taken long for their friendship to return to the warmth and familiarity it had during high school. Their friendship was filled with humor, light teasing, and those occasional deep conversations that made them feel closer.

Just then, the ringtone on her phone broke through the cozy atmosphere as she sat cuddled up with her grandma, watching cheesy Christmas movies on the television. She felt her heart skip a beat, hoping it was her ex. But then reality hit her hard, and she realized it was much more likely to be one of her friends reaching out.

Merry Christmas! she read, smiling at the cheerful message from Rodrigo. Despite her disappointment that it wasn't from her ex, a warm feeling spread through her.

Merry Christmas! she quickly replied. **How is your holiday going?**

It's crazy! There are way too many people in my house right now.

Yeah, I'm at my grandparents' place. There are a lot of people here too, but it's kind of nice.

You're in town for the holidays?

Yeah, until like the 5th of January.

Like, totally?

Yeah, totally... Butthead.

Haha, what are your plans for New Year's Eve?

Lily invited me to a party she's going to with her boyfriend. I really don't want to feel like a third wheel, but I also don't want to sit at home feeling miserable and alone.

Need a wingman?

You'd actually go with me?

Sure! It'd be great to see you after all these years.

Okay, I'll text you the address when she sends it to me.

Cool, enjoy your time with family!

You too! she texted, slipping her phone into her back pocket.

"One of your friends?" her grandmother asked, looking curious.

"Yeah, he's going to go with me to my friend's New Year's Eve party, so I won't have to go alone."

Her grandmother smiled and said, "See, God's plan does not include Alex."

Elena gave her grandmother a gentle squeeze and felt a wave of relief that she had such a wonderful friend by her side.

"Yay! I'm so excited for tonight!" Lily shouted enthusiastically from the passenger seat as Elena climbed into the back. Although Lily was more toned than she had been in high school, and her hair had been cut to chin length instead of flowing to the middle of her back, she was still fundamentally the same person she had been back then—full of energy and hope.

"Did you pre-game without me?" Elena asked, buckling her seatbelt with a determined smile, eager to have a fantastic time tonight.

Lily's boyfriend, Mark, laughed heartily, "Two shots were all it took to get her to this point." Mark, who was a year ahead of them in school, was not someone they knew very well. However, Lily and Mark had crossed paths a few years after graduation, transitioning from friends to a couple in no time at all. He was tall and lanky, with blond hair and a full beard. Mark was rarely seen without a hat and consistently doted on Lily every chance he got.

Lily playfully punched his arm lightly, saying, "Hey! I haven't been drinking lately; I'm a lightweight now. You should be happy that I'm such a cheap date."

"She has a valid point," Elena chuckled. "This is actually better for your wallet in the long run." Elena felt a bit nervous about going out for the first time since the breakup, but knowing that Rodrigo would be there provided her with a small sense of relief.

"Any word from the ex?" Lily asked casually.

Elena knew that this question was coming. It was a common inquiry from everyone she spoke to, but even though she was prepared for it, it still hurt to answer. She tried to convey her feelings to Lily by responding with as few words as possible: "Nope."

"Did you try to talk to him?" Lily asked, her buzzed state diminishing her level of tact by the second—not that she had a great deal of tact to begin with.

"Nope," Elena replied, trying to keep the conversation light.

"Lil," Mark interjected, being more perceptive than his girlfriend, "I don't think Elena wants to discuss her ex right now."

Lily turned in her seat and looked at Elena, her expression softening with a hint of pity in her eyes. "Sorry, hun, I wasn't thinking. Of course you don't want to talk about him. Let's switch topics and talk about Rodrigo instead. You invited him tonight, right?"

"It's fine," Elena said with a small sigh. "I've gotten used to people asking about him, and actually, Rodrigo kind of invited himself, but I don't mind. He makes me laugh, so he'll definitely make tonight more enjoyable. Plus, I won't feel like the third wheel."

Lily faced the front again, nodding thoughtfully. "You two were always close. They would hang out without the rest of us sometimes," she told Mark.

"So?" he asked, clearly confused.

"So, I think they might have been hooking up," Lily said, her voice dropping a little as if the revelation was a secret.

Elena was shocked. Her and Rodrigo? No way! "Why would you think that?" she asked, her voice rising slightly in disbelief.

"What else would you be doing alone together besides hooking up?" Lily shot back, her tone half-teasing, half-serious.

"We would hang out, listen to music, explore second-hand stores, watch the city lights come on at the airport viewing area, and talk about my crush on Eddie and Rodrigo's girlfriend troubles. We never once hooked up—not even close," Elena answered. Although that wasn't entirely true. There had been one almost kiss back in high school, but she doubted he remembered it, so it didn't really count.

"If you say so," Lily laughed, her voice light and teasing.

"Please don't say anything like that to him tonight, Lily. He is the only person helping me get through this breakup. Don't ruin it for me," Elena pleaded, her tone earnest.

"Don't worry, I won't," Lily promised, a reassuring smile on her face.

"She might," Mark muttered under his breath, his eyes twinkling with mischief.

Lily punched him lightly again. "I won't say anything! I'm not that drunk!" she insisted, a mock-seriousness in her tone.

"Yet," Elena remarked quietly, a playful smirk crossing her face.

"Don't make me punch you too!" Lily yelled playfully, her laughter filling the car.

They pulled up to the party. It was at a friend of a friend's ranch, so there was plenty of space for the multitude of cars Elena could see lined up. She felt relieved that the party was so packed; it would make her feel less conspicuous and reduce the pressure to appear 'on' or fake happy if she wasn't feeling it. 'You can do this,' she told herself as she gathered her courage and headed inside.

"You won't be out late, will you, m'hijo?" his mother asked, her voice laced with concern.

This was what he hated most about the holidays: his mother's ability to track his comings and goings and her overprotective nature, which was much harder to ignore. "Ma, it's New Year's Eve. I probably won't be home tonight," he said as he grabbed his coat and car keys from the small table by the door.

"I know it's New Year's Eve," she replied firmly, "but it's dangerous with people driving drunk on the roads. I want you to be careful."

"I'll be careful, Ma," he reassured her, though he could see the worry etched on her face.

She looked at him as he reached for the doorknob, a frown deepening her expression. "I don't believe you."

He laughed lightly, "I know, Ma, but I'm 25 now, and I don't live here anymore, so you'll just have to suffer in silence and pray all night until I return. After all, it's New Year's Eve, and I'm not coming home until tomorrow."

Before he could sneak out completely, she walked into the foyer, kissed his forehead, and then roughly made the sign of the cross in the same spot she had kissed. After crossing him, she smacked the side of his head gently. "Don't be rude to your mother; it's a sin. Have fun, don't drink too much, and be careful."

He kissed his mother's cheek affectionately and headed for his truck, feeling a mix of love and exasperation.

After arriving at the party, Elena headed straight for the kitchen and the alcohol. As a psychologist in training, she understood that alcohol was a depressant, probably not the best substance for her to ingest in a saddened state. However, her non-logical brain took over, and she went with Lily to take a shot. Elena wanted tequila, her usual drink of choice, and there was plenty available. She craved the confidence boost it could give her, even if the effect was short-lived. 'Alcohol is a depressant,' her budding psychologist side reminded her. She poured the shot. 'Fuck it.' In this moment, she didn't need to be a budding psychologist. Hell, she didn't need to be anything more than a regular girl at a small-town party tonight. Clinking glasses with Lily, she said, "To not caring," and downed the shot. She set the glass down and poured another, drinking it in one swift motion, followed by a slice of lime.

The guy next to her exclaimed, "Damn girl! I like your style!" as he downed his own shot of whiskey, bourbon, tequila, or vodka; Elena wasn't paying attention to him or his drink of choice.

During the shot-taking, Mark had been busy mixing up three drinks, and as Elena set down her shot glass, he handed her a red cup filled with some mixture of alcohol and whatever was handy. "I call this the 'New Year's

Scream' because it sneaks up on you and scares the shit out of you, sometimes literally," Mark winked playfully.

"Thanks, Grosso," Lily said as she took her own red cup.

"Yeah, thanks, I think," Elena replied, taking a tentative sip. It was surprisingly good, with no hint of alcohol, which meant it was dangerously misleading—at least it would be if she hadn't heard Mark's description of the 'New Year's Scream.'

"Lily!" they heard from the entrance to the house. It was a cousin of Lily's that Elena sort of recognized but not enough to say hello. She walked past the bustling family reunion and back out the front door. Standing outside by herself for a moment and taking occasional sips of Mark's concoction, she wondered when Rodrigo would show up to save her from her loneliness. Her brief solitude was interrupted by the exit of three men looking for a place to smoke. They immediately noticed her solo status the moment they stepped out of the front door.

"Hey, beautiful. What are you doing out here by yourself?"

"I have a new Mustang; want to see the backseat?"

"Is that a keg in your back pocket? Because I want to tap that."

Elena managed to make it back inside without having to respond to their ridiculous comments. She had learned long ago that it was best not to provoke guys like that. Her encounter with the trio of dude-bros made her think of her ex and how she wouldn't be bombarded like that if she were visibly coupled. So, Elena decided to remain as invisible as she could.

As she looked around the crowded living room, she saw a group of girls re-enacting a synchronized dance their sorority used to perform, while the boys ogled them with obvious interest. Walking into the dining room, she spotted a room full of guys who had smoked so much pot by that point that they were deep in discussion about how a snake and a rat in a nearby aquarium revealed the meaning of life. In the kitchen, a lively group was taking body shots of tequila and vodka, drinking anything they could find to look cool and feel happy.

She peered down the hall, past couples making out against the walls. The bedroom doors were closed, and groups of drunken boys crowded around them, listening intently to some random girl making some random guy moan. She hoped they were both in control when they made the choice to hook up.

He didn't know a soul when he walked through the door. This wasn't too surprising. The people at this party weren't exactly his close-knit crowd, and his social circle wasn't that large to begin with. He wasn't worried, though; he had a knack for making friends wherever he went because he was a chameleon. Like that time he went with Eddie to visit his grandfather in a nursing home and ended up joining a weekly poker game with some of the old vets. He could adapt; he could fit in anywhere. So far, anyway. Standing in the living room, he took a moment to survey his surroundings, looking for Elena. The Elena he knew would be in the thick of a crowd, either telling an animated story or listening with rapt attention. But the Elena he was looking for tonight wouldn't be doing either. She was going through a rough patch, though not as deeply damaged as she might think. He suspected she'd be on the outskirts, alone.

"Boo," he said, sidling up to her. She was exactly where he expected, on the sidelines of the party, observing. This wasn't the Elena he knew, but he figured she'd bounce back with time.

"Rodrigo!" she exclaimed, wrapping her arms around him in a warm bear hug. "I'm so glad you're here!"

"Are you drunk, young lady?" he asked, only half-joking.

She rolled her eyes. "Not even close."

He was relieved but didn't show it. "Planning to change that?"

She shrugged, then hugged him again, maybe a bit more inebriated than she was letting on. "I've missed you."

"I missed you too," he said, laughing as she squeezed him tighter, and he returned the bear hug.

"You need a drink, my friend," she said, noticing his empty hands as she pulled away.

"Maybe, but not a strong one. I have to drive home someday," he replied.

She started pulling him by the arm toward the kitchen. "Someday, but not tonight. Come on—you can't let me drink alone."

He let her lead him along. "Technically, you wouldn't be alone. You're in a house full of drunks."

"Yeah, but I don't care about the rest of them," she said with a smile.

She poured two shots of tequila. "To reunions," she toasted.

"To reunions," he echoed.

"To reunions!" chimed in a drunken man in the kitchen they didn't recognize.

Rodrigo then poured himself a Jack and Coke. "Where's Lily? You came with her, right?"

"She's around somewhere," Elena replied. "She was already buzzed before we even got here, so who knows what she's up to now." She paused, then added, "You know, she thought you and I were hooking up in high school."

"What? Why would she think that?"

"Mostly because we spent so much time together, just the two of us."

He thought back to their high school days. "Yeah, we did hang out a lot on our own. Did you ever see me as more than a friend?"

Elena laughed. "Hell no! I was way too into Eddie to even think about anyone else!"

He rolled his eyes. "Story of my life."

Elena hesitated, then asked, "Did you ever think of me as more than a friend?" A faint blush appeared on her cheeks.

"Nah, I tried not to make it a habit to crush on my friends. Plus, you made it pretty clear you were all about Eddie, so I knew not to bother."

Elena placed her hand gently on his arm. "You were a good listener, even back then," she said, a softness in her voice. She pulled her hand away, but the warmth of her touch lingered.

Rodrigo felt a familiar uncertainty. He went for a classic response, "Obviously."

"Shut up," she laughed, giving him a light punch, which brought a grin to his face.

He held up his drink. "Alright, I've got my drink. Now, what are we going to do?"

Elena glanced around the room. "I don't really know anyone here. I sort of recognize a few people, but only enough to make awkward small talk. Want to go outside?" The tequila had definitely boosted her confidence, making her feel more at ease with Rodrigo beside her. Around him, she didn't need to pretend; he knew her so well that even if she tried, he'd spot her tells instantly and call her out.

"Yes, please," he replied, already moving towards the front door.

Outside, they began to stroll away from the house, leaving the thrum of party music behind. Their breath formed small clouds in the crisp night air as they walked. Elena looked up at the starry sky. "God, I missed this view."

"It's a good one," he replied, heading toward his truck. He dropped the tailgate, climbed up, and leaned back on his elbows, gazing up at the sky.

She followed him up. "I'm having déjà vu."

He chuckled, "Yeah, but back then, in winter, we'd sit inside The Boat. Plus, we'd usually hang out at the airport, so the stars weren't this clear."

"I know, but even then, it was a great view," she replied. "The city lights spread out before us."

Rodrigo took a swig from his red cup, his eyes on the stars. "This is better," he said with a soft smile.

Elena didn't even feel the cold; she was captivated by the stars. She hadn't seen this many in a long time. Back in California, she could count the visible stars on one hand. Out here in the desert, though, that was impossible. The Milky Way stretched across the sky, like a shimmering river in the darkness. She felt a smile tugging at her lips.

Rodrigo glanced over and caught the smile lighting up her face, a sign that maybe she wasn't as broken as she feared. "There's the Elena I know so well," he said, his own grin spreading.

"What?" she asked, looking at him in surprise.

"You're smiling, all on your own, without anyone making you. The real you—the you from before him—is still in there."

She turned to face him, her voice catching slightly. "I'm sure you're right. It's just hard to feel that way right now. He was the love of my life."

Rodrigo looked straight at her, turning serious. "First, this is the first time in our entire friendship that you've actually admitted I'm right about something." He paused, letting her smile. "And second, if he was really the love of your life, he wouldn't have left. When someone truly is the love of your life, it isn't easy to just walk away. But he did, which means he wasn't it."

Elena went quiet, her gaze drifting back up to the vast night sky. "Have you ever been in love?" she asked softly.

"I'm not drunk enough to answer that question," Rodrigo said, taking another long swig of his drink.

Elena smiled to herself, choosing to stay silent—a technique she'd learned in her clinical skills class. The power of silence.

It didn't take long; it rarely did with Rodrigo, who didn't like sitting in silence for too long. "Ugh, fine. No, I haven't," he finally admitted, finishing the rest of his drink.

"What's stopping you?"

He sighed. "I thought I came to this party to wingman for you, not to have a therapy session."

She just waited, a small smirk playing on her lips, which only made him more annoyed.

He sat up, exasperated. "Every girl I've been with has been great, but there's always something missing. I don't even know what it is, and maybe I never will. But honestly, I'm fine with that. Can we be done with all this deep shit now?"

Elena sat up beside him, grinning. "You're so easy." She hopped off the truck bed and headed back toward the house.

"Easy?" he repeated, following her. "What do you mean, 'easy'?"

She made her way to the kitchen to refill her drink. "Don't worry about it. Just get yourself another drink." She loved getting under his skin.

Rodrigo shot her a glare, saying nothing as he poured himself another Jack and Coke.

"Come on, Rodrigo, you know I can murder stare way better than you," she teased, laughing as she sipped her refreshed drink. He kept up the glare. "Alright, challenge accepted." She set her drink down and gave him her most intense stare—the one that said, I'll murder you in your sleep without batting an eye. She was very, very good at it.

"Damn, I forgot how intense your murder stare is. You win," Rodrigo conceded, downing a shot of tequila to calm his rattled nerves. "You're terrifying, you know that?"

Elena laughed as she started to walk out of the kitchen. "But you love me anyway."

"Sure I do," he replied with a playful sarcasm, rolling his eyes behind her back.

The rest of the night was filled with easy conversation, laughter, and playful teasing, just like when they were kids. It felt like no time had passed in their friendship, as if the years apart hadn't left a mark. Being together in person felt just as natural as their phone calls and texts. Lily would wander in and out of their conversations, joining in on the fun. When the countdown began, Rodrigo and Elena shared a friendly kiss to ring in the New Year, grinning like old friends celebrating together.

"Elena, are you ready to go?" Mark asked, breaking into their laughter.

"Ready to go? Mark, the ball barely dropped!" she protested with a grin.

Mark chuckled, "It's actually almost four in the morning."

"Really?" Rodrigo asked, wide-eyed.

Mark held up his phone, and sure enough, the screen confirmed it was nearly four in the morning.

Elena stood up, stretching. "Well, I guess it's that time."

"I can take you home if you want," Rodrigo offered, glancing over at her.

Mark looked visibly relieved. "Actually, that would be a lifesaver. Lily's passed out drunk in the car, and I'd like to get her home before she, you know…"

"She'll be fine," Elena said, waving her hand dismissively.

"I know, but I don't want to risk it," Mark replied, chuckling.

"Thanks for the ride here, then. Tell Lily I love her face when she wakes up," Elena said with a smile.

Mark laughed. "Will do. Later, you two."

Rodrigo turned to Elena. "Alright, so where am I taking you?"

She looked at him, teasing. "Are you even sober?"

"Honestly? I've been drinking nothing but water since that sip of champagne at midnight." He looked a little sheepish.

"Me too!" she exclaimed, eyes lighting up. "I didn't want to end up drunk and sad, so I stopped drinking. But I'm not quite ready to head home yet."

With a light laugh, he draped an arm around her shoulders, guiding her to his truck. "Perfect, because neither am I. Want to go see it?"

"It?" she asked, her tone cautious but curious.

"You know…" he replied, lifting his eyebrows and wiggling them mischievously.

She laughed and gently nudged him away. "You better be talking about the airport viewing area."

He rolled his eyes, grinning. "Obviously."

They spent the car ride reminiscing about their childhood, with Elena choosing the background music. She scrolled through the radio stations, switching whenever a commercial or a boring song came on. Once they reached their usual spot, they fell into a comfortable silence. Together, they watched the stars and city lights, the world around them feeling paused. It was an in-between place—a realm suspended between man-made lights and starlight. The quiet held a kind of magic, making it one of the few places Rodrigo felt at ease with silence. After a while, she leaned her head on his shoulder, and he wrapped his arm around her waist.

"Do you think you'll ever let yourself fall in love?" she asked softly.

He shook his head. "I thought you just fell. Do you think I can control it?"

"You have control over admitting it."

"I guess that's true," he said, pausing thoughtfully. "But love ties people down, messes with them. You know my wandering soul doesn't have the energy for all that." He hesitated, then added, "But if I ever do fall, you'll be the first to know."

She raised her head just enough to look at him. "Shouldn't the girl you're dating be the first to know?"

"Well, technically, yes. But I'll need someone who's been through it to make sure I don't screw it up. You're perfect for the job since you enjoy giving me shit."

"You're ridiculous," she replied, shaking her head.

"But you love me anyway," he teased, giving her waist a gentle squeeze. He paused, then asked, "Do you think you'll ever fall in love again?"

She only shrugged, her expression turning serious. The idea of falling in love again terrified her. Could she really trust her heart to someone once more? Open herself up like that again? Her pulse quickened, and she felt a slight dampness in her palms. She took a slow, deep breath, hoping Rodrigo hadn't noticed her nervousness. They fell into a peaceful silence, watching the stars inch across the quiet desert sky.

"Thank you," she said quietly, just as the first rays of the sun began to break over the mountain behind them, casting a soft glow that lightened the sky by the faintest degree.

"For what?" he asked, glancing at her with a touch of curiosity.

'For being my medicine,' she thought, though she only said, "Obviously, for being my friend."

He gave her a warm smile. "Obviously."

They sat together, watching the sun rise over the city, its light spreading out and creating a beautiful array of colors across the sky as the darkness gradually lifted. Elena felt a bit silly, almost cliché, but she couldn't shake the sense that this sunrise was a sign that her own darkness would soon lift too. She looked over at Rodrigo, and the calm, peaceful expression on his face brought a soft smile to her lips.

CHAPTER 5

January 2012

Ugh, I'm finally home. That drive was soooooo long.
Elena had just arrived back at her place in the Bay after an exhausting, 16-hour drive. She unpacked her car, stretched her aching muscles, and then called her mom to let her know she had made it home safely. Afterward, she quickly texted Rodrigo.

The instant he read her message, he smiled. He'd been a bit worried about her driving all the way back to California alone. Not that she wasn't a good driver or anything, but he knew she wasn't quite back to her old self yet. **Yeah, I bet. Glad you didn't get abducted by aliens in the middle of the desert.**

I know, right?! She paused, fingers hovering over the keys. She wanted to say more—to tell him how much he'd helped her, how good it had felt to see him, and how much easier she could smile around him. But somehow, it felt too deep. **Thanks again for going with me to that party. It was good to see you.**

Obviously, I'm good to look at! ;)

You're a butthead.

I'm your Huckleberry.

She never actually understood what he meant by that, but it always made her smile.

"Elena? Are you home?" her roommate, May, called out from the living room.

Elena walked out of her bedroom, grateful for the chance to take a break from studying. "What's up?"

May was in the kitchen, unloading a bag full of takeout containers. She was petite, stylish, and brilliantly sharp. Her curly hair was always arranged in elaborate braids, and her dark skin seemed to glow from her dedicated skincare routine. They had met in one of their grad school classes, and when they both needed new housing, it was an easy choice to become roommates. They studied together often, supporting each other as they began working with patients.

They were also equitable roommates, each taking turns with cooking and cleaning without any fuss. Tonight was technically May's night to cook, but she had opted to grab food from their favorite Thai place across the street. The mango sticky rice was absolutely to die for. "Dinner is ready!"

They both sat down at the table, but just as Elena was about to dig into her meal, her phone buzzed, alerting her to a new text. She glanced down, not wanting to be rude by checking, but too curious to resist a quick peek. When she saw that it was a message from Rodrigo, her face lit up with a smile.

May, always quick to notice details—a skill honed through her schooling—immediately picked up on Elena's expression. "Who are you texting that put that grin on your face?"

"No one." Elena didn't even know why she lied, but her face grew warm, betraying her with an unmistakable blush.

May frowned, giving her a knowing look. "Why are you lying? You know you can tell me."

Sighing and biting her bottom lip, Elena took a moment to decide there was no harm in telling her roommate about the support her childhood friend had given her. "It's an old friend. We reconnected a few months ago, and he's been helping me through this breakup. He always seems to know how to make me laugh. Since we were kids, he's had that way of making me laugh so easily." She glanced off to the side, lost in memories.

May studied her face for a moment. "Was he ever more than a friend? I only ask because you look a little more than nostalgic."

"I swear, it's just nostalgia. We had so much fun as kids, and we spent a lot of time together outside of our friend group." Her expression softened. "And now, he just… gets me. It's like he knows exactly when I need to hear from him, and then he's there with a silly joke or a memory that makes me smile every time." She looked at May, a bit uncertain, as if she couldn't quite find the right words to explain how deeply Rodrigo understood her, or how safe she felt letting him in.

"Hmm…" May paused, as if weighing her words. "Okay, don't get mad at what I'm about to say, but are you sure it's just friendship? I'm only asking because the look on your face reminds me of how I felt when I first met Benjamin. We were friends, but also… there was more there, deeper feelings, a connection beyond any other friendship I'd ever had."

Elena's hands began to sweat, and her chest tightened. Her stomach twisted in knots, and suddenly, the curry she loved seemed very unappealing. "We're just friends. I mean, he's fun, and yeah, there's been some harmless flirting here and there, but it's never been serious. Besides, I'm too focused on school to be thinking about relationships." She repeated, "We're just friends," her voice squeaking slightly as if trying to convince both herself and May. She took a big spoonful of curried tofu to cover her discomfort. A sudden thought crossed her mind—Could I fall in love again? The nausea rose at the thought. When she finally swallowed around the lump in her throat, she quickly shifted the conversation. "Did you finish that paper for Dr. Hampton?" May kindly let her change the subject.

February 2012

Rodrigo sprawled out on his bed, relaxing with a joint in one hand and a soda in the other, texting with Elena yet again. Ever since he'd responded to her message a few months back, they'd been talking daily. Normally, he wasn't big on texting, calling, or keeping in touch regularly with anyone—but with Elena, it was different. It felt natural. They'd laugh about old times, talk about school, swap music, chat about their days—anything, really. Nothing ever felt forced or like meaningless small talk.

It was effortless. Sometimes she'd mention missing her ex, and he'd respond with stories about the girls who had turned him down, just to make her feel better. She always encouraged him to keep trying, and at first, he'd done the same for her. Lately, though, he'd been less enthusiastic. She'd told him she signed up for a dating app but hadn't done much with it yet. A month or two ago, he might've urged her to go for it, but now? He found himself telling her it probably meant she wasn't ready to date again. That's the right thing to say, isn't it? No deeper meaning.

Valentine's Day sucks! she texted. **My roommate got flowers from her boyfriend. She tried to sneak into her room before I noticed, so I wouldn't feel bad, but I was just about to walk the dogs, so I saw them. I'm happy for her, of course. Her boyfriend is great, and she deserves flowers—but it makes me miss my stupid ex. And I really don't want to go on some dumb dating app for attention or distraction. It just feels desperate, and that is NOT the time to try dating. Ugh!!!**

He stared at her lengthy rant. His first thought—that she didn't need a Valentine, she had him—was an impulse he chose to ignore. That was just his own frustration with Valentine's Day talking. Instead, he remembered how she'd looked on New Year's Eve, sitting at the airport viewing area, gazing up at the stars with hope in her eyes. Her emerald-green eyes had been the first thing he'd noticed about her back in middle school, and now they were hard to shake from his mind. Better not to dwell on that. He took a few more hits from his joint, letting the smoke cloud his thoughts until he felt pleasantly numb. By the time he'd finished, her next message had come through.

How are you doing on this annoying "holiday"?

He realized he needed to text her back before he got too
stoned to remember he was in the middle of a conversation.
But what should he say? Right now, he felt comfortably
numb, which could be its own issue if he wasn't careful.

**Eh, it's whatever. I mean, I'm talking to a cool girl now,
so it can't be that bad, right?**

He barely registered how that text might come across to
her, but he knew it was the truth. As far as his past
Valentine's Days went, chatting with his best friend from
the comfort of his bed was pretty good. It was certainly
better than the time Ellie had ditched him at Olive Garden
because he could only afford the soup, salad, and
breadsticks special. Or that time Ellie ignored him the
entire month before Valentine's Day, only to show up at his
house expecting flowers. Or all those other Valentine's
Days he'd spent completely alone.

Now, he tended to keep his relationships short and
uncomplicated. School was too important to risk getting
distracted by romance. School, career, and maybe even
traveling the world—that was his plan. Flirting with
someone who lived a thousand miles away? No risk there.

No worrying about arguments or getting left behind. He liked it when things were easy. And, honestly, this wasn't too bad at all. Elena should know that much.

CHAPTER 6

March 2012

Hey, what are you up to?

Elena was sprawled out on one of the long couches in her school's student lounge. The room buzzed with quiet activity; other students sat at nearby tables, studying alone, eating, or collaborating on group projects. Someone had broken an unspoken rule and heated up leftover fish in the communal microwave, but aside from that, she enjoyed the atmosphere here. She liked the busyness, the constant flow of students and staff coming and going. If it got too quiet or still, her mind tended to wander, or she'd start feeling drowsy—libraries were just not her thing. And, of course, the lounge couches were far more comfortable.

The message from Rodrigo was a welcome break from the paper she'd been struggling to write.

Trying to write a paper for my Biological Bases of Behavior class. Thanks for giving me an excuse to take a break! What are you doing?

Packing.

Packing? You moving or traveling?

Traveling. Actually, I'm headed in your direction. My brother lives near Sacramento, and his girlfriend just had a baby, so I've got some uncle duties to take care of. I'm on spring break, so it seemed like the perfect time to go.

Congratulations!

Thanks! I thought I could borrow my brother's car and maybe take a day to visit you.

That would be awesome! Just let me know which day.

Saturday?

Perfect. You can park at my place, and we can head into the city.

Sounds good! I'll let you get back to your paper, and I'll see you in a few days.

Elena couldn't wait to show Rodrigo around San Francisco. They were still talking almost every day about everything and nothing in particular. Usually, it was through text, but sometimes they had phone or video chats. The more she talked to him, the better she felt. She still missed her ex, but Rodrigo made the hurt a little easier to bear.

Rodrigo's week with his brother felt like it was dragging on. He enjoyed getting to know his brother's girlfriend better and meeting his brand-new niece. Luckily, he avoided being thrown up on and didn't have to change any diapers. If he was honest, though, he loved it when his tiny niece held onto his finger while she slept in his arms. Spending time with his older brother was nice, too, though they'd never been that close, given the seven-year age gap. But what he was really looking forward to was seeing Elena. Finally, he'd get to see the places she was always telling him about. No more imagining—he'd get to experience them firsthand. And, of course, being with Elena was never a bad thing.

Saturday finally arrived, and Elena found herself standing in front of her closet, unsure of what to wear. She felt so nervous, though she couldn't quite figure out why. It was Rodrigo, after all—he wouldn't care what she wore. Finally, she settled on her usual skinny jeans, a black t-shirt, and a turquoise tank top underneath. She slipped on her knee-high black boots just as the doorbell rang. She checked her hair and makeup in the mirror one last time, then opened the door.

"You made it!" she said as Rodrigo pulled her into a hug that lifted her off the ground. She hugged him back tightly.

"I'm actually here almost on time. Aren't you proud of me?" he laughed as he set her back on solid ground.

"I figured you'd be about an hour late, so being only thirty minutes late is pretty good for you," she teased, letting him inside and closing the door.

"I like your place," he said, looking around her living room. His eyes lingered as he took in every detail of the space. There were two desks, a worn-out couch, a large flat-screen TV, and a couple of bookshelves. The kitchen was small but tidy, and the dining table was covered in books and a laptop.

"Thanks. My roommate was studying, hence all the books on the table. That's her room by the front door, and my room is in the back," she explained, suddenly feeling a bit self-conscious. Rodrigo hadn't been in her home since high school, and this apartment now reflected her personal style.

Rodrigo didn't say anything but went back to take a peek inside Elena's bedroom. It had a smaller television, bookshelves filled with books and movies, and pictures of her with friends—some he recognized from high school and others he didn't. In the middle of the room sat her full-sized bed, set directly on the box springs without a bed frame.

"No bed frame? Where do you hide stuff when guests come over?" he asked, knowing she kept her place neat enough to avoid shoving things under the bed for a quick cleanup.

"Too broke for a bed frame," she replied, giving him a gentle shove. "Besides, you know I'm a neat freak."

He exaggerated her push, flopping onto her bed with a dramatic "Ow! It's rude to beat up your guests. You're a terrible hostess."

"Oh, if you think that was a beatdown, you're in for a surprise," she laughed, jumping onto the bed to tackle him.

He let her pin him down for a moment, enjoying the playful moment as she straddled him, holding his wrists above his head. He was lost in the fun—right until she licked his face.

"Ugh, gross! This means war, you know!" Rodrigo exclaimed, wiping his damp cheek on her bed as he prepared for payback.

The two wrestled, tickling and trying to lick each other's faces like kids again. After a few minutes of playful chaos, they managed to roll off the bed, with Rodrigo ultimately pinning her down on the floor. He grinned and threatened to unleash his infamous "Around the World" move, which involved licking her entire face.

"Okay, okay! You win! Truce! Truce!" Elena cried out, surrendering as she struggled beneath him. Her hair was already a mess from their wrestling match, and she definitely didn't want her makeup ruined too.

Rodrigo looked down at Elena's bright green eyes, which seemed to occupy more space in his mind than he cared to admit. Her face was framed by a halo of short, fiery red hair, and for a brief moment, he felt his heart skip a beat. 'Shit,' he thought. Horseplay like this, now that they were adults, felt a lot more charged than it had when they were kids. He considered kissing her but quickly dismissed the thought. "Okay, truce—but only if you buy me a coke."

"I have to buy you a coke?" she asked, feigning disbelief.

"Spoils of war," he replied, standing up and helping her to her feet.

Elena felt his warm, firm hand around hers and noticed a small flutter in her stomach. 'I cannot get a crush on my friend,' she thought firmly. 'That's just asking for trouble.' Taking a deep breath, she pushed the feeling away. "Fine, I'll buy you a coke. Just let me fix my hair, and we can head out."

"So...in about an hour, then? Should I start a movie or take a nap while you prettify yourself?" he teased.

She rolled her eyes as she stepped into the bathroom, smoothing her hair back down. "Don't be an ass, I'm already done." She turned off the bathroom light, grabbed her coat, keys, and a small purse, then headed for the door. "Come on, butthead."

He laughed, trailing behind her as they went out the door.

They spent the day exploring the city, visiting touristy spots like Chinatown, Fisherman's Wharf, and Golden Gate Park. Each location was crowded with locals going about their daily routines—many jogging—and tourists pausing to take pictures. Rodrigo picked up a keychain for himself in Chinatown and bought an "I ♥ SF" onesie for his niece at Fisherman's Wharf. As the sun began to set, Elena felt the day couldn't end without showing Rodrigo her favorite spot in San Francisco.

"So, where are you taking me now?" he asked, not particularly concerned about the destination. He'd enjoyed the day so far.

"Baker Beach," she said, offering no further explanation

"So, the beach?" he asked.

"Not just any beach—Baker Beach. You get the ocean view and an amazing view of the Golden Gate Bridge. Plus, dolphins swim there sometimes. I've seen them a couple of times now, it's amazing."

Dolphins swimming in the wild? For two kids from the desert, that would be quite a sight. "Alright, let's check out this beach," he said, grinning.

Elena parked and grabbed a blanket from her trunk—the same one she used to carry in her car back in high school. She'd taken it to football games, to the airport's viewing area, and even to the local park where they'd often hang out. With the blanket in hand, she headed across the pale sand, which still held some warmth from the day.

"This spot works," she said, beginning to spread out the blanket.

"You're the expert," he replied, helping her.

They settled down on the blanket, watching as the sun sank slowly into the ocean. Elena, who had always loved the water, felt a deep peace in seeing the sun dip beyond the Pacific's sparkling horizon. Rodrigo, feeling both refreshed and content, leaned back on his arms. When Elena did the same, he felt the heat from her fingertips beside him, sending a small thrill up his arm. 'Shake it off, man,' he told himself. 'You've been single too long—this isn't about Elena.'

Elena gazed out over the water. Although she didn't visit the beach as often as she'd like, each trip felt restorative, as if the retreating tide carried away her worries. The view of the Golden Gate Bridge in the distance reminded her she was no longer confined to New Mexico—a feeling that had haunted her youth. She looked over at Rodrigo, who seemed mesmerized by the waves, his eyes bright with wonder. 'I wonder what he's thinking,' she mused, noticing how close their hands were. Just a slight shift of her pinkie would bring them into contact, allowing her to feel the warmth of his strong hand. 'Knock it off,' she chided herself. 'Don't read too much into this just because he's here and your ex isn't.'

"Hey, is that a fin?" Rodrigo asked, pointing out towards the water.

In the fading light, it was difficult to be certain, but soon enough several fins appeared, bobbing in and out of the waves. "Yeah, the dolphins are here," Elena said, leaning forward eagerly.

They watched as four dolphins surfaced, their fins slicing gracefully through the water. One even leapt from the waves, landing with a splash among the others. "Wow," Rodrigo said, "this might just be my favorite place we visited today."

Elena grinned. "And we're not even done yet."

They watched the dolphins continue to play in the warm light of the setting sun, staying until the last rays disappeared behind the horizon. "Ready to go?" Elena asked, breaking the peaceful silence.

Rodrigo flashed a smile at her. "Where's the next adventure?"

"Come on," she said, reaching out to help him up. He scooped up the blanket as he stood, shaking out as much sand as he could while they walked back to her car.

"If we'd had a beach back home, we would have spent all our time there instead of the airport viewing area," he commented as they walked.

"Absolutely! But hey, the airport viewing area wasn't a bad second choice," she replied with a grin.

They drove to the Mission District, where Elena carefully parallel parked. It was a skill she was still learning, as the need for it rarely came up in New Mexico. Once parked, they got out of the car. "Ready for the last part of our day?" she asked, her excitement clear.

"Bring it on," Rodrigo replied, looking intrigued.

"Alright, so my friend told me about this building nearby with a fantastic view. Only problem is, it's an apartment building with keypad entry, and we don't have access," Elena explained as they walked toward a plain building nestled between a restaurant and other nondescript structures.

Rodrigo gave her a mischievous look, raising an eyebrow.
"So, we're breaking in?"

"Let's try to follow someone in first," she replied, smiling.
"I'd like to avoid a life of crime if possible."

They waited for about ten minutes before a woman stepped
out through a side door. She wore sweatpants and an
oversized concert t-shirt from Britney Spears's 2000 tour.
As she walked a few feet away, she stopped to light a
cigarette. "Perfect," Rodrigo murmured as he turned away
from Elena and approached the woman.

"Hi, excuse me? My friend lives upstairs. He invited me
and my girl over, but he's not answering the buzzer. Any
chance you could let us in after your smoke break?" he
asked, his charm fully on display. His smile seemed even
brighter against his darker skin.

The woman looked at Rodrigo, then over to Elena. Elena
shrugged, feigning embarrassment for intruding on the
woman's smoke break. "Well, okay," the woman said at
last. She set her cigarette down on the sidewalk, walked
over to the door, and unlocked it. Elena quickly grabbed the
door before it closed, while the woman returned to her

cigarette, taking a long, relaxed drag. Elena tried not to think about how many people had peed on that part of the sidewalk.

"Nicely done," Elena whispered to Rodrigo as they entered the building and headed to the elevator.

"The ladies can't resist my smile," he joked, flashing it at her again.

She laughed and pressed the button for the top floor. The elevator stuttered to life and groaned louder as they climbed higher. "I hope this thing doesn't kill us. My friend didn't say anything about the elevator being sketchy."

They watched the floor numbers slowly tick upward until the elevator finally halted at the top. A long moment passed, and they both stared at the unmoving doors. "Um…if you get me stuck in an elevator, you're going to owe me more than a coke," Rodrigo joked, his tone half-nervous, half-amused.

At last, the doors slid open, and they stepped out with a sigh of relief.

"Okay, so we'll take the stairs on our way back down," Elena laughed, though there was an unmistakable tension in her voice.

"You think?" Rodrigo replied, stepping off the elevator. The apartment building was nothing special; the hallway looked like that of a cheap motel. The carpet was gray, though it may have once been beige, and the walls were plain white. Dark brown doors lined the hallway, each with a number. The overhead fluorescent lights provided just enough light to read the door numbers and a sign pointing to roof access.

"I'm guessing this is where we're going?" Rodrigo asked.

"Yeah, the roof has the view," Elena said, immediately regretting the obvious statement. She felt a little silly for pointing out the obvious; of course, they hadn't come here to admire the hallway.

Rodrigo took the lead, inspecting the door. "No alarm," he said, cautiously pushing it open and stepping back, ready to bolt if it went off. When nothing happened, he stepped onto the dimly lit rooftop. "Careful, there's a bit of a drop here," he added as Elena followed him.

Unfortunately, his warning came too late. Elena slipped as she stepped outside, her foot catching on the uneven rooftop. "Ow," she muttered, looking up at Rodrigo, cheeks flushing pink with embarrassment.

Rodrigo immediately looked concerned. "You okay?" he asked, reaching out his hand.

She took his outstretched hand, allowing him to help her up. "I'm mortified, but I think I'll survive," she joked with a small smile.

Rodrigo chuckled now that he knew she was alright. "Tried to warn you," he teased.

"Whatever," she grumbled, brushing herself off. "Let's check out this view—it better be worth it."

They rounded the corner, and both went quiet, momentarily holding their breath.

Rodrigo broke the silence first. "It's definitely worth it." They walked to the building's edge, taking in the glowing cityscape. Distant lights twinkled in the high-rise buildings, and car headlights below created a feeling of movement and life. For a long while, they stood side by side in silence, watching the city below.

Elena stole a glance at Rodrigo, noticing the line of his jaw and the curve of his lips. 'Don't look at him like that,' she scolded herself. 'He's your friend, not a potential for more.'

Rodrigo, meanwhile, found his own gaze drifting toward Elena. He couldn't help but admire the way her green eyes seemed to glow as she looked out over the city. He'd seen that same look countless times—in the small city lights of the airport viewing area, under the endless night sky behind their high school, at the beach earlier today, and now here, on this rooftop. She was beautiful. 'Don't think like that, man,' he reminded himself. 'Stop it.'

After a quiet moment, Rodrigo broke the silence. "You're a psychologist," he said, half-joking.

"Well, almost," she replied, turning her gaze from the city lights to Rodrigo.

"So why is it that when you tell yourself not to think about something, it's all you can think about?"

She wondered what he was thinking. Was it similar to what was running through her own mind? "It's like if I tell you not to think about a pink elephant. Just mentioning it makes the thought pop into your head, and telling yourself not to think about it only makes it more noticeable. Don't think about a pink elephant. No matter how hard you try, it's still there in your thoughts," she explained, still processing the concept herself.

"Hmm, that actually makes sense. You've always been smart, such a school girl," he teased. "I'm sure you've known how to get over your ex since you started grad school. Why did you ask me for help?

"Same reason people go to therapy. When you're too close to your own life, it's hard to see the best path to take. Sometimes you need an outsider's perspective. It's the same reason most therapists see a therapist—everyone could use a little help sometimes."

Rodrigo looked at her, surprised she admitted so freely to needing outside help. "You've just never been…"

The conversation was cut short when the roof door opened, and footsteps approached. "Excuse me, there's no rooftop access allowed. Please head back inside," the security guard said, shining his flashlight on them.

"Sorry," they both muttered as Rodrigo led the way to the door with Elena a step behind. Under the fluorescent lighting, Rodrigo noticed why. When she'd fallen, she'd torn a hole in her jeans, and there was a large, bleeding scrape on her knee.

"Figures," she said, gently touching the scrape to check the damage.

"Elena, why didn't you tell me you were bleeding?" Rodrigo asked, concerned.

She looked down, bending to inspect her shin, too. She suspected there would be a scrape there as well, but her sturdy black boots had taken most of the impact, leaving only a scuff mark. "I honestly didn't think I'd hurt myself this badly. The roof was rough, and there was a bit of a slope right outside the door. I must have slid down that a bit. At least I had jeans and boots on, or it could've been worse."

Rodrigo knelt in front of her to examine the scrape himself. It wasn't too bad but needed cleaning; pieces of roof gravel were stuck to her knee, and her hands looked a bit scraped up, too. "Alright, let's get you cleaned up, my friend."

They took the elevator back down to her car, where Rodrigo offered to drive so she could rest her leg. She accepted, happily taking advantage of the extra control over the music.

When they reached her apartment, he helped her up the stairs despite her protests. "Really, Rodrigo, I'm not hurt that badly. No need to baby me."

"I know you can take care of yourself," he said with a grin. "But why not take advantage of my chivalrous side and boss me around your apartment for a while? I'll clean up and bandage those war wounds, and then we can finally get some food."

She couldn't resist smiling at him, feeling her defenses weaken. She knew she'd never ask for help like this on her own, but honestly, her knee hurt more than she'd let on. She had landed with her leg twisted awkwardly beneath her, and her knee had bent slightly. It wasn't anything serious, nothing that needed a hospital, but it was definitely painful. "Alright, if it'll make you feel better," she conceded with a sigh.

As she started to sit down on the couch and kick off her shoes, Rodrigo called out from the bathroom where he was rummaging for bandages. "You might want to change out of those jeans. I can't roll skinny jeans up high enough to clean your leg properly."

She smirked and teased him, limping slightly toward her room. "Trying to get me out of my clothes?"

"Do you want me to?" he shot back, turning up the flirtation.

'This is dangerous territory,' she thought. She gave a nervous chuckle. "Nope." Closing her bedroom door behind her, she opened her dresser and looked at her pajama options. Normally, she didn't put much thought into it, but shorts and a T-shirt felt risky tonight. 'Oh, whatever,' she decided, slipping into her usual sleep shorts and an old T-shirt before opening the door again.

Rodrigo's eyes instinctively took her in, almost against his will. Even in her comfy pajamas, she looked… really good. He swallowed hard and brought himself back to the task at hand. "Go ahead and sit down," he managed, gesturing to the bed.

She sat, and he began cleaning the bits of roof gravel gently from her scraped knee. They stayed silent as he used a wet cloth, dabbing softly to avoid causing her pain. When he finished, he reached for another cloth and some rubbing alcohol. "This part might sting a bit," he warned, lightly applying it to her knee.

She hissed softly as the alcohol made contact. "Sorry," he murmured.

"No, it's okay," she replied, managing a small smile.

He found a few large band-aids, applied ointment to them, and gently pressed them onto her knee. His strong hands moved with unexpected care, placing the band-aids over her scraped skin. When he finished, his hand lingered, lightly brushing down her calf and sending a spark through her body. "Now, let me see your hands," he said, his voice dipping lower.

"They're fine," she whispered, her voice slightly shaky.

Still kneeling, he gently took her left hand in his, examining it closely. "Alright, this one looks okay. Let me see the other," he said, holding her right hand and noticing a scrape on her palm. He carefully cleaned and bandaged it, just as he had with her knee. He was so gentle with her. She watched him closely, feeling a sudden urge to reach out and touch his cheek. 'Bad idea jeans,' she warned herself.

Rodrigo could feel her gaze on him as he worked. Her skin was so warm beneath his touch, and he had to resist the urge to run his hands over her legs again. 'She's your friend, she's your friend, she's your friend,' he repeated to himself, the words becoming a mantra. As he finished, he looked up at her, his voice husky, "Good… good as new."

"Thanks for the first aid," she said, her right hand still resting in his. He stayed kneeling, his other hand braced on the bed beside her as if preparing to stand but still holding back.

"Yeah, no problem," he replied, but he didn't move. He could feel the warmth radiating from her leg, her hand still soft in his own, and noticed, maybe, a slight tremble.

She looked down into his eyes, feeling a surge of warmth as she thought about how easy it was to spend time with him. This day had been perfect in ways she hadn't expected. She found herself wondering what it would be like to lean in and kiss him, just a simple, gentle kiss. Were his lips as soft as they looked, or would they be a little rough, like his hands? 'You'll regret this,' she told herself, but her resolve began to weaken as she leaned a bit closer. Rodrigo leaned forward, too, their eyes drifting shut as they closed the space between them.

"Hey, Elena!" her roommate, May, called from the front of the apartment, breaking the moment. "How was your friend's visit?"

Both Rodrigo and Elena jolted back, their moment slipping away as they quickly moved apart, each avoiding the other's gaze. Elena stood up, trying to regain her composure. "Oh, it was a lot of fun, except that I fell. Can you believe it? I scraped up my leg." She moved into the living room, launching into the story for her roommate as though nothing had happened.

Rodrigo stayed behind, lingering in her room for a moment to gather his thoughts. 'What did we almost do?' he thought as he gathered the first aid supplies, a strange mix of excitement and regret gnawing at him. Finally, he made his way out of the bedroom and into the living room, where Elena was animatedly recounting their day. He glanced at May, who seemed to be looking at him with a curious, almost knowing smile. 'Had Elena been talking to her roommate about me?' he wondered. Girls tended to talk about guys they were interested in, right? But were he and Elena really in that territory? His mind was buzzing with questions. He looked back at Elena, trying to read her expression, but she avoided his gaze, seemingly focused on her conversation with May.

Deciding to keep it brief, he introduced himself to May, exchanged a few polite words, then turned to Elena. "Well, I should get going," he said, pulling her into a quick hug. She hugged him back, and he could feel the warmth of her embrace lingering as he let go and made his way to the door. "See you around," he added with a smile, then left, heading back to his brother's house, driving a little faster than usual as if trying to outrun the pink elephants in his head.

CHAPTER 7

June 2012

"So, he was like, 'I'm just trying to get an idea of some things we can do together.' I told him, 'This is our first date, and you're already planning to see a movie that doesn't even come out for four months!' Then he said, 'This happens to me all the time! I can't help it if I'm passionate!' Needless to say, we did not go on a second date." She laughed, the familiar sound catching his attention and bringing a smile to his face.

Rodrigo appreciated that Albuquerque had that perfect balance of city feel and small-town charm, where you'd almost always bump into someone you knew. He made his way over to the bonfire where Elena was standing with a few people he vaguely remembered from high school.

"Did you go on another bad date?" he asked, smiling as he approached her.

"Rodrigo!" she exclaimed, pulling him into a tight hug. "What are you doing here?"

He chuckled, noting she seemed a bit tipsy. "Chris is dating the cousin of the guy who lives here, so I tagged along."

"Do you need a drink? I'm drinking vodka and limeade. It's delicious."

"Getting schnockered tonight?" he teased as she led him to the table that served as the makeshift bar. He used the word they'd coined in high school to describe their levels of drunkenness.

Elena laughed, starting to pour him a drink. "I'm barely at 'sch,' so shut up! You need to catch up!"

He took the drink she offered and downed it for her amusement. "You know I'm already stoned, right?"

"I figured, but drunk Rodrigo is more fun," she said, wrapping him in another hug. "I'm so glad you're here. It sucks living so far from my best friend."

They moved over to a couple of chairs at the edge of the gathering, away from the loud music. Rodrigo leaned back, feeling a comfortable buzz from the drink. "I'm your best friend?"

"Well, yeah. I tell you more than I tell any of my other friends. You, on the other hand, don't tell me as much. Maybe that means we're just friends. I don't know; I just feel like you're my best friend. We talk, like, every day."

"Like, totally?" He laughed, deflecting the emotional undertone of her words with humor.

She playfully hit his arm. "Shut up. Who's your best friend, then?"

He thought about it for a moment. He and Elena did talk nearly every day, mostly through texts, and he always found himself smiling whenever he heard from her. They video-chatted at least once a month, sharing laughs, stories, and even the occasional vent session. She confided in him about everything from her bad dates and family dramas to her lingering feelings about her ex. He told her a lot too—maybe not everything, but more than he told anyone else.

"Well?" she prodded, breaking his thoughts.

"Hmm, you are," he admitted with a small smile.

"Why do you sound so surprised? Am I a bad best friend?" she asked, taking another sip from her red plastic cup.

"Why would you think that? I wouldn't keep you around if you were."

She paused, gazing at him for a moment. 'I'm a bad best friend because I think I like you,' she thought, but she kept the thought to herself, shaking her head with a small chuckle. "I don't know, I'm 'schno.'"

"A minute ago, you were barely 'sch.'"

She laughed, waving him off. "Maybe I made this drink a bit stronger than I intended. Don't worry, though—I only plan to get 'schnoc' so I won't have a hangover tomorrow." She had wanted just enough alcohol to feel more confident but not so much that she'd start feeling nostalgic about her ex. Yet, at this level of drunkenness, she felt dangerously close to spilling her secrets—especially the one that made her feel like a "bad best friend."

If she wasn't careful, she might even lose enough of her filter to…

"Elena, come on! We're doing former roommate shots!" someone called from the bar.

"Duty calls," she said with a grin, glancing at Rodrigo before walking back over to her friends.

He watched her walk away, still puzzled as to why she thought of herself as a bad best friend. As she moved, he couldn't help but glance at her legs and the way her shorts accentuated her ass. She had a good figure, and he caught himself remembering the time in her room in California when he'd almost kissed her. 'Pink elephants, man,' he reminded himself, shaking his head as he got up to look for Chris.

Rodrigo and Chris had been friends since high school and still hung out from time to time. Chris had dark brown hair kept in a buzz cut, a lean frame, and skin that showed off his Puerto Rican heritage. He was shorter than Rodrigo, and Rodrigo had tried, and failed, to get him to join him at the gym. Chris, though, always laughed and said, "I like being small—it makes the ladies want to take care of me." Rodrigo had to admire that confidence. He never seemed to feel insecure about his height or build; he simply exuded an effortless charm that drew people to him.

Eventually, he found Chris on the old leather couch in the living room, locked in a make-out session with his latest girlfriend. 'Figures,' Rodrigo thought with a smirk. Spotting a pencil on the nearby table, he tossed it at Chris, hitting him square on the side of the head.

"Hey!" Chris yelped, jerking back.

Rodrigo didn't miss a beat. "Dude, let me bum a cigarette."

Chris, who hadn't paused for more than a second, grinned and pulled a half-empty pack and a lighter from his pocket, handing them over without interrupting his girlfriend's steady trail of kisses along his neck.

"You don't smoke," Chris remarked, eyebrows raised, as he passed Rodrigo a cigarette.

Rodrigo shrugged, taking the cigarette and lighter, "I do tonight." He went outside before lighting it and took a long drag, hoping it might take his mind off Elena's tan legs and tight ass.

Meanwhile, outside, Elena and her former roommates were clinking shot glasses. "To roommates!" they shouted in unison, downing their drinks. Elena chose tequila, her favorite spirit for questionable decisions. After the shot, she looked around for Rodrigo, but he was nowhere to be seen in the backyard.

She wandered into the house and spotted Chris and his girlfriend on the couch. "Nice to see you, Chris," she greeted him with a smirk, still scanning the room for Rodrigo.

Chris didn't look up but raised a hand in a casual wave, which made her laugh and roll her eyes. She continued her search, her feet moving her forward almost instinctively, her heart beating a bit faster as she moved from room to room. She wasn't sure why she felt so compelled to find Rodrigo; she only knew he was the person she wanted to spend the rest of the night with. After a quick glance in the kitchen, she headed out the front door.

As she stepped outside, she saw a figure sitting alone at the curb. Even from the porch, she caught the faint scent of cigarette smoke drifting her way. "You're smoking now?"

she asked as she walked toward him, her pulse quickening just a bit, though she didn't know why.

Rodrigo looked up as she approached but only shrugged. "I guess so," he replied, exhaling smoke as she settled down beside him. She took the cigarette from his hand and took a short drag.

"So, you're smoking now?" he teased, raising an eyebrow.

She laughed lightly and took another quick puff. "Not really. I just take a puff now and then when I'm drinking. If I inhale too much, I'll start coughing like crazy."

He chuckled, taking the cigarette back from her and inhaling deeply.

She wrapped her arms around her knees, drawing them close as she looked over at him. "Not having fun in there?"

He exhaled and leaned back, looking thoughtful. "Not really. I don't know most of the people here. I recognize a few from high school, but none from our old group."

"Except me," she said with a warm smile.

He returned her smile. "Except you."

She looked up at the sky, falling into a comfortable silence. The stars seemed unusually bright, and the quietness outside felt peaceful compared to the noise of the party. Rodrigo glanced over, watching her face as she gazed upwards, her expression soft and calm.

Her face was flushed a pale pink, likely from the alcohol, he assumed. His gaze lingered on her lips, and his thoughts began to race. The silence between them became unbearable. "How's life?" he finally asked, breaking the tension.

"It's okay. I'm trying to date again, more seriously this time, but it's not going well," she replied, her voice a little more downcast than usual.

Rodrigo nodded, understanding. "Yeah, I heard part of your story when I got here. Are you still doing the online thing?"

She let out a small laugh and shook her head. "Yeah. It's lame. Most of the guys I've met are either creepy or boring. I laugh so easily, but I've had dates where I didn't laugh at all. The rest, I end up comparing to my ex, and they don't measure up. I keep waiting for the butterflies, but they never come."

"The butterflies?" Rodrigo asked, his brows furrowing slightly.

"You know," she said, waving a hand as if it were obvious, "when you first meet someone and you can't stop thinking about them, and every time you do, you get that nervous excitement—like a fluttering feeling in your stomach. I keep waiting to feel that with these guys I'm meeting, but it isn't happening. I haven't felt it since my ex."

She paused, trying to ignore the flutter she felt in that moment.

Rodrigo could see the sadness and hopelessness in her eyes, even in the dim light. "You'll feel them again, I promise," he said, his voice soft, trying to comfort her.

She looked at him for a moment, considering how sweet he was being and how much she trusted him. He always knew exactly what to say to make her feel better. She felt a slight flutter in her stomach.

'This is a bad idea,' the sober part of her brain warned. But her drunk brain was in charge, and she couldn't stop herself. She leaned closer to Rodrigo, her eyes locked on his. Closer still. 'Stop!' she told herself, but the distance between them disappeared.

Rodrigo was frozen, watching her lean toward him, not blinking. 'This is not happening,' he thought. 'She's drunk, I need to stop this.' But before he could act, her lips were on his. It was just a brief, innocent peck—a soft press of her lips against his. She pulled away slightly, eyes closed, and he could taste the citrusy lip balm on her mouth— grapefruit, maybe?

"Sorry," she whispered, her lips grazing his as she spoke. "I'm drunk."

Rodrigo didn't know how to react. Part of him wanted to pull her closer and kiss her with more passion than a peck. Another part of him—the rational part—knew that would be a mistake. Better to let it go. But her hand was resting on his thigh, where she had placed it while leaning in to kiss him. It was distracting. Her lips were still close, tempting him.

He flicked the cigarette from his hand, letting it fall into the street, and grabbed her face, kissing her deeply. She parted her lips, and the kiss quickly escalated from a simple peck to something more. Tongues and teeth. She bit his bottom lip and smiled mischievously before diving back into the kiss with urgency. His hands moved to her hair, and her hand on his thigh slid upward, her other hand now resting on his chest.

"Dude!" Chris suddenly called from the house, slamming the door behind him.

Rodrigo and Elena broke apart, their faces flushed. "What?!" Rodrigo yelled, frustration clear in his voice.

"We're leaving," Chris said, walking past them.

Rodrigo glanced at Elena for a moment, still caught in the aftershocks of the kiss. "Why?" he asked, his eyes never leaving her.

Chris grabbed Rodrigo's arm, pulling him toward the door. "Fought with my girl. Let's go. Bye, Elena."

She stood still as Rodrigo was dragged toward Chris's car. "Bye, Chris. Bye, Rodrigo," she said, her voice soft, not taking her eyes off of him. Her fingers brushed her lips, lingering there, unwilling to let go of the warmth left by his kiss.

Rodrigo didn't say anything as he climbed into Chris's car and slammed the door, still not looking away from Elena.

'Shit,' Elena thought to herself. 'I'm going to completely regret this in the morning.' One of her old roommates descended the porch steps and walked toward her, snapping her out of her thoughts.

"Dude, come on, we're playing Beer Pong. I need a partner," he said, handing her a bright green ping pong ball.

"Sure," Elena replied, following him into the house. Might as well try to drink that bad decision away. No good comes from falling for a friend. The butterflies in her stomach were still fluttering, and her lips continued to tingle.

"So, I did see what I think I saw, right?" Chris asked as they drove toward Rodrigo's apartment.

Rodrigo stayed silent, so Chris pushed further, "Cause what I think I saw was you and Elena making out. Like, hardcore making out."

"Drunken mistake, that's all," Rodrigo muttered, his gaze fixed on the passing streetlights. "Loneliness and lowered inhibitions, that's all it was."

Chris shrugged, and the two men fell into an uncomfortable silence. Rodrigo stared out the window, his thoughts drifting back to the only other time in his life when loneliness and lowered inhibitions had blurred the line between friendship and something more with Elena.

He was sitting in class, struggling to focus on his test when he kept hearing a consistent tapping sound. Frustrated, he looked around the room, trying to pinpoint the source. Nothing. No one else seemed bothered by it. The tapping continued until, suddenly, his dream broke as he realized it was coming from his window.

He turned to his bedside clock: 3:04 a.m. It had to be Eddie. Eddie would show up sometimes when he couldn't sleep. Rodrigo climbed out of bed and opened the window without thinking. "Eddie, man, you gotta…" but it wasn't Eddie climbing through the window.

"Elena?"

"I was at a party down the street, but my ride left without me," Elena said, as she finished climbing through the window. "I didn't know where else to go."

Rodrigo steadied her, catching the faint scent of alcohol on her breath. "Who was your ride?"

"This guy I met in drama class. Obviously, we're not going on a second date." She sighed. "I told my mom I was staying with Lily, so I couldn't call for a ride. And I'm really drunk. Didn't want to wake anybody up, so I figured I'd come here since it was so close." She swayed slightly, unsteady on her feet.

Rodrigo grabbed her arms to steady her, feeling a knot of worry form in his stomach. He had never seen her this drunk. *"Why did your ride leave you? How far away was this party?"*

She laughed, her voice a little unsteady. "He tried to feel me up while we were making out, and I slapped him. He got pissed and stormed out," she chuckled again, "I drank a lot, but I won the game."

"What game?"

"King's Cup," she replied. "I didn't have to drink the cup in the middle, but it was a long game, and I drank a lot of beer and shots. Your room is a mess," she added, leaning on him with most of her weight.

"How far away was this party?"

She looked at him, her focus wavering. "Two streets over. Calm down, Dad!"

He led her to his bed. "Why don't you sit down?"

She dropped onto the bed. "Okay," she laughed again, her head swaying slightly.

He couldn't believe how compliant she was being. He thought it was lucky that the guy had left after she slapped him. "In the morning, you can tell me whose ass to kick. He shouldn't have left you there, and he shouldn't have encouraged you to get this drunk."

"I'm high too. Druuuuunk and stoooooonnnnned," she slurred.

'Good thing my parents are heavy sleepers,' he thought. "I didn't think you got high," he said.

"I never did before. It feels weird."

"Lay down and go to sleep. You're going to feel like shit in the morning," he said as he removed her shoes and tucked her in, grabbing a pillow for himself. He laid down on the floor, trying to find a comfortable position. He heard her groan from the bed. "What is it?"

"Thirsty," she murmured.

He stood up and began walking toward the kitchen to get her some water. "You're annoying, you know that?"

"You loooove me," she sang, her voice light from the bed.

He walked quietly through his house, feeling irritated. She was reckless for letting herself get so out of it around strangers. Then again, it sucked that she couldn't have fun without worrying about being groped at a party. He was relieved she had enough sense to make it to his house. Hopefully, Mom will go to church in the morning without trying to drag me with her.

He returned to his room with a glass of water, only to find Elena fast asleep. He set the water down on the nightstand next to her and started to move back to his makeshift bed on the floor.

"Rodrigo?" Her hand brushed his arm, soft and tentative.

"Yeah?"

"I shouldn't have gone to that party alone."

He sat down on the edge of the bed next to her. She looked vulnerable, her eyes wide and slightly wet. "Probably not."

"I wanted to be tough," she said, her voice cracking a little. A tear escaped and rolled down one cheek.

He reached over and gently wiped the tear away with his thumb. "You are tough. You don't need to prove that by putting yourself in dangerous situations."

"I feel so dumb."

"You're not dumb," he reassured her, his voice soft.

"I was scared and alone, but I knew I would feel safe here."

He smiled sadly at her, "I'm glad I could help."

"Could you lay with me? I'm cold."

He noticed her shivering, probably from the alcohol. "Sure, if you think it will make you feel better." He laid down next to her, and she nestled her head on his chest.

"Thanks for being my friend," she murmured, beginning to drift off to sleep.

"Obviously," he whispered, enjoying her warmth and the feel of her head on his chest.

The next morning, he woke to the sound of the front door shutting and his parents getting into their car to go to church. Elena was still curled up next to him. She must have felt him stir, because she slowly opened her eyes and looked up at him. "Hi," she said, shyly.

"How's your head?"

"Pounding," she said, still looking up at him, her hand resting lightly on his chest.

"You were super drunk last night. I was worried," he said, his hand instinctively reaching out to tuck some loose hair behind her ear. He realized that he was alone in his house with a beautiful girl in his bed. His eighteen-year-old brain took over as he looked at her lips. He'd broken up with his girlfriend recently and was still feeling lonely. Now he had a beautiful girl in his bed with him. He was already shirtless, and her hand felt nice on his chest. His hand moved to her cheek.

"Sorry, won't happen again," she said, sitting up and looking down at him.

"Better not," he said, licking his lips, his voice low.

They began to lean toward one another, their faces just millimeters apart, when she suddenly stopped. "Damn it!" She scrambled off the bed and ran toward the bathroom. He heard her retching. Loneliness and lowered inhibitions.

They never talked about their almost kiss from high school. Rodrigo never brought it up because he knew that they weren't really attracted to one another—just lonely. He figured she hadn't brought it up because of embarrassment. It had never happened again, and a few months later, they graduated. He felt that not talking about it was the best option this time too. It was just loneliness and lowered inhibitions again. No sense in making it into something more.

Elena was barely focused on the game of Beer Pong, and her partner was definitely carrying their team. But how could she focus after that kiss? Did it mean anything? Should she bring it up? What if it meant something to her but not him? What if it was just her drunk brain, and she didn't really want it? What if it completely screwed up their friendship? What if he just wanted her to be another one of his hook-ups and nothing more? 'Ugh, why did I have to kiss him? This complicates everything,' she thought. Better to ignore it. It was a drunken mistake. No need to talk about it.

CHAPTER 8

July 2012

Hey

They hadn't spoken in over a month. She hadn't said anything because she was embarrassed about kissing him and worried that he might think she wanted something more than just friendship. Still, she missed him, which inevitably led her to send the simple message: "Hey."

Hey, what have you been up to?

He hadn't reached out because he liked the kiss and wanted more, but he didn't want to ruin the friendship or get involved in a long-distance situation. So, he decided to keep his distance for a while, both physically and electronically.

School, work, bad dates... you know, the usual. You?

That's cool. Where are you working?

It's not really work… I'm not getting paid or anything, but I've started actual training, so I'm working at a therapy clinic a few days a week.

Nice.

He hated how stilted and detached he was acting towards her, but he felt that distance was what he needed right now. He couldn't afford to get involved with one of his friends.

Elena decided to throw herself into her internship. Focus on school and training, it's more important than what's going on with Rodrigo anyway. Besides, today she would be seeing her very first therapy client. She had to be at the top of her game—focused, empathetic, assessing for safety, letting the client know she was an intern… so much to remember.

She walked into the counseling center and found the room she had reserved. Putting her bag down in the chair where she planned to sit, she looked around, making sure everything was set up properly—there were tissues and bottles of water for the client—and then grabbed the informed consent packet that she would review with the client before beginning the session. She took a deep breath and glanced at the clock, which was set unobtrusively next to the chair the client would sit in. Five minutes. You've got this. Today is just gathering information, hearing their story, and making them feel safe. You do that with people all the time.

She took one more breath and then received a call that the client had arrived. She went out to greet them.

The session was, by no means, perfect, but it wasn't bad. At one point, she was stuck on what question to ask next, but she voiced that she was considering her next question and took a brief pause. The client seemed understanding and took the moment to drink some water. Elena felt that it was a successful first session and that she had made the client comfortable enough to share parts of his story. She hoped he would return for the second session.

She reached for her phone and began typing a message to Rodrigo to share her good news, but then she hesitated. He probably doesn't want to talk to me after that stupid kiss, and I don't want him giving short replies or ignoring me and ruining this good feeling. So, she texted May instead. She'll understand what I'm feeling better than Rodrigo anyway.

August 2012

I'm currently on the subway, surrounded by an overwhelming number of preteens. There are so many of them packed into one car that it's impossible to move. It's hot, and the smell is unbearable. How's your day?

Once again, it had been a few weeks since Rodrigo and Elena had spoken. She hated it. She missed her best friend. Small talk hadn't worked last time, so she thought, maybe something that might make him laugh will help break the ice and get us back to the easy back-and-forth we used to have.

Gross, stinky preteens are the worst. My day's been good, just relaxing at home.

Nice, I'm jealous.

'Stupid drunken kiss ruined everything,' she thought as she tucked her phone away, knowing he wouldn't respond. She didn't want to extend the awkwardness, the same awkwardness she felt in their last exchange, even through a simple text message.

Rodrigo had been at the library when Elena texted again. He knew she was trying hard to fix things, to get back to how they were before the drunken kiss. But it was harder now. When he thought about her, all he could think about was that kiss and how complicated everything could get if they started down that road. He didn't like complicated. Avoidance seemed like the easier path. Besides, he was studying. The new semester had just begun, and he wanted to start fresh, no procrastination this time! He had even bought himself a planner. He hadn't opened it yet, but it was something, at least more than he'd ever done to try and organize his life. Elena would be proud.

Damn it! I'm not supposed to be thinking about Elena.

Okay, back to geology. Focus, man.

He took a deep breath and returned to his reading. A cute girl sat down at the far end of the table, unpacking a laptop.

He smiled at her when she looked up, and her cheeks turned a faint shade of pink. See, better to focus on the here and now, on the simple things. He went back to his reading, glancing at the girl occasionally, but not feeling the same rush of excitement, he thought he would.

September 2012

Elena had a decent-sized caseload at her internship now and was feeling more confident in her abilities to help people. She was sitting in the student lounge at school, finishing up her final project for her Cognitive Behavioral Therapy class, and looking forward to the summer quarter coming to an end. She and her classmates planned to go out to dinner tonight after their last exam to celebrate surviving another quarter. She was beginning to feel like she had found a real sense of community in California now, that it was finally starting to feel like home. A feeling she never thought would be possible for her after Alex ended things and she felt like she didn't belong anywhere.

Her classmate Bobby walked in and waved as he headed over to heat up some food. Elena smiled to herself as the sense of community grew stronger.

October 2012

Halloween. A holiday Rodrigo normally forgot about until kids started ringing his doorbell, sticky-faced and adorable in their costumes. But this year was different. He had a date with the cute girl from the library. They'd been casually seeing each other since that first meeting, not frequently—both were juggling jobs and classes—but enough to have a weekly date. Tonight, they were headed to a Halloween party her friend was throwing.

He dressed as a "lumberjack," which, in his case, meant jeans, a black T-shirt, and work boots. To add a touch of costume, he threw on a faded red flannel shirt he'd found at the thrift store and topped it off with a black beanie. His date was dressed as a cat. It was simple and classic, though about as uninspired as his own lazy costume choice. 'Eh, whatever,' he thought. At least he was getting out of the house, though he wished they had a bit more of a spark. Witty banter wasn't her thing.

Out of curiosity, he'd checked social media earlier and saw that Elena had posted pictures from a night out in the city, dressed as a sexy pirate. Her bright smile in those photos only made him feel the lack of connection with his date more.

November 2012

Happy birthday, old lady!

Old?! 26 isn't old!

Haha

Even though he was keeping his distance, Rodrigo didn't want to miss her birthday.

You know I'm going to be in town for Thanksgiving in a few weeks. Maybe we could hang out?

Sure, let me know when you get in.

Maybe if we hang out, things can get back to normal, he thought, but even as he hoped, he knew he wasn't ready to face her. Especially now that things with the cat girl had fizzled out.

November 22, 2012 – Thanksgiving Day

I'm in town, you free on Saturday?

Elena's heart leapt with hope as she hit send. Maybe if we hang out, he'll see that the kiss was a drunken mistake. I'm not in love with him, and we can just be friends again. She sat on her grandmother's couch, trying to ignore the butterflies in her stomach as she waited. Her aunt and mother bustled around the kitchen, cooking Thanksgiving dinner.

But Saturday came and went with no response from Rodrigo. She wasn't entirely surprised, so she'd made plans with Mary and Lily just in case. They were always good company and brought a mix of nostalgia and current laughs into the conversation. The night passed in a blink whenever she was with them.

December 2012

Hey, sorry I missed you at Thanksgiving. I lost my phone. Will you be coming back for Christmas?

Yeah, I'll be back on the 22nd until the 5th. You want to get together and catch up?

"She's coming back for Christmas and wants to hang out," Rodrigo told Chris, passing the joint and lighter over.

"You can't avoid her forever. Go, hang out with her. If she kisses you again, go for it—who cares? Besides, it's been what, over a month since you got laid, right?" Chris took a drag, always an expert at keeping things casual.

"Yeah, I guess," Rodrigo replied, but deep down he knew it wasn't just about that. He genuinely missed their friendship—the banter, the light-hearted flirting. Those awkward, small-talk texts just weren't the same.

Yeah, that'd be cool, he typed back to Elena. But the moment he hit send, the familiar feeling of hesitation crept back in. Avoidance still seemed easier. Who had the energy to deal with complicated feelings, anyway? Maybe he'd just text the cat girl again.

December 31, 2012 - New Year's Eve

Elena hadn't heard from Rodrigo since he'd promised to meet up with her during her recent trip to New Mexico. Christmas had come and gone without a response to her simple "Merry Christmas" text. Frustrated and feeling brushed aside, she decided to head to her friend's annual New Year's Eve party and drink until she didn't care anymore. But, of course, that plan backfired—it only made her bolder.

Happy New Year, butthead!

Across town, Rodrigo was just as drunk. His neighbor had stopped by with a bottle of tequila, and between the two of them, they'd already downed half of it. 'Screw it,' he thought, feeling a surge of confidence and deciding to reply.

Happy New Year to you! Enjoying it so far?

Yeah, now that you're finally talking to me again.

I was never not talking to you.

Could have fooled me.

Sorry I've been kind of flaky lately.

More like a lot flaky. I'm used to you being a little flaky, but you really took it to a whole new level this time.

I know, I'm sorry. But you and I are like... Mario and Princess Peach, or Jack and Sally, Buttercup and Westley, Fry and Leela, Peanut Butter and Jelly…

What are you saying? Her heart raced as she reread his message, suddenly feeling much more sober. Did he want them to be together? Did their kiss actually mean something to him? Why was he taking so long to answer?

Rodrigo stared at his phone, rereading his own words. What was he saying? That they belonged together? That hadn't been his intention… or had it?

Her phone buzzed, and she felt almost too anxious to read what he'd finally sent. Would this be the message that would change their friendship forever?

I don't know what I'm saying, I'm drunk. Maybe I'm more like Bowser, Oogie, Humperdink, Bender, or

anchovies. Yeah, that makes more sense, lol.

Rodrigo had always been full of pop culture references when he was drunk. She decided to play along.

Yeah, those seem more accurate, lol.

Rodrigo sighed with relief, grateful that Elena had chosen to brush off the implications of his earlier text. To avoid further temptation to say something he might regret, he decided to turn off his phone for the night.

CHAPTER 9

April 2013

Elena arrived at the small dance club with her friends from school, immediately feeling a wave of insecurity. People were dancing everywhere, and most of them looked like they knew exactly what they were doing. She'd always loved watching people dance but could never figure out how to make her own body move as freely as they did. 'I don't fit in here,' she thought, her face heating up with embarrassment and an almost overwhelming urge to leave. She hated feeling like this. Usually, she could fake confidence until it became real, but tonight, she wasn't in the mood to pretend. Grabbing a vodka soda with lime from the bar, she found an empty spot against the wall, out of the way, where she could watch the scene unfold as her friends showed off their dance moves.

She focused on a group of twenty-somethings on the dance floor. They wore a mix of styles that made her think bohemian hipster. They danced freely—and badly—but clearly didn't care what anyone thought. She chuckled to herself at their wild, uncoordinated moves. They reminded her of people in old Woodstock videos, dancing as if nothing else in the world mattered. Their loose style didn't exactly fit the remixed pop blasting from the speakers, but it didn't seem to bother them in the slightest.

It had been months since she'd last spoken with Rodrigo. Their small talk had fizzled out, feeling awkward and empty after a year of deep, daily conversations. Still, tonight she felt lonely, and she missed their easy banter. She wanted to laugh with him again, even if just for a moment.

So, I'm at a club, and there are these people dancing like hippies to remixed pop music. They look ridiculous. I wish you could see it.

Rodrigo hadn't heard from her in months. He was never great at reaching out, especially when he was uncertain about his feelings. But it was nice to see a message from her.

If I was there, we could show them our awesome moves on the dance floor, give them a run for their money, and not care what anybody thought of us.

It was the perfect response, exactly what she needed to hear, but it didn't make her feel better. It only made her miss him more, a tight feeling forming in her throat. Could they ever get back to when everything was easy?

Yeah, that would be nice.

She spent the rest of the night trying to enjoy herself, awkwardly dancing with her friends, but her thoughts kept drifting back to Rodrigo, imagining how much fun it would be to dance together, carefree.

He didn't respond further. What else was there to say? He wanted so much for things to go back to how they were before the kiss, but as more time passed, he suspected that it might be impossible. It had been nearly a year of this awkward, small-talk texting. They hadn't even tried phone or video calls since that night. Maybe with more time and distance? But that thought seemed foolish, too—they barely talked as it was, and they were already a thousand miles apart. How much more time and distance would it take?

"...I mean, the Twilight movies really are, like, the movies of our generation, don't you think?" Rodrigo's date said, interrupting his thoughts.

Right. He was on a date. He should be paying attention to her, not thinking about Elena. It was probably rude to have responded to Elena's text mid-date, but he didn't see this going anywhere serious with the girl from his bio lab. They had almost nothing in common, and she couldn't seem to stop talking about Twilight. Chris had convinced him that dating other people was the best way to move on from the kiss and maybe return to being friends with Elena. So, here he was, sitting in a small Mexican restaurant, nibbling on tortilla chips, while his date had been talking about Twilight for what felt like twenty minutes straight before she finally paused to breathe.

"Rodrigo?" she asked, noticing his wandering attention.

"Uh…I've never actually seen them," he admitted, grimacing slightly as he realized how obvious it was that he hadn't been listening. To his surprise, she smirked at him.

"Then why don't we go back to my place and watch them?" He hoped that was code for hooking up, because he had zero interest in sparkly vampires. Luckily for him, she was cool with smoking weed, which made the sparkling vampires way more entertaining.

CHAPTER 10

October 2013

"Hey Frank," Elena called out to the older man standing on the BART platform. He was waiting for the train, staring absently across to the other platform, his gaze unfocused and distant. Frank was a tall and stout figure, his hair a thick, pure white, giving him a distinguished appearance. He leaned on a wooden cane with a horse-head handle—more of a style statement than a necessary walking aid, though it did offer him a bit of stability, especially as arthritis continued to worsen with age.

"Elena, is that you?" Frank asked, turning his head toward her voice, his face lighting up with recognition.

"Sure is. How are you doing today?" she replied, her tone warm and friendly.

"Not bad, not bad," Frank responded with a shrug. "Could definitely use some caffeine though," he added, half-joking.

Elena grinned and placed a small cup of coffee into his

outstretched hand. "Good thing you ran into me then," she said, her voice light.

Elena had been riding the same BART train with Frank for a few months now. She had first met him when he tripped while boarding one day, and she happened to catch him before he fell. After helping him to a seat, Frank had struck up a conversation, asking her about herself—her name, what she did, where she grew up, and so on. When she told him she was training to be a therapist, his eyes lit up. He excitedly shared that his wife had been a psychologist but had passed away the previous year. Elena had felt an immediate connection with him over this shared understanding of the field. From then on, whenever she saw him, she made sure to stop and chat. Over time, she discovered his love of coffee, and he learned about her passion for music. They had developed a little routine: she would bring him a coffee once a week, and in exchange, he would bring her a burnt CD that his son had helped him create—a compilation of music from "his time." Elena had started to look forward to seeing her train buddy.

One of her favorite things about public transportation was the sense of routine it created. People tended to ride the train at the same times each day, and more often than not, they boarded the same cars. While most commuters didn't engage with strangers, Elena had always made an exception for Frank.

"So, how are your classes going?" Frank asked, always eager to hear about her progress.

She smiled. He always seemed genuinely interested in her life as a budding psychologist. "They're going well so far, but we're only in the second week of the quarter. Ask me again in six weeks, and I might give you a very different answer," she said with a playful wink.

Frank laughed heartily. "You'll do just fine," he assured her with confidence.

"Thanks, Frank. How's work treating you?"

Frank worked as a stockbroker in the bustling financial district of San Francisco. Although he could have retired over a decade ago, he once told Elena that he loved the thrill of the stock market too much to walk away just yet.

Their train arrived just as he answered, "Oh, you know how

it is. When stocks go up, I'm a hero. When they go down, I'm a villain. It's all just a gamble, which is exactly how I like it." He chuckled as they boarded the train and made their way to their usual spot near the doors.

"How's the dating life going?" Frank asked with a grin. "You know, my son is available."

He'd been trying to set her up with his 40-year-old, divorced son at least once a month.

"Frank, you know I don't have time for a dating life right now," Elena responded with a light laugh. "School is my main focus. Plus, your son's a bit too old for me."

"Good for you. Education should always be the priority!" Frank nodded approvingly. "And you're right, my son is a bit too old for you, but he's a good man if you ever change your mind." His eyes twinkled mischievously, letting her know he wasn't entirely serious.

They chatted about his health, her latest music discoveries, and his upcoming travel plans with his son, until Frank's stop arrived. They both stood, preparing to navigate through the crowd. Elena always helped clear a path for

Frank to ensure he didn't trip again.

"Hope the stocks treat you well today," Elena called after him as he stepped off the train.

"See you tomorrow, young lady."

"Bye, Frank."

After Frank exited, Elena looked around for an empty seat, though as usual, none were available by the time he got off. So, she leaned against the wall by the doors. Today, she found herself standing next to a tall, handsome man in a suit. He had well-kept blond hair, long enough to be styled but short enough to look professional, sky-blue eyes, and a strong jawline. His suit looked impeccable—tailored to fit him perfectly. The only casual item about him was his laptop bag, slung over his shoulder with the strap across his body.

He smiled at her as she fumbled through her bag, searching for the headphones she knew were buried deep within. Elena was the type of person who over-prepared, always carrying more things than she'd ever need: protein bars, deodorant, medications for headaches, allergies, and nausea, a water bottle, schoolwork, a book, a small first aid kit, a mirror, sunglasses, and a collection of other assorted items she only ever used occasionally. She almost missed the man's smile, but it was hard to ignore—it was a warm, genuine smile, showcasing perfect, straight white teeth, with a dimple on his right cheek.

"I think that's really cool," the man said, breaking the silence.

"Huh?" Elena asked, still distracted by her tangled headphones. Her fingers finally found the earbud cord, which, of course, was a tangled mess—as always.

"I think it's really cool, how you talk to that man. You and I seem to ride the same train most days. I've seen you talking to him for months now. I think that's kind of you."

Elena felt her cheeks flush. She quickly tried to untangle the headphones, hoping her body language would signal that she wasn't interested in chatting. "Thanks," she mumbled, "it's really no big deal, though. He's just a nice guy, and his wife was a psychologist, and I'm training to be one, so we bonded over that. Like I said, it's nothing special."

She could feel herself rambling, and inwardly, she cursed the way she sometimes felt compelled to explain herself too much.

"Come on, most people on the train don't talk to the strangers around them, even though we all follow a similar enough morning routine that we start recognizing each other. Not only do you talk to this guy every day, but you even bring him coffee."

"Wow, you've noticed a lot about me."

He smiled knowingly. "Not just you," he said, subtly pointing towards two teenagers making out in the back of the train. "Those two have broken up at least twice on the morning train. That lady over there," he gestured to a woman knitting in her seat, "has knitted four scarves and a hat in the last three months. The guy sitting by the window is studying to be a teacher, and that man over there speaks Mandarin but is trying to learn Spanish."

Elena raised an eyebrow, surprised that he was as much of a people-watcher as she was.

"I know, it's a strange hobby," he admitted with a grin, "but

I don't like to be on my phone all the time, so I pay attention to what's happening around me. Plus, I'm a lawyer, so I tend to notice the small details."

"Those kids? They've broken up three times on this train," Elena said with a smirk. "I had the pleasure of sitting in front of them during the last one." She rolled her eyes at the memory.

"Ah, so you do it too. I knew we'd have something in common." He reached out his hand with a grin. "I'm Jake."

"Elena," she replied, smiling as she shook his hand.

CHAPTER 11

It was the night of Jake and Elena's first date. He had chosen a steakhouse in the Financial District of San Francisco, which meant it was upscale—and way out of her comfort zone. May had helped her pick out an outfit that met the dress code requirements and even styled her hair, as Elena was too nervous to make the side bun work the way she wanted it to. "I don't know why I didn't ask him to pick a different restaurant. I'm so nervous going to such a fancy place. I just know I'm going to spill water down my dress and embarrass myself." Elena babbled as May placed the final few embellished bobby pins in her hair.

May giggled and gave her a reassuring smile. "You'll be fine. Just take deep breaths and only have one glass of wine. And remember, if it goes well, you get to pick the next place."

Jake had offered to pick her up from her house, but she preferred to cross into the city on her own, even though it meant taking BART. He seemed like a nice enough guy through the texting they'd done all week, but people had said that about Ted Bundy too—and look how that turned out. She texted Jake to let him know she was on the train, and barring any delays, she should be there in twenty minutes. He let her know he'd meet her at the station, and they could walk to the restaurant together. With her phone still in hand, she considered texting Rodrigo. She missed him, and part of her anxiety about her date with Jake was because her mind kept returning to the kiss she and Rodrigo had shared, despite how much time had passed since then. Maybe this date was exactly what she needed to get her mind off of Rodrigo. It had been a year and a half since that kiss, after all. She hadn't seen him since and hardly spoke to him anymore. Jake could be the person to help her move on.

She put her phone away without texting Rodrigo and watched the world pass by until the train headed into the tunnel and into the city. When she stepped off the train, she straightened her blue dress, glad she'd chosen comfortable wedges that matched it, making walking a little easier. As promised, Jake was waiting for her at the station, a single red rose in his hand. He smiled as she approached, and she felt her cheeks heat up. He looked stunning in his suit, more relaxed than his work attire since he wasn't wearing a tie. She wondered what he might look like in jeans, a t-shirt, and boots. Did he even own jeans?

"You look wonderful," he said, leaning down to kiss her cheek, before handing her the rose. He offered his arm for her to take, and she did. "The restaurant is just around the corner."

She focused on the sidewalk, worried there might be a crack that could trip her or cause her to roll an ankle in her wedges. "Great, I'm starving." His arm was steady, and she could feel muscles under her hand. "Do you come here often?"

His voice was smooth and confident. "My firm has a lot of corporate clients, so we often have meetings over lunch or dinner. This is one of the places we bring folks, so I'm a bit of a regular. The food is excellent though."

They reached the door, and he grabbed the handle before she could, holding it open for her. As they entered, the hostess immediately recognized Jake and pulled two leather-bound menus from the hostess stand, which looked more like the front desk of a spa than the hostess stands

Elena was used to. "Hello, Mr. Shaw, we have your table ready for you. Please follow me."

The restaurant was packed, and everyone was dressed in their best attire. Elena was glad for May's fashion advice; she didn't feel out of place in her outfit. However, she did feel out of place in other ways, particularly when it came to her bank account. She usually dreaded checking her balance, knowing it would be low. Living off student loans and some limited funds from her mother and grandparents meant a lot of ramen for dinner and never steak. Jake pulled her chair out for her, and she sat down, scanning the menu the hostess had handed her. She tried to ignore the prices, since Jake had insisted that no matter what, dinner was his treat. Still, her eyes couldn't help but drift over to the prices. She could pay for two weeks' worth of groceries with the amount he was about to spend on this meal. Her heart rate quickened, and her face flushed as she began to feel self-conscious.

"What's looking good to you? I think I'm going to go with the Wagyu steak and salad," he asked, eyes still on the menu, seemingly unaware of Elena's growing nervousness.

"Umm, I, uh, maybe, um…" she stammered, feeling her cheeks flush. She hadn't expected the prices to be so high and felt out of place.

Jake's gaze shifted to her, his tone gentle. "Everything okay? If you're not seeing anything you like, I know some off-menu items the chef makes that we could try."

Elena took a deep breath, calming herself. She pushed aside the little voice telling her she didn't belong here. "Sorry, the prices just surprised me, that's all. I think I'll go with one of the pasta dishes—the black truffle mushroom looks good."

He gave her an encouraging smile. "Great choice—that one's delicious, definitely one of my favorites." After a quick chat about wine preferences, they ordered a bottle of Cabernet Sauvignon, along with their meals.

Then came the classic first-date "interview," as Elena thought of it. Jake asked about her family and offered sincere condolences upon learning her dad had passed away when she was younger. She found out that he had a close-knit family, with two younger siblings making him the eldest. He shared stories of growing up in San Francisco, where his family often traveled during the summers, allowing him to see much of the world. She opened up about her own New Mexico roots and explained, in general terms, how she ended up in California without getting into too many details about her ex, Alex. He spoke of his career as a corporate lawyer and the family tradition of law that he was proud to continue. She mentioned her long-standing dream of becoming a psychologist, admitting she wasn't sure how she'd even learned about the profession as a child, given that no one in her family had finished college, let alone pursued a doctoral degree.

Their conversation flowed as they laughed and enjoyed their meal, and Elena felt a sense of accomplishment for not spilling anything on her blue dress. Despite her initial discomfort around people from a higher social class, she relaxed as she and Jake discovered shared interests and values. They both adored dogs and loved reading. Road trips fascinated them equally, and they shared a curiosity about space. Though he enjoyed skiing—a sport Elena had never tried and wasn't sure she'd like due to her aversion to cold weather—and wasn't into video games like she was, their other commonalities more than made up for the few differences.

For dessert, they split a raspberry cheesecake, and Jake paid the bill without hesitation. Elena caught a glimpse of the receipt and felt a quiet admiration as she noticed he'd left a generous 20% tip.

On the way home, Jake offered to drive her, and she happily accepted, relieved to avoid a late-night ride on BART. They chatted during the drive, and he let her choose the music, discovering yet another shared taste in tunes. Elena was surprised by how much she enjoyed herself; for the first time, Rodrigo wasn't on her mind.

When they arrived at her apartment, Jake walked her to her door. Before she turned the knob, she reached up and kissed him, a soft and confident gesture that left them both smiling. "I had a great time tonight," she said, lingering a moment longer. "But next time, I get to choose where we go."

Jake's smile widened, his gaze warm and genuine. "Deal." He watched her step inside before heading back to his car, and she felt a surge of excitement to tell May how the night had gone—ignoring, for now, the missing butterflies.

CHAPTER 12

November 2013

He knew she was in town because he'd seen her check in on social media at a local pub with some friends. He wondered why she hadn't told him. 'Probably because every time she tells you she's in town and tries to make plans, you flake,' he admitted to himself. 'She's probably given up on trying to see you. Plus, you two barely talk anymore since the kiss.'

The memory of their time together drifted back, making him smile. He thought about all their childhood moments and more recent conversations, especially that night on the rooftop in San Francisco. She had become his "pink elephant"—a thought he couldn't let go of. And it wasn't even just about the kiss, though, okay, that was part of it. It was a good kiss, but it was more than that. Before the kiss, they'd texted every day, talked on the phone, or video chatted often. She'd been his best friend, and he missed that more than anything. Nobody else in his life knew him as well as she did. 'Maybe she'll give me a chance if I make the plan,' he thought.

He stared at his phone, willing it to make up his mind for him, or maybe for her to text him first. "Eh, what's the worst that could happen? She says no?" he asked himself aloud. But the idea of her turning him down made his stomach drop. Pushing the thought aside, he lit up a joint, took a deep drag, and quickly typed out a message.

Hey, I saw you were in town. It'd be cool to see you if you have some free time tonight.

He hit send, his heart thudding as he watched the screen. Waiting, he took another hit off his joint, trying to shake off the nervousness he felt but didn't want to examine too closely. Again, like a persistent pink elephant, the memory of her kissing him popped up in his mind. He could almost feel her hand on his chest and taste her grapefruit lip balm 'Damn, best not to think about that,' he told himself.

He checked his phone again—full bars. The message had gone through without a hitch. Still, he felt the urge to check his connection one more time. Standing up, he wandered over to the kitchen, hoping a snack might distract him. He opened the fridge and stared at its contents without really seeing anything he wanted. Leaning against the open door, he looked back at his phone on the couch. Nothing. He heard the faint sound of a message notification in his mind and quickly glanced at the phone to see if it had lit up. Still nothing.

Sighing, he closed the fridge and walked back to the phone, glancing at the time when he sent the message and the current time. Three minutes. It had only been three minutes. He was never one to sit around waiting for a reply like this. Normally, he could go hours, sometimes even days, without responding to people. But here he was, staring at the phone. Four minutes.

Meanwhile, across town, her phone had buzzed a few minutes ago, but she was in the middle of dinner and didn't want to be rude. It was probably her cousin asking when she thought she'd be heading back to the house where she was staying. Or maybe it was Jake, checking in to see how her trip was going. Both could wait. She was caught up in reminiscing with Mary and Lily, enjoying every moment of their conversation.

For a split second, she wondered if the message was from Rodrigo, but she quickly dismissed the thought. 'There's no way he'd text me just because I'm in the same state as him,' she thought.

"So, any new guys, Elena?" Mary asked, raising her eyebrows. Elena's friends loved hearing her single-life horror stories, and her recent dates had at least provided them with plenty of entertainment.

"Sort of. I started dating this guy, Jake. We've only been out a couple of times, but we're getting along really well. There's potential there," Elena said, relieved to finally have a successful dating story to share. She noticed her friends looked a bit disappointed—not that she had good news, but because they seemed to miss hearing her single-girl adventures.

"Do you have a picture of him?" Lily's disappointment faded quickly, replaced by curiosity.

Elena pulled out her phone to show Jake's social media profile picture. When she unlocked the screen, a new message notification caught her eye. Rodrigo had messaged her after all. She smiled to herself as she read it, seeing he was actually trying to make plans. A flutter of excitement rose in her stomach, and she let out a nervous laugh, which she passed off as jitters about showing her friends Jake. Rodrigo could wait a little longer for a response—he often made her wait hours to reply. For now, she pulled up Jake's profile for Mary and Lily to see.

"Cute," Mary commented.

"Ooh, and a lawyer," Lily noted as she leaned in, curiosity taking over as she began scrolling through Jake's profile. Mary peeked over her shoulder, both of them fully engrossed.

Elena snatched her phone back with a grin. "Alright, that's enough snooping, you two."

Lily shrugged. "You know I'll just look him up when I get home."

Elena rolled her eyes. "I'm sure you will, but at least this way I don't have to watch. And please keep your findings to yourself. I'd like a few surprises left. You tend to uncover the blood type, family history, and shoe size of anyone someone's ever known when you go into detective mode."

"Everyone needs a talent," Mary teased. "Speaking of talent, I have choir practice soon, so I need to get going."

"Yeah, I should get my Black Friday shopping haul home before my Jeep gets broken into," Lily said, grabbing her keys and purse.

After they paid the check and hugged goodbye, they headed to their respective cars.

Once Elena started her car, the heater blasting to warm up the chilly interior, she replied to Rodrigo's message with a simple, **Where?**

Rodrigo knew exactly where he wanted to meet. It was quiet, easy to reach, and had the best view. It was their place: **the airport viewing area. I'll meet you there at 9, he texted back.**

He grabbed his keys and jacket, heading out the door even before she replied. He felt confident she'd say yes, and he needed some time to get there on time. Just as he drove down his long driveway, her reply arrived with a simple smiley face.

As he navigated the highway, a wave of doubt crept in. There was a reason he'd been keeping his distance from Elena this past year and a half. They were friends, and he didn't want to risk ruining that. Sure, there was a spark between them, but he'd always told himself not to let it go further. After all, friendship mattered more than a fleeting moment, right? But then, he couldn't get their kiss out of his mind.

Besides, were they even close friends at this point? They hardly talked anymore. As he weighed it all, he realized that what mattered most was that he missed her. Whatever happened beyond that, they could figure out later. Right?

She circled the airport parking lot, her mind racing with doubts. Should she really be doing this? Meeting Rodrigo at the viewing area felt like a risk—one that could lead to something she'd wanted for a long time, but might also cost her a part of herself. She and Jake hadn't talked about exclusivity, but did that unspoken status give her the right to spend time with someone she felt such a strong attraction to? And what if Rodrigo was the one she was meant to be with? Would she regret not going more than actually going?

Her playlist shifted, and an acoustic version of one of her favorite songs by her all-time favorite band began to play. The timing threw her off, especially when the lead singer's voice seemed to ask her when she would allow herself to be happy. The song took her down memory lane, recalling all the moments she'd shared with Rodrigo over their fifteen years of friendship. They'd had plenty of happy times, with just a few frustrating conversations sprinkled in to keep things interesting. Rodrigo made her feel happy, excited, fearless. With a deep breath, she finally turned her car toward the entrance to the airport viewing area. "I'm going to let myself be happy tonight, whatever that means."

He spotted her car as it pulled into the quiet airport viewing area and slowly made its way to the corner of the lot where he was parked. His truck was the only other vehicle there, and in the twenty minutes he'd been waiting, no other car had passed by. It was a cold night, with the sky dark and thick, hinting at an impending snowstorm. The eerie quiet and the oncoming storm felt like omens. Was this a bad idea? Was that why she was so late? She was usually punctual. Maybe she was having second thoughts too.

Turning off his truck, he stepped outside, leaning casually against the passenger door, trying to appear relaxed despite the nerves coiling inside him. When she got out of her car, her smile made his heart pound.

"I wasn't sure if you were coming," he said, doing his best to sound nonchalant.

"Yeah, honestly, I wasn't either," she admitted with a slight laugh. "I drove past the turnoff a few times before finally making up my mind. I hope you haven't been waiting too long."

"No, just got here a few minutes ago myself," he lied, suppressing the urge to tell her that he felt he'd been waiting for her his whole life. That felt too corny and would completely ruin his calm, casual act. This was supposed to be about reconnecting with an old friend, after all. "So, what made you finally decide to come?"

She took a deep breath, telling herself to be brave. "It's going to sound silly, but I was listening to this song, and one of the lines asked me when I was going to let myself be happy. And I thought about you. Since we were kids, every time we've hung out, talked on the phone, texted, or video chatted, I've felt happy. So even if tonight is the last time we see each other, I wanted to give myself the chance to add more happy moments to my life…with my friend." She added "friend" at the last moment, unsure if he wanted anything more.

For a moment, he was speechless. Her words echoed something he'd been feeling himself, though he hadn't needed a song to realize it. He only knew that whenever he thought of her, he found himself smiling. Finally, he laughed, finding his voice. "That doesn't sound silly at all—it sounds pretty familiar." He shivered slightly and gestured to his truck. "It's freezing out here. Want to sit in the truck while we wait for the snow?"

"Sure," she said, reaching into the back seat to grab a familiar blanket. He recognized it immediately—it was the same one she'd kept in her car all through high school. This was the blanket they'd taken to the beach during his visit to California, the one they used at football games, at the park, and here at the airport viewing area.

He opened the passenger door and helped her climb into the truck, noticing the warmth of her hand against his own, now rougher with time. He climbed in beside her, started the engine, and turned the heater up. She spread the blanket over her lap and then reached over to cover his as well. Leaning in close, he caught a hint of her perfume. He had the urge to kiss her, but hesitated—she'd called him her "friend" after all.

After adjusting the blanket, she looked out the windshield. "This brings back memories. You and me, sitting in a car, looking over the city late at night, when we should've been home."

He laughed. "Yeah, we came out here a lot back then." 'But this feels different,' he thought, 'because now I really want to kiss you.'

She turned to him, her face softening. "It's nice… being here with you again." He sensed there was something more she wanted to say, but the words seemed to catch in her throat.

Just then, the first snowflakes began to drift down onto the hood of the truck. He saw her shiver slightly. "Still cold?"

"A little," she admitted, giving a small, nervous chuckle. "I guess I'm not used to the snow anymore—I've been in Cali too long."

He reached over, hesitating for a moment, before putting his arm around her shoulder. "This better?"

She looked up at him with a warm smile. "Yeah, it is. Thanks."

But her phone suddenly buzzed, interrupting the moment. She glanced at the screen and silenced it, sighing. "I guess I can't escape to the past for too long," she mumbled to herself.

"The past?" he asked, picking up on her tone. He wanted to ask who'd called, but wasn't sure he wanted to hear the answer.

"That was…my present. Maybe my future. I'm not sure yet. At least for me, it's still uncertain," she admitted, gesturing out at the view in front of them. "But being here with you, like this, reminds me of my past." She glanced at him, her expression unreadable.

"Oh." He could only assume it was her boyfriend. Instinctively, he began to pull his arm back.

Her heart pounded, and she felt a wave of panic rising. She took a steadying breath, deciding to clarify. "Please don't pull away. That wasn't my boyfriend. Just someone I've been on a few dates with—nothing serious, at least not yet. But…there's a chance it could be, eventually. Unless…" She hesitated, knowing the next words would be impossible to take back. "…Unless there are other possibilities." She was grateful for the darkness in the truck, hiding her blush.

He took her hands, his gaze steady. It was now or never. "I'm just not sure if I can be an option. Not long-term, not with you in California and me here."

She traced her thumbs over his knuckles. "I get it. Long-distance isn't something I want either—it's never worked for me. But I also don't want regrets. Leaving here tonight without asking if there's a chance… even if it's only for right now… that would be something I'd regret."

He looked at her, a conflict of emotions tightening in his chest. He didn't want to let her go, yet he feared that if he held on, one of them might end up hurt. For a moment, he glanced away, his eyes landing on the softly falling snow and the glow of city lights outside the windshield. Finally, he murmured, "Fuck it," and pulled her close, capturing her lips in a kiss.

At first, the kiss was gentle and uncertain. But when she wrapped her arms around his neck, it deepened, becoming an expression of everything unspoken between them. He cupped the back of her head, then eased her down onto the seat, her fingers weaving through his short, dark hair. She nibbled his lip, bringing in a hint of the playfulness they'd always shared. Her laughter blended with his sigh as the moment grew more intense.

He kissed along her neck, feeling her hands slip under his shirt, and a small moan escaped her lips. He straightened briefly to shrug off his jacket, and she did the same, tossing the blanket to the floor. Her hands found the hem of his shirt, and in one swift movement, she pulled it off, her fingers trailing over his chest. She leaned forward, running her tongue along his skin and playfully nipping at his chest, a soft bite that made him shiver.

She licks his chest and bites his nipple. "Mmm, you're devilish," he breathes, voice low, unbuttoning her jeans.

"You like it when I'm devilish," she says, nibbling his other nipple. He pauses just long enough to pull off her shirt and unhook her bra. She reclines against the seat again as he leans over, sucking and licking one nipple while his hand gently massages her other breast. Small moans escape her as he blows on the breast he was licking before he takes it into his mouth, pushing it as deep as her large breasts allow. She tries to reach for the button and zipper of his jeans, but he grabs her wrists with one hand.

"I'm not done with you yet," he murmurs, kissing her stomach and continuing his path down to her unbuttoned jeans. He moves her hands toward her now unoccupied chest. She begins massaging her breasts as he works to remove her skinny jeans, a challenging task in the cramped truck. As he tosses the jeans onto the truck floor, he slips his hand inside her panties, feeling the warmth and wetness already there. He slides one finger inside her, causing her to writhe and moan. Slowly, he pulls his finger out and slides her panties down, kissing her legs as he moves downward until she's free of her clothes. He kisses her inner thigh before slipping two fingers inside her.

As he moves his fingers in and out, he licks, flicking that most intimate spot. She writhes with pleasure, and he grabs her ass with his free hand to steady her. His mouth and fingers work in unison, sending her into a wave of pleasure, causing her to cry out. Slowly, he slides his fingers out, giving her one last kiss on the inner thigh. She lies still, breathing heavily, watching him remove his jeans and boxers. He is hard and ready. She licks her lips, her gaze fixed on him.

"That look on your face," he shudders.

"My turn," she says, pushing on his chest until he leans back against the driver's side door. She kneels over him, taking as much of him into her mouth as she can. She licks the tip and sucks, sliding her hand up and down his shaft. Her other hand gently caresses his balls. He thrusts his hips, finding a rhythm. She plays with his balls as he fucks her mouth. He pulls her hair hard, making her cry out in pleasure.

"If you don't stop, I'm going to go, and I'm not done with you yet," he says with effort.

He lays her back down and slides into her. She is wet from earlier but still tight. He thrusts into her, and she moves her hips in time with his. Their rhythm returns quickly. He kisses her, and she digs her nails into his firm ass. She licks her bottom lip as he kisses her neck. Her breathing quickens as he nears the edge, losing his rhythm. She cries out in pleasure just before he does. He collapses on top of her, still inside, as they catch their breath.

"Wow," she whispered, her hands resting lightly on his back.

"Yeah," he murmured, still unmoving, his head resting against her chest. She gently tilted his face toward hers and kissed him softly, a quick, tender peck. He slowly pulled out of her, the motion making her shudder once more. They lay side by side on the truck's seat, the space between them warm and comfortable.

"I definitely don't regret that," she said with a soft laugh, her voice light with contentment.

"Me either," he replied, brushing a lock of hair from her face. He pulled her on top of him, capturing her lips again in a deep kiss. After a few moments, she reached for the blanket that had fallen onto the passenger side floor and draped it over them. Once she finished, she rested her head on his chest. They lay together in the truck, silent, only the sound of the snow gently falling outside filling the space. Neither one of them wanted to break the quiet, unwilling to disturb what felt like a perfect moment. But slowly, the cold began to seep in as the snow continued to accumulate.

Elena shivered, her breath turning visible in the chill air.

"Yeah, it's getting pretty cold. Maybe we should go?" He asked, his voice soft, though he didn't want to part just yet.

She hesitated. She didn't want to leave, but at the same time, she didn't want to seem too eager or needy. She wasn't sure what to do next. Should she go home and let this night be, or should she ask him to stay a little longer? She knew if she went back to her cousin's house, sleep would be impossible. But what if she asked him to spend more time together, only for him to turn her down? She wasn't sure how she'd feel if he didn't want that.

"Elena?" he interrupted her spiraling thoughts. His voice was gentle, understanding. "Do you maybe want to come to my place? It's a little far, but I really don't want to go to sleep yet. It'd be nice to have some company."

Relief washed over her, and she laughed softly to herself. He'd made the first move again, and she couldn't help but feel grateful. "Can we drop my car off on the way?" She asked, eager for more time with him.

"Sure, I'll follow you there," he said, and they began to pull their clothes back on. She climbed out of the truck, shivering as she made her way back to her car. Once inside, she cranked the heater up to full blast, trying to warm herself from the cold air.

'Holy shit,' she thought to herself, a small smile tugging at her lips. 'I just had sex with Rodrigo—in his truck, in the middle of winter.' It all felt so surreal, but the smile wouldn't fade. What does this mean? What am I supposed to tell Jake? Am I driving too slowly? It's been forever since I've driven in snow. I hope I don't wreck my car—that would be embarrassing. What's going to happen when we get to his place? I kind of hope we have sex again, but would that ruin the first time? Oh my god, I need to stop obsessing and focus on driving in this damn blizzard.

CHAPTER 13

Rodrigo felt a wave of relaxation wash over him as he followed Elena to her cousin's house, where she was staying while she was in town. He'd imagined being with her countless times, but reality had far surpassed his daydreams. Everything about their night felt so right, as though they'd been building toward this moment for a long time. He wasn't sure what it would all mean by morning, but that was a problem for later. For now, he focused on the road and watched as her little car made its cautious way through the falling snow, each turn and careful maneuver stirring a hint of worry in him. What if she skidded on the icy surface? But she drove with patience and precision, slowly making her way to a small brick house. When they finally arrived, a flurry of nerves hit him, surprising him with their intensity. Butterflies—he'd heard Elena describe them for years, but this was the first time he really understood what she meant.

Rodrigo quickly hopped out of his truck to help her across the slick sidewalk. The icy surface was treacherous, but she managed to climb back into the truck without incident, and he walked around to his side, wondering where the night might lead. As he settled into the driver's seat and started the engine, he glanced over and noticed she was sitting on the passenger side, leaving a wide gap between them. He'd hoped she would slide over to sit next to him, close enough that he could hold her hand or drape an arm around her shoulders.

"What are you doing way over there?" he asked with a teasing smile, trying to mask his disappointment with playful banter.

Elena's thoughts were a whirlwind of uncertainty. The cozy, intimate cocoon of the truck had been comforting before, but now that they were back on the road, reality felt stark and overwhelming. She didn't know how to act around him anymore. Should she sit closer, cuddle up, and make the forty-five-minute drive to his place feel like an extension of their earlier connection? Or would that seem too forward, too presumptive, like she suddenly thought they were a couple? She wanted to keep things cool, to act like their friendship hadn't completely shifted after their kiss and everything that followed. Her mind raced through possible responses. Each one felt wrong, too forced, or just plain silly. The silence dragged on, pressing down on her chest. She had to say something—anything—before it became even more awkward.

But Rodrigo seemed to sense her struggle. He reached across the seat, his hand open and inviting. "Come on, if you sit next to me, you'll keep me warm." His voice carried just the right amount of teasing warmth, the easy confidence she envied. How did he make it all seem so effortless? She took his hand and, with as much grace as she could muster, scooted across the bench seat until their legs were touching. His arm slipped around her shoulders, pulling her close. The warmth of his touch chased away some of her doubts, and for a while, they sat in companionable silence.

Yet, predictably, her thoughts started racing again. What did all of this mean? Would things change once they reached his house? And what about Jake? Did Jake think they were exclusive? How would he react if he found out? Did it even matter? And what did it say that she was worrying about Jake right now? Should she tell Rodrigo about Jake? Would he be willing to move to California? What if they all crossed paths one day…?

"Hey, can I put on some music?" she blurted out, desperate to quiet her spiraling thoughts and find a way to stay in the moment.

"Silence too much for you?" he asked, glancing at her with a hint of curiosity.

"I'm a city girl now," she said, feigning casualness. "I'm more relaxed with a little background noise." It was a lie, but it was easier than admitting how unsettled her thoughts really were.

Without missing a beat, he reached over and handed her the auxiliary cord to the radio. "Here," he said. "You can plug this into your phone and play whatever you like."

"You're giving me control over the radio?" she asked, surprised and a bit delighted. Most people she knew would hesitate at least a little before giving up control of their music.

"Sure, I trust you," he replied, and she could see the faint outline of his smile in the dim light.

She took the cord, her fingers brushing against his for just a moment, and plugged it into her phone. As she scrolled through her music library, she felt a flicker of nostalgia. Her thumb paused over a familiar song—a track that immediately transported her back to high school.

In her mind, she was suddenly back in Rodrigo's mother's cozy office. The room always smelled like fresh-baked bread, cakes, or something equally warm and comforting. They'd spent countless hours there, listening to music on the family's computer. Rodrigo's voice echoed in her memory.

"Here, I love this song!" he'd said, grinning as "Joy to the World" by Three Dog Night began to play. He'd started dancing in his chair, carefree and full of energy.

"Me too! It's so fun!" she'd agreed, laughing at his enthusiastic moves.

"Then this is our song," he'd declared, still swaying. "It makes us both smile."

She had laughed again. "I think there are very few people who don't smile when they hear about Jeremiah the bullfrog."

"Yeah, but everyone else isn't here right now listening to it with us. So, it's our song."

"Deal." Her smile had been wide and genuine. "By the way, are you and Eddie going to the game this Friday?" She'd tried to sound casual, but she'd wanted to know if she'd see Eddie.

He'd shrugged, a hint of frustration crossing his features. "I'm supposed to take Ellie out Friday night, but honestly, I'm not feeling it."

Ellie was Rodrigo's on-again, off-again girlfriend. This latest chapter of their relationship had lasted three months. It was their third attempt at being together, and it seemed rocky at best. "You two seem to fight more than you get along," Elena had said, raising an eyebrow. She hadn't seen them truly happy in months.

"I know," he'd admitted. "I should break up with her, but it kind of sucks being single."

"You say that to your forever single friend," she'd teased, rolling her eyes.

"Yeah, but you're so good at being on your own," he'd said, his tone softening. "Don't tell anyone this, but I really don't like being alone. If I break up with Ellie, I'm afraid I'll end up single forever."

"Oh, shut up. You will not," she'd said firmly.

"How do you know?" he'd challenged.

"Here's how," she'd replied with mock seriousness. "We'll make a pact. If neither of us is married by the time we're 40, we'll marry each other." She'd grinned at the idea of having her best male friend as a backup plan. Forty felt like a lifetime away; they had nearly 25 years to figure things out.

"So, we're each other's backup plans?" he'd asked, his smile returning.

"Exactly."

He'd laughed, the sound light and easy. "Okay, deal."

The first notes of "Joy to the World" erupted from the speakers, jolting Rodrigo slightly as the upbeat melody broke the silence.

"Oh, I love this song. I haven't heard it in so long," he says, his smile widening as the familiar tune plays. "See? I knew I could trust you to play some good music," he adds, laughing softly, the memory of a hot summer day at his house and a marriage pact flashing in his mind. He doesn't bring it up, though. Discussing marriage with someone he just slept with for the first time feels... well, like a terrible idea. Especially when he doesn't see himself ever getting married.

It's funny to think about how much they've both changed. He used to be so afraid of being alone, and now he finds himself cherishing the solitude. It gives him freedom, something he never imagined he would value. He owes this newfound independence to Elena. She's the one who showed him how amazing it is to truly know yourself—to feel completely comfortable in your own company.

But what does it mean that they slept together? Has it ruined over a decade of friendship? He still doesn't know.

'Eh,' he thinks, dismissing the thought. 'I'll worry about that later.'

They rode the rest of the way in comfortable silence. Elena busied herself with scrolling through songs, occasionally landing on something unfamiliar but perfectly fitting the mood. Rodrigo chuckled to himself; music was the only time she let go of control, switching tracks on a whim. In high school, he'd driven with her often, tasked with flipping through her massive CD binder, searching for whichever tune caught her fancy. He had always loved seeing this spontaneous, almost chaotic side of her—it was such a contrast to her typically careful demeanor. Her "musical attention deficit disorder," as he jokingly called it, suited her.

They pulled up to the small adobe house he had inherited from his grandmother—a definite work-in-progress. For a brief moment, he felt self-conscious about its unfinished state.

"I'm a little surprised, but this place suits you perfectly," she remarked, her voice warm.

"You think so?" he asked, his eyes scanning the scattered construction materials in the yard.

"The way you described it, I was picturing a tiny shack in the woods. But this feels like a home. I can imagine you working on it, putting your touch on everything."

Her words made him swell with pride, though he doubted she could see his flushed cheeks in the dim light. Smiling, he helped her across the snow-dusted yard and into the house, where he had recently installed a new door. "I've been learning a lot about remodeling. I'm on a first-name basis with everyone at the hardware store now. Makes me feel pretty grown up."

She grinned, appreciating the pride he took in his work. The questions that music had temporarily quieted rushed back, though, filling her with nervous energy. What would happen once they were inside? Would they have sex again? Should they? Would it change everything? She silently berated herself: Oh my god, just stop overthinking!

"I want a very grown-up tour, then," she said, hoping her voice didn't betray her nerves.

"Right this way, my lady." He cringed internally—My lady? Seriously? He mentally kicked himself for sounding like a character in a bad historical drama. How am I going to recover from that? He led her into the house, trying to regain his composure.

'He's made all the moves tonight,' she realized, 'from texting her to meet up, to their first kiss, to bringing her back here.' Determined to take a little initiative, she stopped in the foyer, their clasped hands halting his progress. She took a deep breath, willing herself to sound confident. "You know what? I don't think I'm up for a tour right now." Her voice was husky, and her mouth felt suddenly dry.

"Oh…okay." He furrowed his brow, momentarily worried she might be too tired to continue whatever this night was turning into.

She decides to seize the moment—something she rarely does. She grabs his face and kisses him deeply, her lips lingering on his. He hesitates for only a brief second before returning the kiss. Their lips meet again, this time with an intensity that knocks things over as he pulls her toward his bedroom. They kiss with abandon, fumbling down the hall. Shoes are kicked off, jackets discarded, and with barely a break, they begin to shed the outer layers of clothing. She reaches for his pants, unbuttoning and unzipping them, her fingers working quickly. He pulls off her shirt and reaches behind to unclasp her bra.

They finally reach the bedroom, their clothing marking a trail behind them. Out of breath, they pause, coming up for air. He pulls off his shirt while she removes her pants. For a brief moment, they stand facing each other, before he grips her waist and lifts her onto the bed with confidence. She enjoys his take-charge attitude—he always seems so calm, so in control.

She lies back on the bed, gazing up at him, savoring the view as he strips off his boxers. He pulls off her thong, then climbs on top of her, kissing her deeply as his hands work to bring her pleasure again. She enjoys him taking charge, but he's already done that tonight. So, she sits up, gently pushing him back against the headboard.

He sits on his knees, and she begins to kiss him, running her hands over his body. His fingers brush through her hair as she takes her time, letting her touch him as she pleases. She caresses him with her tongue, her touch slow and teasing, and he moans softly. She pauses, looking up at him, sensing his need.

"Don't stop," he breathes, the urgency in his voice clear.

"I won't," she replies, climbing into his lap, sliding him inside her with ease. Using the headboard for leverage, she moves against him, rolling her hips with a rhythm that builds between them. She kisses him again, her lips finding his as he fondles her breasts, and the moment grows even more intense. He moans again, pulling her hair gently. She grabs his muscular arm, feeling the goosebumps rise on his skin—she knows he's close.

His reaction is enough to send her into a wave of pleasure, and they come together, a rare and beautiful moment. She stays close, keeping him inside her, savoring the intimacy as they kiss again.

"I like it when I stop overthinking," she sighs softly.

"Mmmm…" is all he can manage, his body still pulsing with the aftershocks of their shared pleasure.

She slowly pulls away, lying beside him. He collapses next to her, his arm naturally draping across her body. He sighs again, a soft, contented sound.

"Mmmm…" he murmurs once more.

"You've said that already," she laughs.

"All… can… mmmm…" he sighs, smiling contentedly.

She returned his smile, feeling a mixture of disbelief and joy. How could this night be real? Was it some vivid dream? But, did it even matter if it was? Then, as her mind was prone to do, questions began to creep in: What about tomorrow? Could they just go back to being friends? What if… No. Stop. Don't overthink. "I think I'm starting to overthink things," she admitted, her voice tight with nerves. "Can you distract me?"

"Distract…huh?" He was slipping into a blissful post-coital daze, ready to drift off into sleep, wrapped in her warmth. He could have stayed like that for hours, but her words pulled him back. Overthinking—it was a familiar issue for her. Hadn't she moved past that? "Okay, distraction…" he mumbled, fighting to stay awake.

"Yeah, so I don't ruin the night by thinking too much," she added, a touch of pleading in her tone.

"Right… let me think…" He could feel himself slipping again, exhaustion tugging at him. But he knew he couldn't let her overthinking take over. Not tonight. Elena had always been prone to spiraling thoughts. He realized with sudden clarity that he wanted to be the man who helped her through that. What could he do to pull her away from her thoughts? "Tell me how we first met," he suggested, a smile playing at the corners of his mouth.

The request surprised her. Of all the memories they shared, she struggled to recall their very first meeting. Middle school, for sure, but what was the exact moment? Did they have a class together? Did Eddie introduce them? She searched her memory, distracted by the proximity of his lips. How did we meet?

"What class do I have next?" Eddie asked, his brows furrowing slightly as if he were truly puzzled.

"It's been two weeks, Eddie. You still don't remember?" Elena replied, unable to hide a hint of exasperation mixed with amusement.

"I get confused," he said with a shrug and a disarming smile that only made him more endearing. It was easy for Elena to overlook his lack of focus, partly because she suspected it was a ploy to strike up conversations with girls. Eddie was her lab partner, so she had no choice but to engage with him to complete their assignments, even though talking wasn't her strong suit. Their partnership had grown to the point where they exchanged greetings whenever they crossed paths in the courtyard. She would have been genuinely surprised if he didn't already know they had science together after lunch. *"We have science next,"* she said, a hint of a nervous grin tugging at her lips.

"Where is that again?" he asked, a glint in his eyes suggesting he was enjoying this game more than he let on.

"Come on, I'll walk you there."

Before they could move, a voice called out from behind Elena. *"Eddie, you going to football practice tonight?"*

"Yeah, are you?" Eddie turned to respond, momentarily forgetting their conversation.

"Nah. Can you let Coach know I have a doctor's appointment?" the voice replied, casual but with a hint of urgency.

"Sure thing," Eddie said easily. The boy who spoke stepped into Elena's line of sight.

"Hey, Elena," he greeted her, his tone friendly and familiar. She recognized him vaguely but was surprised he knew her name.

"Hi," she responded softly, feeling a flush of shyness. New people always put her on edge.

"You know Elena?" Eddie asked, glancing back and forth between them.

"Yeah, we've got math together," Rodrigo replied, flashing a warm smile.

Elena's stomach twisted. She recognized him too but hadn't worked up the nerve to speak to him before now. He had noticed her, remembered her name, and she felt a pang of *guilt. Social interactions had never been her strong suit. The only reason she talked to Eddie as much as she did was because he always took the lead. It was clear she needed to improve her people skills.*

Elena recounted to Rodrigo the story of how they had first met. She felt a bit foolish reflecting on how shy she had been back in middle school. These days, she still sometimes appeared shy, standoffish, aloof, or even rude—depending on who you asked—but her behavior wasn't due to fear as it had been years ago. Now, she preferred to observe and assess social situations carefully before figuring out the best way to make new connections.

"That's how we met, huh?" Rodrigo said, his voice carrying a teasing edge.

"Wait, was that not the day we met?" she asked, suddenly second-guessing herself.

"Um…" he hesitated, clearly stalling for dramatic effect.

"It wasn't?!" Elena's face flushed with embarrassment. The thought that she had misremembered such a significant moment with someone so important to her made her cringe.

"No, it wasn't," he said, smiling playfully. "But hey, thinking about it made you stop overthinking everything else for a second, right?"

"Maybe for a minute," she admitted, a small smile tugging at her lips. "But now you've got me scrambling to remember when we actually did meet."

"Don't worry about it. It's cool," Rodrigo said with a mock-serious look. "I guess I'm just not as important to you as you are to me. You should probably leave."

"Ugh, I hate you," she replied, giving him a playful shove, their laughter breaking the momentary tension.

"I seriously can't believe you thought that was our first meeting."

"Then why don't you tell me the real story?" she challenged. "Jog my memory."

"Nope."

"Why not?" she asked, sounding almost offended.

"If I don't tell you, you'll obsess over it. You'll think about it so much you won't have time to overthink what this night actually means."

He had a point, though his teasing only made her more curious. "Okay, since you brought it up—what does this night mean, then?"

"It means that…that…shit, I have no idea," he said, suddenly feeling butterflies in his stomach, jolting him back to reality from their lingering closeness.

"I really don't want to lose you as a friend," she said earnestly.

"Same. But I don't do long-distance relationships, and neither do you."

"Yeah, you're right. So…what does that make us? Just two friends who had sex?"

"I guess that's all we can be," Rodrigo replied, his voice tinged with reluctance. "Neither of us are going anywhere anytime soon, right?"

"I'm not. I've got school and my internship—I love it, and I'm good at it. You've got this house, your family, your school." She sighed deeply. "Still, it feels like we're more than just friends."

"Maybe," he conceded, "but…"

"But…"

"Here's what I know," he continued more seriously. "You've been one of my best friends since seventh grade. I want you to keep being one of my best friends. I like hanging out with you—and I *really* like seeing you naked and doing dirty things with you. If we can keep doing that? Awesome. But even if we can't, I still need us to be friends."

"Agreed," Elena said, letting the silence linger for a moment before breaking it with a mischievous glint in her eyes. "You know, we have seen each other naked before."

"What?! No way! If that happened, I would definitely remember!" he exclaimed, feigning shock.

It was the summer before their junior year of high school, and most of their friend group was actually in town. While they had access to a few cars, their lack of money for gas kept them tethered to their small town, unable to make the drive to the nearby city. With no parties happening that night and two hours already spent lounging around at the park, they decided to drive aimlessly while brainstorming what to do next. Lily took the wheel since it was her car.

Mary sat in the passenger seat, as always. She loved being in charge of the music and absolutely despised cramming into the back seat with three others. That left Rodrigo, Elena, Eddie, and April squeezed into the back. Eddie ended up in the middle, sandwiched between the two girls, with Rodrigo to Elena's left. Fortunately, all four were slim enough that the cramped arrangement wasn't as bad as it could have been.

"How about we go to the music store?" Mary suggested, adjusting the radio dial.

"They close in like ten minutes," Elena replied, glancing at the clock.

"We could go back to my place and watch a movie or something," Lily offered casually.

"Maybe," April said hesitantly. Her black hair now sported two thick pink streaks—a rebellious summer choice made possible by the school's ban on unnatural colors during the academic year.

"We could play Yellow Light," Eddie said suddenly.

"Yellow Light?" Lily echoed, her curiosity piqued.

"It's simple," Eddie explained with a grin. *"Whenever we hit a yellow traffic light, everyone has to shout 'Yellow Light!' The last person to say it loses a piece of clothing."*

"That's not a real game," Mary protested, her unease evident.

"It totally is!" Rodrigo jumped in. *"Eddie's older brother used to play it all the time."*

"Well, unless someone has a better idea, we might as well give it a shot," Elena said, trying to sound confident even as her stomach churned with nerves.

"I'm in," April said, determined to outshine Elena as the group's most daring member.

"Sure," Lily agreed easily.

"I guess I'm in, too…" Mary conceded reluctantly, her lack of enthusiasm apparent to everyone.

"Okay, but if you lose everything, you can't back out," Eddie declared, a mischievous sparkle in his eyes. Elena had a strong suspicion that he was quite pleased to be flanked by two girls.

For the next half-hour, they drove around, yelling out "Yellow Light" whenever necessary. As it turned out, the boys were losing. All of them had shed their shoes and socks, though the girls' losses were more severe since they wore flip-flops. April, Mary, and Elena had already lost their shirts, while Lily remained victorious, having only lost her shoes. Meanwhile, Rodrigo and Eddie were down to just their boxers. Approaching another traffic light, Lily slowed the car, willing it to turn yellow. As if on cue, it did, and Eddie was the last to yell.

"Damn it!" he shouted, frustrated.

"You lost at your own game!" Elena laughed, unable to resist poking fun.

"Dude, nobody wants to see your junk," Rodrigo snickered, relieved he wasn't the one in Eddie's predicament.

"I'm not getting naked," Eddie said defiantly.

"You have to. It's your rule," Lily pointed out, unable to hide her amusement.

"Yeah, remember? 'You lose, you get naked,'" Elena quoted back, grinning.

"What if we all go to the park and get naked together?" April suggested with a defiant smile, clearly eager to prove she was the boldest.

"Why?" Mary asked, bewildered.

"To make Eddie feel less embarrassed, obviously," Rodrigo laughed.

"Fine. I'll get naked if everyone else does," Eddie conceded.

They drove to a small park near Eddie's house, tucked behind their high school. It featured a modest play structure with slides, ladders, and a bridge, all surrounded by patchy grass. The park had always been their refuge—a place to talk, play childhood games, or seek solace on difficult days. As Lily parked, a tense silence fell over the group.

"Okay, here we are. Time to get naked, I guess," Lily said, cutting the engine.

"No peeking," Mary reminded everyone quickly.

They all agreed. No peeking.

"We are such a weird group of friends," Elena muttered, starting to unbutton her shorts.

Nervous giggles echoed as they each stripped down, covering themselves as much as possible. Elena stole a quick glance at the boys and blushed, not disappointed by what she saw.

"This is exactly why no one should live in a small town," Elena joked, trying to ease the tension.

"Oh man, I totally forgot all about that crazy night. I can't believe you actually peeked after you promised you wouldn't," Rodrigo said, chuckling as he remembered that evening and the sneaky glances he stole at her too.

"Wait a minute, are you telling me you didn't peek at me? Come on, I could feel your bare skin against mine. You must have taken a look," she teased, raising an eyebrow.

"I would never do such a thing. I'm a perfect gentleman, you know," Rodrigo replied with a mischievous grin.

"Yeah, right. You were a sixteen-year-old boy with raging hormones. You totally peeked, and we both know it!"

"Okay, okay, you got me. I peeked," Rodrigo admitted, throwing his hands up in mock surrender. "But can you really blame me? There I was, stark naked, sitting next to a gorgeous girl who was equally undressed. It was too tempting to resist."

"You thought I was gorgeous?" she asked, her voice softening with surprise.

"Well, yeah, of course. But you were into Eddie back then, and I had this silly rule about not crushing on my friends. It seemed like a good idea at the time," he explained, shaking his head at his younger self's logic.

"I'm really glad you decided to change that ridiculous policy," she said, her eyes twinkling with affection.

"Me too," he replied softly. He leaned in and kissed her tenderly, then gently pulled her on top of him again, savoring the feeling of her body against his.

"You want to go again?" she asked, feeling a familiar excitement building inside her.

"Fuck yes," he growled playfully. "Thinking about naked you in high school reminded me that I have the real deal now, all to myself." He guided her hand to his growing arousal, his breath catching in his throat.

"Damn, boy," she whispered, her voice husky with desire. Slowly, teasingly, she positioned herself and slid him inside her for the third time that night, both of them sighing with pleasure as they connected once again.

After they finished, they lay side by side, gazing up at the ceiling, each lost in their own thoughts. Rodrigo was trying to muster the energy to move his legs enough to go to the kitchen and fetch some water. Elena, on the other hand, was wondering if she had a hairbrush stashed away in her purse to tame the wild mess her hair had undoubtedly become after three passionate rounds of lovemaking.

"Thirsty," Rodrigo finally mumbled, pushing himself up with some effort to head towards the kitchen.

Elena watched him go, savoring the view of his tight, naked ass. "Yum," she whispered appreciatively. Sitting up, she began to attempt combing her fingers through her tangled locks, trying to work out some of the knots that had formed.

For the first time, she took a moment to really look around his room. It was a bit messy, with clothes scattered on the floor, a few well-worn books piled on the nightstand, and some boxes waiting to be unpacked stacked in the corner. His laptop sat on the dresser, as though he had been working on it in bed earlier. Despite the clutter, it felt like a home – lived-in and comfortable.

As Elena continued to comb through her hair, she didn't notice Rodrigo watching her from the bedroom doorway, a soft smile playing on his lips.

"Hey gorgeous," he said, startling her slightly. She looked absolutely stunning sitting naked in his bed, and he took a mental snapshot of the image, wanting to remember this moment forever. "Here, rehydrate," he added, handing her a glass of cold water.

Elena took a small sip before her thirst hit her full force, and she ended up gulping down half the glass before coming up for air. "Wow, I didn't realize how thirsty I was. Thanks," she said gratefully.

"Sure thing," Rodrigo replied, climbing back into bed and immediately wrapping his arm around her. Elena instinctively cuddled up next to him, fitting perfectly into the crook of his arm as if they were two puzzle pieces meant to be together.

"What do you want to be when you grow up?" Elena asked, her voice soft and curious.

Rodrigo chuckled, "When I grow up? Aren't I grown up now?"

"You know what I mean," Elena said, playfully poking his side. "When you're done with school and have to venture out into the big, bad real world."

"Well," Rodrigo began, his tone becoming more serious, "after I graduate, I want to apply to grad school and get my master's in environmental engineering. I dream of traveling around the world, helping people, especially when it comes to water and air pollution control. I want to save lives by saving the environment, you know? What about you?"

"After I get my license, I would love to have my own practice or work in community mental health," Elena replied thoughtfully. "I want to help people who can afford therapy so that I can also assist those who can't. And, well... I'd also like to get married and have a family someday. Do you ever think about having a family?"

As soon as the words left her mouth, Elena regretted them. Now he was going to think she was hinting at wanting to marry him and have his babies. Damnit, this was getting too serious too fast.

"I don't think I'll ever get married," Rodrigo said, his brow furrowing slightly. "I don't really see the point, it's just a piece of paper. Why do I need to prove that I love a woman by telling the government about it? And as far as having kids? There are already over 7 billion people on this planet, and it can't sustain that kind of population. I might consider adoption someday, but probably not having my own biological children. Plus, I want to travel the world for work. That kind of lifestyle wouldn't really be compatible with a wife and kids."

Noticing the disappointment flickering across Elena's face, Rodrigo decided he needed to change the subject. "Hey, do you remember that night after one of the football games?" he asked, his tone lightening.

Elena, grateful for the shift in conversation, replied, "Which night after a football game? There were, like, a million of them."

"Like, for real?" Rodrigo teased, putting on his best Valley Girl voice.

Elena pinched his side playfully. "Oh, shut up, butthead. Tell me about the specific night you're thinking of."

Rodrigo's mind drifted back to that night, the memory as clear as if it had happened yesterday. He had been waiting for Eddie to finish showering after the football game. That was the downside of getting rides from someone on the football team – you had to hang around for them after everyone else had left.

"You ready?" Eddie had asked as he left the locker room, his hair still damp from the shower.

"Yeah, but I'm not ready to go home yet," Rodrigo had replied, feeling restless.

"Me neither. Want to go to the park?"

"Sure."

The two boys had walked to Eddie's truck, where he tossed his football gear into the bed before they climbed inside. The park was in the neighborhood behind their high school, so they didn't have far to travel. In less than five minutes, they were there, eagerly jumping out of the truck and walking across the dewy grass towards the play structure surrounded by sand.

Using one of the ladders attached to the structure, they climbed up and sat on the bridge that connected the two halves of the playground. For a few minutes, they sat in comfortable silence, enjoying the cool night air.

Finally, Rodrigo broke the quiet. "I saw Elena and Lily at the game."

"Oh yeah?" Eddie replied, his interest piqued.

"Yeah, you know Elena has a crush on you, right?" Rodrigo said, immediately regretting his words. He and Elena had talked about her feelings for Eddie, but he wasn't, technically, supposed to say anything.

"She does?" Eddie asked, sounding intrigued.

"Yeah, she told me," Rodrigo admitted, figuring he might as well be honest now that he'd let it slip.

"That's cool, but I wouldn't want to get in your way," Eddie said, his tone careful.

"What do you mean?"

"I don't know. You guys hang out all the time. It kinda seemed like maybe you two had a thing going on."

"You're crazy," Rodrigo scoffed, though a small part of him wondered if there was any truth to Eddie's words.

"Whatever you say, man," Eddie shrugged. "For me, though, she's just a friend. A hot friend, but still just a friend."

They fell quiet again, each lost in their own thoughts. Rodrigo found himself pondering Eddie's words. Did he like Elena as more than a friend? He'd never really considered it before, but now the idea was planted in his mind.

As they sat in contemplative silence, headlights suddenly swung past them as a car pulled into the parking lot.

"I hope that's not the cops," Eddie said, tension creeping into his voice. They had been chased out of the park once before by the police, since technically the park was closed after dark.

Two figures crossed the grass, and as they reached the sand, Rodrigo could make out that it was Lily and Elena.

"This is crazy," Lily said, her voice carrying in the still night air.

"I thought you guys were going home after the game," Elena said, surprise evident in her tone. Rodrigo had told them as much when he ran into them earlier.

"We were going to, but neither of us was tired yet," Eddie explained with a shrug.

"Cool," Lily said as she and Elena climbed onto the structure and sat down next to the boys on the bridge. Elena had brought along the big blanket that she always carried in her car, and the four of them spread it across their laps to ward off the chill of the November air.

As they huddled together under the blanket, Rodrigo couldn't help but feel a spark of something – excitement, nervousness, or maybe a mix of both – as Elena's arm pressed against his. He wondered if Eddie was on to something about his feelings for Elena.

"Oh yeah, I totally remember that night. It was so weird that we ran into you guys there. Oh, and by the way, thanks a lot for spilling the beans to Eddie about my crush!" Elena said, playfully nudging Rodrigo's side.

"Come on, you know you secretly wanted me to tell him," Rodrigo teased back, a mischievous glint in his eye.

"Maybe, but it didn't matter apparently," Elena sighed dramatically. "So, he thought you liked me back then, huh?"

"I guess so," Rodrigo shrugged, trying to appear nonchalant.

"Did you?" Elena asked, her voice softening with curiosity.

He paused for a moment, his brow furrowing in thought. "I might have. I don't know. I really tried not to think of you like that. You liked Eddie. What chance did I have?"

"I guess we'll never know," she chuckled, leaning in to plant a soft kiss on his lips.

They continued to talk like that for the rest of the night, their words flowing easily between them. They reminisced about old times and talked about their hopes for the future. Whenever the topic of their present situation came up, they would skillfully avoid a deeper conversation by losing themselves in each other's embrace. Both realized that this was a form of denial, but neither was willing to change the status quo, too afraid of shattering the delicate balance they had found.

As the first rays of sunlight began to peek through the windows, they found themselves in his living room, wrapped in a big, cozy blanket. They sat in comfortable silence, holding one another close as they gazed out of a large window, watching the sun rise above the snow-covered landscape.

For once, Elena wasn't overthinking everything. The sunrise was too breathtaking to allow her mind to wander. The sky transformed into a canvas of vibrant oranges, soft pinks, and warm yellows as the sun slowly emerged over the horizon. The pristine snow dimly reflected the colors in the sky, creating a magical, shimmering effect. The world around them was quiet – the kind of profound silence that only comes in the middle of nowhere when snow blankets the ground.

After the sun had fully risen, they dressed without exchanging a word. There was no tension in the air, just a calm serenity that enveloped them both. They didn't want to break the spell of their quiet world, but they knew that Elena had to return to say her goodbyes and prepare for her drive back to California the next morning.

Still wordless, they walked hand in hand across the melting snow to his truck. Rodrigo helped Elena into the cab, and she immediately slid to the middle seat, wanting to be as close to him as possible. Once he started the truck and put it into gear, he slipped his arm around her, pulling her close.

Rodrigo expected Elena to plug in her phone and start some music, as she usually did, but they remained in comfortable silence during the drive back to the city. Elena wanted to remain in their bubble for as long as she could. She committed every detail to memory: the feel of him next to her, the warmth radiating from his body, the steady rhythm of his breath, and his familiar, comforting scent. She didn't know if they would ever share a moment like this again.

Rodrigo, too, was savoring every second. He soaked up her essence – the calmness she radiated that would make her an excellent therapist someday, the silky feel of her hair against his cheek, the comforting weight of her body leaning into his, and the faint, floral scent of her perfume that lingered in the air.

They reached her cousin's house all too soon. Rodrigo parked the truck across the street and turned off the engine. Neither moved for a moment, both trying to think of a way to prolong their goodbye. Eventually, he gave up, got out of the truck, and walked around to the passenger door to help her out.

"So, last night was fun," Elena said with a nervous laugh as she took his hand, carefully stepping onto the melting snow.

"That's what you're going with?" Rodrigo chuckled, raising an eyebrow.

"What else should I say? That last night was absolutely amazing and it really sucks that I have to go back to my house a thousand miles away because it would be incredible to have more nights like that?" Elena blurted out, her words tumbling over each other.

"That works," Rodrigo said softly. "You're an awesome friend, you know that?"

"You're not so bad yourself," Elena replied, her voice warm. "I better get inside. My ten-year-old cousin is already going to judge me for being gone all night."

"He judges you?" Rodrigo asked, surprised.

"Well, he acts like an overprotective parent sometimes," Elena explained with a laugh. "He'll say, 'Where were you last night?' and even though I think he's trying to be funny, it still feels a little bit like I might get in trouble."

"If he's watching, then he won't like this," Rodrigo said mischievously as he put his arm around her waist and kissed her deeply, with more passion than a friend should ever use. Elena reluctantly broke away from the kiss before they got carried away. "I better go," she said, her voice slightly breathless.

"Okay. I'll talk to you later, dear friend?" Rodrigo asked, his tone playful but with a hint of uncertainty.

"If you really are my friend, then you better talk to me later," Elena replied as she started to cross the street to her cousin's house.

"Wait!" Rodrigo called out suddenly, not ready to let her go.

She turned around, a mix of hope and curiosity on her face. "Yeah?"

Rodrigo scrambled to think of something to say, not wanting to look like a lovesick fool. "When are you coming back?"

Elena laughed, relief evident in her voice. "Christmas, obviously!" She turned back towards the house and carefully made her way across the icy patches in the shade, trying to ignore the flutter of excitement in her chest at the thought of seeing him again in just a month.

"See you then, friend!" Rodrigo called out.

"See you then, friend," Elena replied without turning, a small smile playing on her lips.

"You're more than a friend," Rodrigo whispered to himself as he watched her walk away.

"We're more than friends," Elena murmured under her breath as she walked through the door into the warmth of her cousin's house. As soon as she shut the front door, she heard a familiar voice call out,

"Where were you all night?" from down the hall. She couldn't help but laugh at her younger cousin for being so predictable.

CHAPTER 14

December 2013

"How was your Thanksgiving?" Elena's friend, Emilia asked as she plopped her well-worn backpack down on the table in the cozy coffee shop where they met each week to study. Emilia was definitely a free spirit, a whirlwind of energy and authenticity. She knew exactly who she was and never apologized for it. Elena always described her as a modern-day hippie with a Latina twist.

Emi's beautiful brown skin seemed to glow with life, and her voice could easily fill a room. They had met as undergrads in New Mexico and had both ended up in similar graduate programs in the Bay Area. To Elena, Emi was like the sister she never had – someone she could be completely honest with, call out on her bullshit, and trust to do the same for her when needed.

Elena's cheeks immediately flushed a deep pink, and a smile she couldn't suppress spread across her face.

"OMG! What happened?!" Emi exclaimed, her eyes widening with excitement, hoping Elena would dish out a juicy story.

"Nothing really," Elena mumbled, suddenly unsure if she wanted to share her time with Rodrigo. For some reason, she worried that talking about it might tarnish the magical moments they had spent together.

"Come on, girl. I've known you long enough to know when something's up with you," Emi pressed, leaning in closer. "And you sound so coy – I've never heard you be coy before. I didn't think it was something you were even capable of doing, if I'm being honest. I've also never seen you smile like that. You're practically glowing like a Christmas tree with that smile. Something happened. Something big."

Emi's voice, as usual, carried throughout the entire coffee shop. This wasn't unusual – Elena was pretty sure Emi had been this loud since birth.

"Okay, yeah, something kind of happened," Elena admitted, her voice barely above a whisper. "But I don't know if I want to tell anyone about it, and I definitely don't want to broadcast it to the entire coffee shop, so please, keep it down."

"I'm not yelling," Emi protested, "my voice just happens to project well. Why wouldn't you want to tell me?" She made a conscious effort to lower her voice, leaning in even closer.

"I don't know. It's like it's sealed in this perfect little bubble, and if I talk about it, it won't be as special anymore," Elena explained, her fingers nervously tracing the rim of her coffee cup.

"Hmm, okay," Emi said, her curiosity piqued but respecting her friend's hesitation. "If you don't want to tell me, I won't push." She resigned herself to never hearing about whatever happened to Elena over the Thanksgiving break. Opening up her laptop, she put in her earbuds and turned up her music. She knew Elena well enough to know that given enough space, she'd eventually open up.

Elena mirrored her friend's actions, putting in her own earbuds and starting up her music. She tried to focus on the article in front of her, but her mind kept wandering back to Rodrigo. She wondered what he was doing, if he was thinking of her too. After a few minutes of futile attempts to concentrate, she realized she wouldn't be able to focus until she either talked to Rodrigo or talked about her time with him.

With a deep breath, Elena pulled out her earbuds. Emi, who had been waiting for this moment, immediately followed suit without hesitation.

"Okay, so you remember me telling you about my friend Rodrigo?" Elena began, her voice soft but determined.

"Yeah, the guy you've been friends with for like forever, and you've been flirting with through text since you and Alex broke up?" Emi replied, barely containing her excitement.

"Exactly. Well, he and I hung out over the break…"

"And?" Emi interjected, too eager to hear more.

"I'm getting to that," Elena said with a hint of annoyance. "So, we met at the airport viewing area. We used to hang out there all the time as kids and talk about life and watch the stars and stuff. Anyway, we met there and sat in his truck talking for a while, and then it started to snow."

"Oh man, that sounds kind of romantic," Emi sighed dreamily.

"Anyway," Elena continued, "it started to snow, and then Jake called…"

"Did you answer it?" Emi interrupted again, her eyebrows raised.

"No, Jake isn't my boyfriend, and Rodrigo and I were having a moment or something," Elena explained, a small smile playing on her lips.

"Okay, so Jake called, you ignored it, and then?" Emi prompted, leaning forward in anticipation.

"Rodrigo and I started making out, and one thing led to another…" Elena trailed off, her cheeks flushing again.

"You guys smashed?!" Emi exclaimed, her voice echoing through the coffee shop.

Elena cringed, looking around nervously. "Ugh, I hate when people call having sex 'smashing.' I know that's what it is, but it sounds so impersonal. Also, thanks for making everyone in the room pay extra attention to our conversation now," she added, noticing people trying (and failing) not to look at their table.

"So, you guys didn't have sex?" Emi asked, making an effort to lower her voice again.

"I'm a lady. A lady doesn't discuss those sorts of things," Elena replied, her attempt at being coy betrayed by the sparkle in her eyes.

"So, you guys totally did it," Emi stated matter-of-factly.

Elena's resolve crumbled. "Several times, yes," she admitted with a shy smile.

"Nice!" Emi said with emphasis, giving Elena a playful nudge.

"Ugh… anyway… so we did it in his truck, and…"

"How was it?" Emi interrupted once more, unable to contain her curiosity.

Elena's smile widened, her eyes taking on a dreamy quality. "It was the best sex I've ever had."

"Wow," Emi drawled, elongating the 'ow' with a mix of surprise and admiration.

"I know. And after, we went back to his place and talked and..." Elena paused, struggling to find the right words. 'Made love' sounded too cheesy, 'fucked' felt too harsh, and she absolutely refused to say they 'smashed'. Finally, she settled on, "well, you know... we connected all night. And then we watched the sun rise together."

"That sounds incredibly romantic," Emi said, a hint of envy in her voice.

"It really was an amazing night," Elena replied, her eyes taking on a dreamy quality as she smiled wistfully.

"So, are you two like, dating now?" Emi probed, leaning in closer.

Elena's smile faltered slightly. "No. Neither of us is willing to do long distance. We're just friends," she said with forced determination.

"Yeah, right. You're just friends that had a lot of sex and amazing conversation all night long," Emi scoffed. "You know, if this was a movie, you two would totally fall in love," she added, only half-joking.

"Good thing this isn't a movie, huh?" Elena retorted, trying to brush off the comment.

"Have you talked since?" Emi pressed, not quite ready to let the subject drop.

"Every day," Elena admitted.

Emi raised her eyebrows at her friend, clearly skeptical about the whole 'just friends' situation.

"We've always talked every day, or at least almost every day," Elena defended. "Nothing has changed!"

Sensing her friend's discomfort, Emi decided to change the subject. "Well, I'm glad you had fun for Thanksgiving. I was interrogated by seven different relatives about why I was still single. My Tia Isa even tried to set me up with her assistant teacher."

"So, why not go out with the assistant teacher?" Elena asked, grateful for the shift in conversation.

"She's 47," Emi deadpanned.

Elena burst out laughing, once again drawing the attention of the other café patrons. "I'm sorry, dude. At least your family is trying to be helpful," she said, wiping tears of mirth from her eyes.

"I guess so," Emi replied, rolling her eyes with a snicker.

Meanwhile, 1000 miles away, Rodrigo passed the pipe and lighter over to his friend Chris. Chris had recently broken up with yet another girlfriend and had called Rodrigo to help him move into the denial stage of grief by smoking weed. Rodrigo was more than happy to oblige.

Chris took a long hit and passed everything back to Rodrigo. "How was Thanksgiving, man?" he asked, his voice slightly strained as he held in the smoke.

Rodrigo smiled to himself, memories of Elena flooding his mind. "It was good," he replied simply.

"Yeah, mine too. I scored a new TV on Black Friday," Chris said, finally exhaling.

"Nice," Rodrigo mumbled as he grabbed a handful of cereal from the box sitting between them and shoved it in his mouth with a satisfying crunch.

"What'd you do?" Chris asked, reaching for the cereal box himself.

"I hung out with Elena," Rodrigo replied, trying to sound casual.

Chris's eyes lit up with interest. "That's cool. Did you get it in?"

Rodrigo's smile widened as he took another hit and handed the pipe and lighter back to Chris. "Yep," he said, letting the smoke curl out of his mouth.

"Nice," Chris nodded approvingly.

A few weeks later, Elena found herself pulling out of her apartment complex parking lot, ready to embark on her

drive back to New Mexico for Christmas. She always
drove, claiming it was because flying was too expensive
and leaving her two dogs in a pet hotel was a hassle. But in
truth, she loved being on the open road with nothing but her
music, her thoughts, and the stars for company.

As she headed towards the freeway, her mind began to race.
Would she see Rodrigo again? If they did meet up, what
would happen between them? Could it possibly be as
magical as it was at Thanksgiving, or was that just a one-
time fluke? And what about Jake? Should she take the
initiative and make plans with Rodrigo, or wait for him to
say something?

She pondered this last question longer than the others. If
she left it up to Rodrigo to make plans... well, he wasn't
exactly known for his planning skills. He was more of a
spur-of-the-moment kind of guy. So, she could spend the
week freaking out, wondering if he was going to suggest
hanging out, or she could take matters into her own hands.

Decision made, she decided to call him on her way out of
town. It was late, but he was usually up at this hour
anyway. One ring... what if he didn't answer? Two rings...

God, I love driving at night. Three rings... "Hello?" a distracted Rodrigo answered.

"Oh, hey. Sorry to call so late, are you busy?" Elena asked, suddenly feeling nervous.

"Hey Elena. I'm never too busy to talk to you," Rodrigo replied, his voice warm.

"Stop using bad lines on me," Elena laughed. "You sound like you're at a party or something."

"Yeah, Chris wanted to get a drink, so I came to town. We're at some bar downtown, I didn't pay attention to the name. What's up?"

"Nothing really, I'm just starting my drive to New Mexico," Elena said, trying to sound casual.

"What? It's already nine o'clock there, why are you leaving so late?" Rodrigo asked, concern evident in his voice despite his attempt to hide it.

"I like driving at night. Then it's just me, the stars, and the truckers. The roads feel safer somehow. I know it's weird, but it's my favorite time to drive through the desert," Elena explained, a smile in her voice.

"So, are you calling so that I keep you from falling asleep on the road?" Rodrigo teased.

"Not yet, I'm wide awake now. I was actually calling because I was wondering what you were doing for New Year's Eve." Elena held her breath, hoping he was free.

"I don't have any definite plans yet. Chris wanted to hang out, but I could bail on him for the right reasons," Rodrigo laughed, thinking to himself that she was the perfect reason to bail on Chris.

"Well, maybe we can hang out. My friend is throwing a party at nine. Maybe we can get together before and grab dinner and then go to the party?" Elena suggested, her heart racing. This is not a date, she kept repeating to herself. It couldn't be a date. He's your best friend. Your best friend that you had a lot of sex with a month ago. She shook her head, trying to dispel the butterflies in her stomach.

"Yeah, that sounds pretty awesome. I'll pick you up at your cousin's at..." Rodrigo paused, thinking for a moment, "seven?"

"That works for me. I'll see you then," Elena replied, excitement bubbling up inside her at the prospect of seeing Rodrigo again.

"Yeah, and if you get sleepy, don't call me. I'll probably be in bed dreaming," Rodrigo joked.

"You're hilarious," Elena laughed.

"But seriously, if you get tired, call me. I'll annoy you so much that I'll keep you awake," he added, his tone more serious.

"Cool. Have fun with Chris," Elena said, still chuckling.

"Drive safe," Rodrigo replied before hanging up.

As he put his phone down, Rodrigo's mind was racing. New Year's Eve. What the fuck was this going to look like?

"Who was that?" Chris asked as he handed Rodrigo a shot of tequila.

"Elena," Rodrigo replied, downing the shot without flinching. They were sitting at the bar, mostly because they wanted easy access to the drinks. Plus, it was a Monday night, so the bar was relatively quiet. There were a few people playing pool at a couple of the tables spread throughout the dimly lit room.

"Another round?" the bartender asked. She was around their age, with dark brown hair in a stylish pixie cut, light blue eyes that sparkled in the low light, and a sleeve tattoo on her left arm. Rodrigo couldn't make out all the details of the tattoo, but he could swear he saw a monkey riding a walrus.

"Sure, you buying?" Chris asked the bartender, a mischievous glint in his eye.

"Only if you're packing vag in those pants. I don't do dick," she retorted with a hearty laugh as she poured two more shots, her hands moving with practiced ease.

Rodrigo couldn't help but chuckle at his friend's expense. "Hitting on a lesbian again, Chris? How many is that now? Three in the last week?"

"Shut up, dude!" Chris protested, his face reddening slightly. "I haven't been hitting on a bunch of lesbians!"

"Whatever you say, man," Rodrigo said, shaking his head and laughing some more. He had to admit, Chris's obliviousness was pretty entertaining.

"You're a dick," Chris grumbled stoically as he downed his own shot and promptly ordered two more, determined to drown his embarrassment.

"So, why did Elena call?" Chris asked, eager to change the subject. "Does she want the D?"

Rodrigo's smile faded, replaced by a look of annoyance. "Don't be an asshole," he said, his tone sharper than before. "She's coming back to town and wants to hang out."

"Yeah, 'hang out,' I'm sure," Chris said with a knowing smirk. "You gonna get it in again?"

Rodrigo sighed, feeling a mix of frustration and discomfort. "Dude, it's not like that."

"What's it like then?" Chris pressed, genuinely curious.

"We're friends, that's all," Rodrigo insisted, though even he wasn't entirely convinced by his own words.

Chris scoffed. "You guys fucked. Girls don't know how to just be friends once the pussy is involved."

"You have a foul mouth," the bartender interjected as she set their third round of shots in front of them, her disapproval evident in her tone.

"You love it," Chris said to her, winking playfully.

The bartender rolled her eyes. "You're just lucky I like getting tips, and the drunker you are, the looser your wallet," she quipped.

Feeling embarrassed by his friend's behavior, Rodrigo turned to the bartender. "I'm sorry for his behavior. He's been rejected one too many times lately. I promise, he'll tip well," he said, hoping to smooth things over.

"He better," she replied with a pointed look at Chris. She stayed close, wiping down the bar, her curiosity seemingly piqued by Rodrigo's conversation about Elena.

"Anyway, we are just friends, but... I don't know. Getting it in again would be nice," Rodrigo admitted, though it felt like an understatement. In reality, he couldn't stop thinking about Elena. Her laugh, her smile, the way she made him feel when they were together. "I want to make this visit a good one," he added, mostly to himself.

Rodrigo realized that Chris was probably the wrong person to be talking to about this. His friend wasn't exactly known for his emotional intelligence or sensitivity. Not that Rodrigo had feelings to discuss. He and Elena were just friends after all. At least, that's what he kept telling himself.

"Well, she had a good time fucking you the last time she was here, right?" Chris said, his words slightly slurred from the alcohol.

Rodrigo sighed inwardly. Chris really wasn't good at understanding the complexities of relationships. "Of course she did. You're talking to the king," Rodrigo replied, giving Chris the macho response he expected to hear.

As the words left his mouth, Rodrigo felt a pang of frustration. Sometimes it sucked being a guy, always having to maintain this facade of emotional detachment. All he really wanted was to talk about how he was feeling about Elena. Sure, the sex had been amazing, but the conversations they shared were even better. Just spending time together felt right in a way he couldn't quite explain.

He wanted to confide in someone about how Elena was one of his best friends, but after Thanksgiving, things had shifted. He longed to express his fears about potentially losing her as a friend if he pursued something more, and how he felt that if he didn't take that risk, he might regret it forever.

But here he was, a guy in a bar with his buddy, and guys weren't "supposed" to talk about feelings. So instead, he made jokes and sexual innuendos, all while his heart and mind were a whirlwind of conflicting emotions.

The bartender, her curiosity piqued, listened intently to Chris and Rodrigo's conversation about Elena and Rodrigo's potential love life while she expertly poured drinks and tidied the bar. Her eyes occasionally darted between the two men, picking up on the subtle nuances in their interaction.

Suddenly, Chris's phone buzzed. He checked it quickly, his eyes lighting up. "Hey, I just got a text about a party back home. Wanna go?" he asked, looking up at Rodrigo.

"In Los?" Rodrigo asked, using the familiar shortened version of their hometown's name. The nickname brought a flood of memories rushing back.

"Yeah, Dave's picking me up in a minute. You in, or what?" Chris was still glued to his phone, thumbs flying as he continued his text conversation with Dave.

Rodrigo hesitated, weighing his options. "Naw, I think I'm going to have one more drink and head home," he decided. He didn't want to drink too much, just in case Elena called and needed someone to keep her awake during her long, solitary drive.

"Lame," Chris scoffed as he tossed some cash down on the bar. "Later, loser."

Before Chris could leave, Rodrigo grabbed his arm, stopping him. He quickly counted out the money Chris had left for the bartender. Only after he was satisfied that the tip was sufficiently generous did he release his grip. "Later, man," Rodrigo said, giving a small nod as he signaled for the bartender.

"What can I get you?" she asked, approaching with a friendly smile.

"Can I get a Guinness and a water," he said with a weary sigh, the weight of his thoughts evident in his voice.

The bartender's smile widened, a glint of intrigue in her eyes. "Okay, but only if you tell me about this girl. And don't give me all the bullshit you told to your friend. I want the real story."

Rodrigo's eyebrows shot up in surprise. "There is no story," he insisted, though his tone lacked conviction.

"I've been bartending for a while, and I'm pretty good at reading people," she said, leaning in slightly. "I suspect that you were holding a lot back from your friend."

Rodrigo studied her face, trying to decide what to do. It was none of her business, after all. "Why would I tell a total stranger something I won't tell one of my friends?" he asked, curiosity mixing with caution in his voice.

The bartender shrugged, a knowing look on her face. "Because I'm a bartender. People always tell the bartender their problems when they're drinking alone. Plus," she added with a wry smile, "who else are you going to talk to?"

She had a point, Rodrigo had to admit. Plus, it probably would be easier to talk to a stranger about what he was feeling since it was unlikely that he would see her again. "Okay, deal," he conceded with a small nod.

The bartender's face lit up as she handed him his beer and set a glass of water down on a coaster in front of him. "Okay, start at the beginning," she prompted, settling in to listen.

Rodrigo took a deep breath, his mind wandering back through the years. "Wow, the beginning, huh? The beginning was being twelve years old, walking into my first day of middle school," he began, a nostalgic smile playing on his lips. "She was the first girl I noticed in the classroom because of her sparkling green eyes." He laughed softly to himself, the memory vivid in his mind. "She was also the palest girl in the room."

The bartender leaned in, clearly intrigued. "So, you had a thing for her since then, huh?" she asked, her voice gentle and encouraging.

Rodrigo paused, taking a sip of his Guinness as he gathered his thoughts. He wanted to take advantage of this unique situation and be as honest with himself as he could be. "From that moment, I was intrigued by her," he began slowly, "but I don't think I let myself like her like that until more recently."

The bartender leaned in, her curiosity piqued. "What kept you from liking her as more than a friend back then?"

"For the longest time, she had a thing for my best friend," Rodrigo explained, his voice tinged with a hint of regret. "She trusted me enough to talk to me about it. I didn't want to get in the way of that, in case he felt the same way. I also didn't want to make a habit of crushing on my friends."

"But that first day, you didn't know about her crush on your friend, and she wasn't your friend yet either," the bartender pointed out. "Are you sure you didn't have a thing for her then?"

Rodrigo furrowed his brow, delving deeper into his memories. "That's the thing about hindsight," he mused. "I wanted to get to know her, learn more about her. She was so quiet, and yet I could tell she was focused and observant. I wanted to know more." He paused, taking another sip of his beer. "Maybe I liked her then, but that's not what I would have called it at the time. I'm not sure I would call it that now, either."

The bartender excused herself briefly to get an IPA for another customer. When she returned, she picked up the conversation seamlessly. "So, you kept your distance romantically?"

"Yeah, but she has always been one of my best friends," Rodrigo said, a warm smile spreading across his face. "She would tell me anything and, I mean, I didn't always open up as much as she did, but I always knew that I could, that I could trust her. She just has that way about her." His eyes lit up as he continued, "She's going to school to be a psychologist, you know. She's gonna be good at it, too."

"So, when did you start to have feelings for her?" the bartender probed gently.

Rodrigo's expression softened. "A couple of years ago, she got back in touch with me because her boyfriend had dumped her, and she was having a rough time with it. She told me that I always help her to feel better when things are shitty for her." He smiled ruefully, "She does the same for me, if I'm being honest."

The bartender nodded encouragingly, urging him to continue.

"I guess it happened then," Rodrigo admitted. "Although, I don't really know if I can pinpoint the exact moment. Maybe it was before that, maybe after. All I know is that after we slept together at Thanksgiving, I really couldn't get her out of my head."

"And she doesn't live here," the bartender stated, more of an observation than a question.

"Right," Rodrigo confirmed. "She's on her way into town now. We're supposed to see each other on New Year's Eve."

The bartender had to step away for a few moments to pour cocktails for a group of undergrads playing pool at one of the many tables spread throughout the bar. While she was away, Rodrigo's mind wandered to New Year's Eve. He wanted to make it special but didn't want to overdo anything in case Elena wasn't in the same place emotionally that he was. She had already suggested that they go to dinner, but where? He could do casual, get some pizza or a burger. Or should it be classier? She was a city girl now; maybe pizza wasn't good enough?

When the bartender returned, she picked up right where they left off. "So, you'll see her on New Year's? How are you gonna play it?"

By the time she had asked, Rodrigo had his plan almost set. A confident smile played on his lips as he replied, "I only have a short time with her, so I'm going to make it count."

"You going to go big on the romance?" she asked, her eyes twinkling with interest.

Rodrigo's smile widened mysteriously as he pulled out his wallet, paying for the drinks and leaving a generous tip. "Thanks," he said, leaving the bartender hanging as he stood up to leave.

As he walked out of the bar, Rodrigo felt a mix of excitement and nervousness bubbling up inside him. He had a plan now, and he was determined to make the most of his time with Elena. Whatever happened, he knew that New Year's Eve was going to be a night to remember.

CHAPTER 15

Elena had spent a lovely Christmas with her family, texting Rodrigo occasionally. She had informed him that her friend's New Year's Eve party would be a great chance to dress up, so he wouldn't stand out if he decided to wear jeans and a t-shirt. Her cousin was helping her finish her hair, which she had styled into a simple, messy side bun.

 To make it a bit more interesting, she added a couple of twists on the side of her head. She wore a strapless emerald green dress that stopped just above her knees, a dress that perfectly complemented her eye color in a way no other outfit could. Her nude wedges not only gave her a bit of extra height but also offered comfort, allowing her to wear them for longer than heels would. She accessorized with simple stud earrings and a large, fake diamond ring shaped like an octopus.

Then, there was a knock on the door, and her heart skipped a beat.

"You look great," her cousin told her, giving her an approving glance.

"Thanks," Elena replied, trying to calm her racing heart.

"Have fun," her cousin added with a mischievous wiggle of her eyebrows.

Elena laughed and shook her head as she headed for the door. Unfortunately, her little cousin beat her to it.

"And what are your intentions with my cousin?" he asked Rodrigo, mimicking something he had seen in a movie.

Rodrigo responded effortlessly, clearly unbothered by the kid's antics, "I plan to be a perfect gentleman. I'll pay for dinner, escort her to the New Year's party, and make sure she has a safe ride home."

Her little cousin looked skeptical but relented, "Okay, you can take her then."

Elena came up behind him and gave him a playful hug. "Thanks for protecting my honor, buddy," she said with a grin. She grabbed her winter coat, which, unfortunately, took away from the beauty of her outfit. Still, it couldn't be helped, especially with the 25-degree weather. Snow was probably on its way.

Once they were outside, Rodrigo gave her a nervous but warm hug, inhaling the scent of her perfume, his anxiety making the embrace slightly stiff. "You look amazing," he said, his voice filled with admiration.

Elena stepped back to take him in. He was dressed in a simple dark gray suit with a white shirt and a dark silver tie. "You clean up nice yourself," she remarked, raising an eyebrow. "I didn't even know you owned a suit."

The truth was that he had bought it for her, specifically for this night. He wanted her to think of him as more than just that 12-year-old boy in khakis and a blue polo shirt. He offered her his arm, and when she accepted it, they walked toward his truck. She carefully climbed into the truck, doing a little maneuvering to avoid flashing anyone. After settling into the middle of the bench seat, he climbed in, started the engine, and turned the heater on high, directing the vents toward her.

Elena's curiosity couldn't be contained any longer. "So, where are we going?" She hadn't been told where they

were having dinner, but she assumed, given their dress for
the party, that it would be somewhere nice.

"You'll see." He drove toward downtown, and after a short
drive, he pulled up in front of a small, upscale restaurant
that offered a variety of dishes, including several vegetarian
options for Elena to choose from.

"Wow, I've always wanted to come here, but I never had a
reason to," she said, impressed. It was much nicer than she
had expected.

They were seated right away, and he took her coat, pulled
out her chair for her, and, as promised to her younger
cousin, acted like a perfect gentleman. It was clear to her
that he had researched some food and wine options before
choosing this place. He highlighted the items with the best
reviews for her and ordered his own meal and drink with
only a brief glance at the menu. His speech seemed
practiced, almost rehearsed. Elena looked around the
restaurant, feeling a pang of nostalgia. She missed the times
they'd hang out at his place, eating tacos or pizza and
joking around. The conversation had flowed effortlessly
back then. Now, his nervousness was making her feel

nervous, too.

After they placed their orders, he leaned back and asked, "How was your trip?"

"It was fine. I saw a trucker whose entire rig was decked out in Christmas lights, and my dogs tried to make friends with another dog at a truck stop."

"That sounds fun. I always get a kick out of seeing truckers decorate their rigs."

"Yeah, it was really something. How's your place coming along?" she asked, trying to sound casual. But deep down, she felt awkward. She missed their usual playful banter and the easy flow of conversation. Was she the one making it feel strange, or was it him?

He shifted nervously and replied, "Thanks for asking. It's going well. I finally got around to installing the new flooring in the kitchen." He cringed internally. Who was this formal version of himself? He needed to snap out of it.

The clothes, the fancy setting—none of this felt like him. And judging by her expression, it wasn't her either.

Their efforts to keep the conversation going fell flat. As they ate, the tension bubbled beneath the surface. At one point, he was so anxious that he accidentally knocked over his water glass. As she reached over to help him clean it up, her hand trembled, causing her fork to clatter onto the floor. It felt like every pair of eyes in the restaurant was drilling holes into them. They apologized profusely to the waiter, fumbling through the cleanup with red cheeks and forced smiles. When they finally resumed eating, they did so quickly, eager to escape the suffocating awkwardness.

Once back at his truck, he exhaled deeply, feeling the weight of formality lift. "I think a fancy restaurant might've been a bad idea," he admitted, turning to her. "I thought it would make us feel grown up, but honestly? I'm not a fancy guy. I felt so out of place. I'm sorry if I was being weird."

She let out a sigh of relief, her shoulders visibly relaxing. "It wasn't just you. I felt completely out of place too. Anytime I'm in a place like that, I feel like everyone can see right through me—as if they somehow know I grew up in a single-wide trailer. We were both being weird. We should have just kept it simple, gotten a pizza, and eaten at the airport viewing area." She laughed, releasing the last of her pent-up nerves. "Let's go to this party and bring in the New Year right."

He hesitated for a moment before turning to her, eyes soft but determined. "One thing first," he said, voice low. "I've wanted to kiss you since I picked you up, but I was too nervous."

A smile spread across her face, and when they kissed, it was slow and sweet. With each passing moment, the nerves melted away, leaving only warmth. As their lips parted, he let out a deep breath and smiled. "Okay, now I feel better. Let's do this."

They spent the party together, laughing and reminiscing about old times. They found small excuses to touch—a brush of their hands, a playful nudge. Although others milled around, Elena and Rodrigo had finally shaken off the awkwardness from earlier in the night, becoming so engrossed in each other that it felt as if the world had faded away. People would join their conversation briefly but would eventually drift off, sensing that the two were in their own bubble. Elena's cheeks ached from smiling, and when the clock struck midnight, they kissed deeply, each silently hoping this could be their tradition every New Year's from now on.

"So, I have one more surprise for tonight," Rodrigo whispered as the room erupted in cheers and confetti marked the start of a new year.

Intrigued, she tilted her head, a playful gleam in her eyes. "Oh? Another surprise?"

"Come on," he said, lacing his fingers with hers. They slipped out of the party without a word to the other guests, as if sharing a delicious secret.

They climbed back into his truck, and he drove a short distance, eventually pulling up in front of a modest but charming hotel. It wasn't fancy, but it was cozy—perfect in its simplicity. "I figured we could stay here, so we wouldn't have to drive all the way back," he explained, looking at her with hopeful eyes.

She kissed him softly. "It's perfect." Together, they checked in at the front desk, anticipation building with every step they took toward their room. Once inside, Rodrigo hung the Do Not Disturb sign on the doorknob and closed the door behind them. For a moment, they simply looked at each other, savoring the quiet intimacy of the moment. She slipped off her shoes and reached for the zipper at the back of her dress.

"Wait," he said, catching her hand gently. "I have one more thing for you—before that beautiful dress comes off and I lose the ability to think straight." He pulled a photograph from the inside pocket of his suit jacket and handed it to her. It was a black-and-white picture of the two of them from senior prom. They hadn't gone as a couple, but she remembered Lily snapping the shot, though Elena had never actually seen it.

"How did you get this?" she asked, her voice filled with wonder as she examined the picture. Even then, they looked so natural together. Rodrigo had worn a modern take on a classic Zoot suit, complete with a hat and suspenders, while her strapless turquoise dress with black embellishments had made her feel elegant. Her hair had cascaded over one shoulder, catching the light beautifully. Seeing the image again brought back a flood of memories—the mix of joy and melancholy of knowing high school was ending but feeling ready for what lay ahead.

Rodrigo peered over her shoulder, a smile softening his features. "Lily gave it to me before graduation," he explained. "She said it was the best picture she ever took of me. It might even be the only picture of the two of us together."

Elena placed the photo carefully on the dresser. Standing on tiptoe, she kissed his cheek. "This is such a thoughtful gift. Way better than what I have for you." She grinned mischievously and reached into her purse, pulling out a pair of handcuffs.

Rodrigo's eyes lit up with a mix of amusement and anticipation. "Your gift is perfect," he said, his excitement unmistakable.

January 2014

Elena had a few days left in New Mexico before she returned home. She and Emi decided to grab a drink together before they both went back to their routines. It was comforting to have someone who understood both the New Mexico and California sides of her life. To Elena, Emi wasn't just a friend—she was family, and the bond felt even stronger whenever they shared time together in either place.

They stood at a bar downtown, waiting their turn for drinks.

"That bartender with the pixie cut is cute," Emi said, throwing a flirty glance in the bartender's direction.

"You should get her number," Elena teased with a playful nudge.

Emi shook her head, a wry smile on her lips. "She's just eye candy. Besides, it would completely ruin my Auntie's mission to find my one true love. Did I mention she finally set me up with someone my age? Problem is, I had already dated her—two years ago, no less. Thankfully, we both laughed it off, but talk about a mismatch!" Emi's dating stories always made Elena think of her own past romantic misadventures. "But enough about my epic failures in love. How did things go with Rodrigo?"

Elena's face brightened. "It was really good. But it can't happen again. I mean, I'm still dating Jake, and I keep putting off the 'define the relationship' talk, but I can't avoid it forever. Jake is...he's the safer option. He lives in California, he wants a family, he's got a steady job. He's sweet, and when I'm with him, I feel...stable."

"But you're in love with Rodrigo."

Elena sighed, torn. "I don't know what I feel for him. I try not to let myself go there because we want different things out of life. With him, I'm happy in the moment, but leaving gets harder every time. I have my life in California— school, the internship in the fall, and you. My future is there. His is here."

"I see," Emi said with a melancholy smile. "I just want you to be happy, Elena. If that means Jake, then I'm on your side."

"Thanks, boo." Elena paused, her eyes softening as she remembered. "Did I ever tell you about how Jake and I first met?"

"Yeah, on the train when you were helping Frank that day."

Elena sighed, a touch of sadness in her voice. "Yeah, I miss Frank." She had recently learned from his son that Frank had passed away peacefully in his sleep.

Emi nodded sympathetically. "He seemed like a sweet person. So, I know how you and Jake met, but you've never told me how you and Rodrigo met."

Elena rolled her eyes but couldn't hide a small smile. "Someone's obviously on Team Rodrigo."

"I'm on Team You," Emi said with a playful shrug. "But I still want to hear the story."

Elena chuckled. "Well, I'm on Team You too. But, okay, according to Rodrigo, my memory of our first meeting is completely wrong. I thought it was when I was walking with his friend Eddie. Turns out, he insists we actually met in math class." She paused, her gaze drifting as she tried to piece together fragments of a distant memory. "And…"

"What?" Emi leaned in, curious.

Elena's eyes lit up with a flash of realization. "I do remember now." She looked at Emi, a mix of nostalgia and amusement playing across her face. "It was the first day of school, and…" Elena launched into the story, her voice growing more animated with each word.

It was the first day of middle school—a day of new uniforms, changing classes, fluctuating hormones, and unfamiliar faces from other schools. Elena wore the mandatory khakis and navy blue polo shirt, her long brown hair pulled into a tight ponytail. At 5'4", she was taller than many of her peers, a height she had maintained since fifth grade. She doubted she would grow any taller. Though slim, she still carried a bit of baby fat, and puberty was adding curves she wasn't yet comfortable with. The uniform didn't help; it only added another layer of awkwardness.

Her first class of the day was algebra. She scanned the room, ultimately choosing a seat behind a girl she vaguely recognized from sixth grade. Should she be brave and say hello? Or wait for the other girl to speak first? What if the girl didn't remember her—or worse, disliked her? As Elena wrestled with indecision, a boy seated behind her tapped her on the shoulder.

"Do you have a pencil I could borrow?" he asked casually. He seemed so at ease—no hesitation, even on the first day at a new school, clad in a restrictive uniform. He was taller than most boys their age, nearly her height but clearly still growing. Thin and a bit gawky, he nonetheless carried himself with confidence. With his dark skin, short dark hair, and dark eyes, he fit right in with the rest of New Mexico. By contrast, Elena's pale complexion made her feel as if she stood out.

"Um, yeah, here," she replied quietly, reaching into her meticulously organized backpack. Each subject had a matching notebook and pencil set. Fortunately, she had extras and didn't need to split any sets. She pulled a spare blue mechanical pencil from the front pocket and handed it to him, wondering, 'Who doesn't bring a pencil on the first day of school'?

"Thanks. I forgot mine," he said with a grin. "I'll try to remember to give this back at the end of class."

"Um, don't worry about it," she murmured shyly, wishing she could talk to strangers with his effortless ease. Not wanting to get in trouble, she turned back to face the teacher, who seemed ready to begin the lesson.

"Cool. I'm Rodrigo," he said just before she turned away.

"Elena."

"Aww, how cute. I can just picture you as an awkward pre-teen," Emi teased, grinning after hearing the story.

Elena's smile turned wistful. "Yeah. Who'd have thought I'd be pining for that boy so many years later?"

"Serious question, though," Emi paused for dramatic effect. "Did you ever get the pencil back?"

Elena laughed, shaking her head. "Never, but I think he's more than made up for stealing it."

At that moment, the bartender arrived with their drinks, and they returned to join their other friends.

A few days later, Elena was driving home. She couldn't get Rodrigo out of her mind. Her thoughts drifted as memories of their time together replayed like a song stuck on repeat: him taking her hand as he helped her into the truck, their knees touching at the party, that first kiss in his truck, him stealing her octopus ring, their hotel night, the thoughtful black-and-white photo he'd given her, standing on her tiptoes to reach his lips, the cold feel of handcuffs as he explored her desires, his tender "Are you okay?", And her response, "I'm dead in such a good way" after bringing her to climax with his mouth, him pressing deeper into her, whispering for her to stay, falling asleep in his arms, waking up and never wanting to leave, their parting kiss, her fingertips lingering on his lips, his scent clinging to her skin, the bittersweet ache she felt.

She wanted him. She hated that she wanted him. Rodrigo lived a thousand miles away, and their lives were going in different directions. He longed for adventure, to follow his wandering soul across the globe. Meanwhile, she was getting more serious with Jake. It shouldn't matter how Rodrigo made her feel. But no matter how much she tried to convince herself, she couldn't stop thinking about him— and those butterflies just wouldn't go away.

He reviewed the application one more time. New York University. Grad school. It was farther away from Elena than he already was. But he knew it was what he wanted and needed to achieve the work he had always dreamed of doing. Work that could take him across the world. It was the life he had always imagined for himself. But as his finger hovered over the 'Submit' button, an image of Elena flashed in his mind—standing in the doorway of her cousin's house, wearing that green dress that made her eyes even brighter. He hesitated. Maybe I can change what I want my life to look like. Maybe I can settle down, go to school in California. Be with Elena. She wants marriage and a family someday—I could do that. Could I do that? Is there a way to have both? He didn't have an answer. A knock at his door interrupted his thoughts. Before standing up, he hit 'Submit' and walked to the door, doubt already creeping back in.

"Hey, neighbor." It was Luke, a friendly older man from a few houses down who had been close with Rodrigo's late grandmother. Occasionally, Rodrigo helped him with repairs around the house. "I have a big favor to ask. I need help moving some wood from the shed to the house before the snow gets any worse. Could you lend a hand?"

Rodrigo nodded. "Sure thing. Let me grab my shoes, and I'll head over."

At Luke's house, Rodrigo met Ana, Luke's granddaughter. She had short dark hair, warm brown eyes, and a bright smile. Together, they moved the wood inside, chatting and getting to know each other as they worked. When they were done, Luke insisted on treating them to dinner as a thank-you. By then, it was clear to both Rodrigo and Ana that it was a setup. Rodrigo figured if Elena could date people in California, he could date someone too. Maybe it would help distract him, at least for a while. Dinner with Ana was pleasant—good food, easy conversation, and her laugh was nice—but he kept waiting for butterflies that he knew would never come.

Elena and Rodrigo continued their near-daily texts and occasional phone or video calls. He told her about NYU, trying not to dwell on the disappointment he saw in her eyes at the thought of him moving even farther away. She told him about her internship. They never mentioned their dating lives, nor did they discuss what was between them. The conversations grew less flirtatious as they both entered relationships with other people. Elena convinced herself it was for the best; staying just friends was less complicated. But it didn't stop her mind from drifting back to their moments together. Rodrigo told himself that if Elena was happy, that was enough for him. Yet, deep down, there was a nagging fear that he was about to lose the best thing that had ever happened to him. And he wasn't sure he was ready to let that happen without a fight.

CHAPTER 16

April 2014

"This is it," Rodrigo thought. "It's been three and a half months since you've seen Elena. It's now or never. Soon she'll be in love with Jake, and you'll have missed your chance." He texted her:

I know you'll be in town for Easter. Want to hang out, get dinner or something?

She replied quickly, as she always did:

I'm already in town. How about tomorrow night around 7?

Pizza and viewing area?

See you there. You get the pizza.

The thought of seeing her made him feel as if he was crawling out of his own skin. The next twenty-two hours stretched before him like a lifetime. He tried everything to pass the time—reading a book, finishing homework, watching a movie, even going to the gym—but nothing could distract him for long. In the end, he decided to drive to his parents' house, figuring the change of scenery would help. It didn't. Not when one of the songs Elena had recommended came up on his playlist, sending his thoughts spiraling back to her and what it would be like to see her again after three months of nothing but texts, phone calls, and video chats. He arrived in his hometown far faster than the speed limit would have allowed, the urgency within him making every minute feel unbearable.

It was close to two in the morning when he pulled up outside his parents' house. Waking them at this hour felt wrong, so he kept driving, aimlessly at first, until he ended up where he always did when he came home. He went to see Eddie.

The night air was cold for April, but at least the wind—so typical of New Mexico in spring—had died down, sparing him the chill. He parked the truck and paused, reproaching himself for not making these visits more often and for always coming at night. He knew why. Elena would understand too. Pain was something they both preferred to endure in private. Stepping out of the truck, he walked through the quiet cemetery to section G, plot 197. The place was deserted, which was a relief; every so often, he ran into teenagers hoping to scare themselves with nighttime graveyard visits. He, Eddie, Elena, and their friends used to be those teenagers once. He reached Eddie's grave and brushed away the few leaves that had gathered on the headstone.

"Hey man. How's it going? I know, stupid question. I've been good. Finally graduating this year. I know, I'm slow, but it was hard to give up that financial aid check, you know?" Rodrigo chuckled softly. "Before you left, you told me you hoped I'd find someone to love, like you did with Claire. I think I have." He paused, a small, self-deprecating smile on his lips. "You'd never guess who, though," he said, his voice lowering. "Actually, if you were still here, you'd call me an idiot and say, 'Of course it's Elena.' It's been her for longer than I even realized." Rodrigo shook his head. "You told me Claire made you a better man just by being in your life. I think Elena's done that for me too. I hope I make her better. At least a little."

He took a deep breath, his words weighed with uncertainty. "I want to tell her. I'm meeting her tomorrow. But I've never said it to a girl and actually meant it. Honestly? I'm terrified." He looked down at the ground, searching for comfort. "I wish you were here, man. You'd kick my ass, tell me to stop being an idiot and to man up." He hesitated, feeling a wave of doubt. "But there's this other guy. I don't know how I measure up." He exhaled, long and slow. "I miss you, brother." Rodrigo sat there, lost in the silence, until his joints began to ache from sitting too long and the sky turned pale with the approaching dawn. He stood, brushed off his pants, and walked back to his truck. It was time to rest before seeing Elena.

After making plans with Rodrigo, Elena's nerves were on edge. She tossed and turned all night, unable to quiet her thoughts. She was excited—she had missed him—but she also feared what might happen. The attraction she felt for Rodrigo was so strong it made her anxious. Would she be able to resist the impulse to kiss him when they met? She wasn't a cheater, and she and Jake were exclusive now. And she was happy with Jake. She repeated it to herself like a mantra. You're happy with Jake. You're happy with Jake.

But deep down, she wondered if she was trying to convince herself.

What if Rodrigo tried to kiss her? The thought sent a shiver down her spine. Could she stop herself from kissing him back? She knew Rodrigo would respect her boundaries if she told him to stop. But would she be strong enough to draw that line? Was seeing him even a good idea? Meeting at "their spot"—the airport viewing area—was probably not the smartest move. It was where they had first been intimate. The memory alone made her pulse quicken. Being in the same place would be a mistake. But if she suggested changing locations, Rodrigo would get suspicious. Would he think it was because she couldn't trust herself there? Or that she didn't want to remember their time together? Her thoughts spun in circles.

"Ugh!" she groaned.

"What?" her cousin, Bernadette, asked from the other room.

"I didn't say anything," Elena replied too quickly.

"Pretty sure I heard an 'ugh!'"

"That was out loud?"

"Yeah. You okay?"

"I'm fine. Just…making myself nervous for no reason."

"Stop overthinking!" Bernadette called, laughing as she walked back to the kitchen.

"I'm not!" Elena protested, but Bernadette was already gone.

The day dragged on, each hour seeming longer than the last. Butterflies churned in Elena's stomach. When Jake called to tell her about the Easter gifts he'd bought for his nieces, she tried to sound calm. But she worried he would detect guilt in her voice, even though she hadn't done anything wrong—except plan to see a man she wasn't sure she could resist. 'Shit. I'm an asshole,' she thought bitterly. She made an excuse to end the call before she blurted out something she'd regret.

'If I feel this guilty about thinking of Rodrigo, maybe I shouldn't meet him,' she reasoned. With her mind racing, she called Jake back.

"Hey Honey, I just wanted to let you know I'm having dinner with my friend Rodrigo tonight," she said when he answered.

"Okay," he replied, sounding a bit puzzled. "But you don't need my permission to see your friend."

"I know," she said quickly. "But he's a male friend—a straight male friend—and it's just going to be me and him at dinner. I wanted you to know in case it made you feel weird or anything." She spoke with a mix of hope that he would be concerned and hope that he wouldn't care.

"Babe, I trust you," he said easily. "Rodrigo's been your friend since you were kids. He's practically family to you. Go and have fun." There wasn't a hint of hesitation or worry in his voice.

"Okay," she said, feeling a mix of disappointment and relief.

"I'm glad you called back. I wanted to tell you something else earlier."

"Yeah?"

"I love you," he said casually, as if it were the simplest thing in the world.

"You do?" She felt shock ripple through her. The L-word. She'd exchanged "I love you" with her ex after just a few weeks of dating, so why did hearing it from Jake after six months catch her off guard? Maybe it was because she wasn't sure if she felt it, too.

"Yeah, I do."

"Oh. I, um… I… I love you, too," she stammered. Did she? She wasn't sure, but it was too late to take it back now.

"Have fun. I'll see you in a few days," he said before hanging up.

"Yeah, in a few days," she murmured, still stunned, speaking into the empty air. She sat there for a moment before noticing the clock on the nightstand. Great. Now I have to leave to meet Rodrigo, and I've had no time to process what just happened. She grabbed her purse and keys, moving in a daze to her car.

Once outside, she unlocked the door and climbed in, sitting with the key in her hand, paused halfway to the ignition. What just happened? Did I tell Jake that I love him? I did. Do I love him? He makes me happy. I can see a future with him. What will Rodrigo think? It doesn't matter. I'm not with Rodrigo. He's my best friend. Is he my best friend? Yes. I tell him everything. Should I tell him Jake loves me and that I, apparently, love Jake? Do I love Jake? What about Rodrigo?

Her mind raced. Rodrigo isn't my boyfriend. But I do love Rodrigo—as a friend. What about more than a friend? No. We live a thousand miles apart. But what if we didn't? He wants different things from life than I do. What if he didn't? I'm with Jake. But what if I wasn't? But I am. Am I in love with Rodrigo?

Her phone buzzed, interrupting the torrent of thoughts. She pulled it from her purse and saw Rodrigo's text: **Picked up a cheese and green chile pizza. Heading to the airport viewing area.** She realized she'd been sitting there for fifteen minutes, lost in thought. At least Rodrigo was always late. Shaking her head to clear the confusion, she put the key in the ignition and started the car, heading toward the viewing area.

He watched her pull up in her car and felt an overwhelming urge to run away. Was he really going to go through with this? He heard Eddie's voice in his mind, telling him not to be a chicken shit. Right. I can do this. What's the worst that could happen? She laughs in my face? She says, 'That's nice, but I just want to be friends'? She's actually a lesbian? She's in love with Jake? Yeah, that last one would be the worst. So, what if she loves Jake? She could still love me, too. No regrets, right?

She got out of her car and grabbed the blanket from the backseat, not giving a second thought to the last time she used it. Or at least, that's what she tried to convince herself. As she lifted the soft, multicolored blanket out of the car, her mind flashed back to the time she and Rodrigo had made love in his truck. The memory hit her like a wave, and she couldn't help but smile to herself, though guilt quickly followed. 'This is going to be a mistake,' she thought, but there was no turning back now.

He got out of his truck, holding the pizza and a six-pack of beer, and helped her spread the blanket out in the bed of the truck. They both climbed in without exchanging a word. Neither of them was able to speak; the anxiety between them was too heavy. He cracked open a beer and handed it to her, while she placed a slice of pizza and a container of ranch dressing on a plate and passed it to him. They ate in silence, both hoping the other would break the stillness.

"Mmmm… I really miss this pizza," she couldn't help but say.

"I'm glad I picked the right one," he replied with a nervous laugh, attempting to ease the tension.

"Pretty much anything with green chile is the right choice," she said, taking another bite of the ranch-smothered pizza. The nervousness in his voice only made her anxiety spike, and the enjoyment she had been feeling from the pizza began to fade.

They continued eating the rest of their meal in tense silence. Neither could escape the feeling of butterflies in their stomachs, which made it hard to focus on eating. Why is he being so quiet? He's never this quiet. Why is he nervous? Her own nerves were intensifying, knowing that his discomfort was adding to hers. I have to break this silence. He's not saying anything. Somebody has to speak up to ease this weird tension.

"I like hanging out with you like this. Casual suits us better," she said, trying to lighten the mood and referencing their awkward dinner on New Year's Eve.

"Yeah, me too," he agreed, remembering how awkward he'd felt at the restaurant, trying to act like someone else. Once again, they fell into silence.

"So, how's life?" she asked, borrowing one of Eddie's old conversation starters—anything to cut through the awkwardness.

The reminder of Eddie was just what he needed. He thought of his old friend, took a swig of beer, and gained a little courage. "Actually," he began to say at the same time Elena spoke up.

"Oh! I almost forgot to tell you," she said with excitement. "I remember the day we first met."

"Oh yeah?" he asked, his curiosity piqued, wondering if she remembered the day correctly this time.

"Yeah, it was the first day of middle school, first period. I was so nervous and shy, sitting behind Mary, trying to work up the courage to say hi to her, when this very confident boy asked me to borrow a pencil. I remember thinking, 'What kind of person doesn't bring a pencil to the first day of school?' I was also kind of jealous of how easy you made it look to talk to someone you didn't even know. I was so shy back then."

"That didn't last long, though," he said, happy that she remembered the day so clearly now.

"Sort of," she replied, smiling. "It wasn't until graduate school that I became comfortable talking to strangers like that. Honestly, it can still be a little hard for me. You were always better at that than I was."

"Well, that day was special," he said, deciding now was the moment to speak up. He took a deep breath. "I'm glad you finally remember that day. I remember it perfectly."

Rodrigo walked into the classroom, his eyes scanning the room, trying to see if he knew anyone. He recognized no familiar faces, and the seats were quickly starting to fill up. As he looked around one last time, his gaze landed on a girl in the middle of the row closest to the windows. At first glance, she didn't stand out much—she wasn't the prettiest girl in the room. But then he saw her eyes. They were an astonishing shade of bright green, and they seemed to sparkle as the light hit them. Without giving it much thought, he made his way to the desk behind her and sat down. He sat quietly for a moment, unsure what to do next, but all he could think about was getting a better look at those mesmerizing green eyes. He gently tapped her on the shoulder and asked if she had a pencil. Her reply was quiet, almost a whisper, but it intrigued him further. In that moment, he knew that he had to learn more about the girl with the captivating green eyes.

"You had me intrigued from the very first day," Rodrigo began, his voice steady but warm. "That moment when you turned around, and I saw your beautiful green eyes, I just knew I wanted to talk to you. And then, after you spoke, I don't know what it was—something about you made me feel like I had to get to know you. As the years passed and we became closer, you never stopped amazing me. Your brilliance, your growing confidence, your genuine desire to make the people around you happy, your humor, and, of course, your beauty. I'll never forget those rare moments when I saw you let go of control—like when we'd drive around in your car, just the two of us, and you'd make me pick out a CD for us to listen to. You'd have me find one song, and then, before I could even finish listening to it, you'd send me off to pick the next one. I loved that. And I love those times when we text and, even more, the rare times we get to hang out and talk like this. It reminds me so much of how things used to be. I would listen to you talk about wanting to change the world by helping people, and you inspired me to want to help people too. You were always so good at being on your own, so happy with your own company."

Elena was speechless. She had never realized he thought of her that way—brilliant and beautiful. She tried to think of something to say, but everything that came to mind felt cliché. Just as she began to struggle for words, Rodrigo continued, his voice softer now, but full of emotion.

"Remember how we used to go downtown to that thrift store and just wander around? You would go off on your own, happily searching through things, as if you didn't need anyone else there. Or those times when I'd call you, and you'd be sitting outside on your porch, alone, reading. You never sounded lonely, not even once. You were so good at being independent. I learned how to be okay with being alone because of you. You've made me a better person, and you've been doing that since we were kids. Since 7th grade algebra, you've inspired me to always be better."

Elena wanted to tell him that he had made her a better person too, but before she could talk herself into being as brave as Rodrigo was, he continued to pour his heart out, making her sound even more amazing. She could feel her face flush, and she knew that even in the dimming light of the twilight, he'd be able to see the redness creeping onto her pale cheeks.

"You always say that I help you feel better when you're feeling like crap, but you do the same for me," he said, his grip tightening slightly as he took her hands in his. "You're my best friend, Elena, and you have been for a very long time. And when we kissed at Thanksgiving… something changed for me. Something clicked. You are my person. Despite all my efforts to avoid saying this, to avoid meaning it, you've made me feel it, and I mean it, Elena." He looked deep into her eyes, and as he did, he saw the blush on her cheeks. He felt her hands tremble in his. His heart raced, knowing what he had to say next. "Elena… I'm in love with you."

She looked at him for a long moment, desperately trying to find her voice. She had heard the way Rodrigo told her he loved her, every word wrapped in sincerity and meaning. He had laid out all the reasons why he loved her— beautiful, heartfelt reasons that left her breathless. She wanted to respond with words just as beautiful and eloquent. But instead, tears welled up in her eyes. 'Don't cry—whatever you do, don't cry,' she commanded herself. Those three words—I love you—sat heavily on her tongue. Say it. Tell him. You know he makes you better too. You know he's your person too. You know you love him too.

Just say it! Say it! Say it! A tear escaped despite her efforts to hold it back. Tell him! Stop stalling and just say it! I love you too!

Her heart was screaming at her to let the words out—to tell him how deeply she felt the same. To tell him about all the moments that made her fall in love with him slowly over the years and then all at once during Thanksgiving. To tell him all the ways he had made her a better person. How her confidence had blossomed from emulating his example. How she learned to be calm and collected, even in the face of despair in her therapy sessions, because of the strength she admired in him. Her heart begged her to let him in, to let him love her and love him back with everything she had. "I…" Just say it! A tear slid down her cheek. "I…" Another tear fell. "I…can't." Her head betrayed her heart, and tears streamed down her face like tiny rivers. It would never work anyway.

"You can't?" Rodrigo asked, his voice breaking as though he had taken a physical blow. The shock and pain in his eyes were unmistakable, as if the heavyweight champion of the world had punched him in the gut.

"I can't love you like that," she said, barely above a whisper, suddenly feeling like that shy, nervous middle school girl again. She shifted, moving towards the tailgate of the truck.

His hands tightened around hers, pleading for her not to walk away. "Please, don't leave. Just tell me what you mean."

"You're my best friend," she said softly, allowing him to hold her hands as she remained rooted in place, trapped between him and the tailgate.

"So?" he asked, searching her eyes for any trace of hope.

"So, I don't want to lose that," she replied, unable to meet his gaze.

"You're worried that if you tell me you love me, you'll lose me? Aren't you afraid that you're already losing me now?" he challenged, his voice thick with emotion.

"You're making me feel like a terrible person," she murmured, finally lifting her eyes to meet his.

"No, you're making yourself feel like a terrible person. I think you love me too. If you didn't, you wouldn't be this conflicted."

She hesitated, then moved closer, cupping his cheek in her hand. She wanted so badly to kiss him. "We want different things from life," she whispered, her voice trembling.

"So?" he asked again, his eyes pleading.

"Can we please drop this? Pretend it never happened?"

"You really think we can just forget this? That I can forget telling you I love you, only for you to shut me down?"

"Please?" she begged, tears streaming freely down her face.

"Why!?" he shouted, the pain in his voice echoing around them.

She stared at him for what felt like an eternity. 'You're about to ruin your entire life', she thought, but she couldn't stop herself. She wiped her tears, looking him straight in the eyes. She cleared her throat to ensure that her next words would be unmistakable. "I'm in love with Jake."

They were both silent, him staring at her in disbelief, while she tried to shut down her emotions, looking away to hide her pain. The warmth in her gaze disappeared, replaced by a cold, detached expression. She could feel the hurt she was causing him, knew it was cutting him deeply—but she couldn't stop it. She had loved fiercely once before, and it had nearly crushed her. For a long time, it did crush her. The idea of loving someone like that again, only to lose them, was more than she could bear. She didn't think she would survive it this time. She knew she wouldn't survive losing Rodrigo in that way. He was the one who had helped put her heart back together the last time. If she lost him, who would be there to pick up the pieces?

It felt safer—necessary—to give her heart to someone like Jake. Her mind took over, shielding her fragile heart. Even though her heart broke anyway, she convinced herself it was better this way—a lesser wound compared to what loving Rodrigo might cost her in the end. She told herself this was a small ache compared to the agony that awaited if she allowed herself to fall for him completely. Deep down, her rational mind argued that Rodrigo was destined to travel the world, to pursue a life that could never truly be hers. He would never marry her or give her the children she dreamed of. And even if he tried, settling down would make him unhappy—resentful of a life that would feel like second best. This decision was for both their sakes, she repeated internally, trying to believe it.

"Can we please forget this ever happened?" she asked, her voice now flat and devoid of emotion.

"We can try," he replied, though they both understood the truth: trying to forget was futile. This would break them apart.

"I should go," she whispered, climbing out of the truck.

He didn't move to stop her. Neither spoke a word of goodbye. She slid into her car and drove off without looking back. Rodrigo lay down in the bed of his truck on the blanket she had left behind. It was the same blanket that had been there for so many of their memories—the one that saw them growing up together, the first time they made love, and now, the one that witnessed their final goodbye. He let out a laugh, harsh and broken—more of a choked sob than anything resembling humor. No regrets? He felt like a fool. I ruined everything. She ruined everything.

Damn it, this hurts. Now I've lost the only person who ever took away my pain.

He stayed there, staring up at the stars, trying to hold back his tears.

Meanwhile, she drove away, the weight of her decision pressing down on her chest. What am I doing? Not far from where she left him, she had to pull over. The tears blurred her vision, making it dangerous to keep driving. You love him! Turn around and make this right! She rested her forehead on the steering wheel, torn apart by regret. She willed herself to turn back, to go to him and take it all back. She searched for a sign, anything to tell her she was about to make a mistake by leaving him behind. At Thanksgiving, the radio had played a song that pushed her towards him. Now, the mournful tune filling her car seemed to echo her fears, whispering that everything fades away eventually.

She could have taken it as a sign to seize the happiness she could, even if it was temporary. But instead, she chose the safer interpretation: to guard her heart. Losing Rodrigo, no matter how it happened, was inevitable, she convinced herself. It was better to walk away now than face the heartbreak later. Numb and broken, she drove to her cousin's house, feeling like a shell of herself.

CHAPTER 17

May 2014

It's been one month since you told me you loved me. One month since I walked away from you. One month since I lost my best friend. It's been a month of forcing myself to smile even though my heart feels shattered. A month spent lying to everyone around me whenever they ask how I'm doing. "I'm great," I say, fighting the tears that threaten to give me away. It's been one month of wanting to reach out to you, of resisting the urge to dial your number because I know I shouldn't. One month of wishing I'd told you the truth. One month of longing to go back. One month of hating myself for letting you slip away. If someone were to ask me if I love you, the answer would be painfully simple: "Obviously."

Elena re-read the words she had poured into her message, her fingers hovering over the send button. "Just hit send," she whispered to herself, her heart pounding in her chest.

"Hey, beautiful," came Jake's voice, pulling her back to reality as he walked through the door of their shared apartment.

Startled, Elena quickly deleted the message, the words disappearing with a single click. She closed her laptop as if closing a chapter she could never quite finish. "Hey, handsome. How was your day?" she asked, forcing a smile.

He leaned over the back of the couch and planted a soft kiss on the top of her head. "Long. But I'm home now, so it's already better."

She set her laptop on the armrest and stood up, wrapping her arms around him. "I'm glad you're home. What do you feel like for dinner?"

He returned her hug, squeezing her gently. "You pick," he replied, resting his chin on her shoulder.

Elena buried her face into his shoulder, hoping to drown out the nagging pull of the computer and the words she had tried so hard to bury. The ghost of that message replayed over and over in her mind.

"Hello?" Lily answered hesitantly, her tone cautious. She didn't recognize the number flashing on her screen.

"Lily, it's Rodrigo," he said, surprised at himself for making the call.

There was a brief pause before her shocked response came through. They hadn't spoken in years, so her surprise was warranted. "Rodrigo? Wow. Hey, how are you?"

He shifted uncomfortably, feeling the weight of his impulsive decision. "Umm... well..." He faltered, second-guessing himself. This was a mistake, he thought, feeling foolish.

"Out with it, Rodrigo," she said, cutting through his hesitation.

"I just... missed you, that's all," he lied, trying to mask the real reason he had called.

"Uh huh," she replied, clearly skeptical. "We haven't spoken in years, and back then, we barely said more than 'hi.' What's really going on?"

"I'm telling the truth. I missed you," he repeated, though he knew it wasn't entirely convincing.

A long silence followed. He could hear faint music playing in the background, signaling that she was still on the line, waiting him out. It was a clever tactic and one he recognized. He sighed, realizing he couldn't evade her perceptiveness. "Fine," he admitted, reluctantly. "Elena and I had a fight, and I guess... I miss having a connection to that time in my life." It wasn't the full truth, but it wasn't a complete lie either.

"I knew it!" she exclaimed. "I asked Elena about you the other day, and she quickly made up some excuse to end the call. So, tell me, what happened?"

Of course, she would want to know. But he couldn't bring himself to tell her. "How're things with you? Tell me everything," he deflected.

"Fine, but you'll open up eventually," Lily said, with a knowing smile that reflected their deep connection, despite their time apart.

'Probably,' he mused, while half-listening to the details of Lily's current life.

The day I walked away from you, is the day I most regret. Above all things, you were my best friend. You got me through more tough times than I can count, and I burned it all to the ground. I thought I would die without you in my life, but I keep breathing, my heart keeps beating, I keep going. I always thought of you as my medicine, but I'm surviving without you. That's the problem though. I'm merely surviving. My heart beats, my breath comes in and out of my lungs, but I'm not living, and it's my own damn fault. I should have told you I love you...

'Send,' she thought, her finger hovering over the mouse for what felt like an eternity. 'Or maybe not,' she reconsidered, deleting yet another unsent message.

You know that I hate you, right? Since the day you turned away from me, lied to me and yourself. I thought

it hurt after Eddie, but this…is worse. I had you then. Now, I'm alone. May always be that way. Probably for the best. And of course I don't really hate you, I love your stupid face, and your overly pale skin, your shining green eyes, your wit, the way you call me a butthead. Damn, I miss you. This is hard, has been hard. May stay hard for a long time. May be hard until my stupid heart stops. Maybe I should have never said 'I love you'…

'Dude, what would sending this even accomplish? You'll just come across as desperate,' he chastised himself, deleting the words yet again.

I spoke to Lily recently. She mentioned you're still with Ana. That's… good. I'm genuinely happy for—

'Stop it. You have no business sending this. You were the one who walked away. He has every right to move on. This message would only be a selfish act of jealousy—and could give him the wrong idea.' She closed her eyes and hit delete.

You were the damn sun! The force that pushed me through endless grey winters, pounding summer monsoons, and the darkest nights. Every morning, you gave me a reason to rise, warmth to feel on my skin. And now, I hate you for stealing that away from me. Worse yet, you've turned me into some dramatic emo kid. I hate you for that too.

'Come on, you can't send this. You still have the sun—literally. You live in the desert; it's sunny 310 days a year. Snap out of it!' Frustrated, he tossed his phone onto the couch and decided to run under the real sun instead.

July 2014

She didn't want to spend her summer break in New Mexico, but skipping her usual trip home would have raised eyebrows. Avoiding reminders of him turned out to be harder than she expected. He seemed to be everywhere—in the stars scattered across the night sky, in aimless drives around town, even in the hues of sunsets and sunrises. When Lily texted, inviting her out to dinner with

Mary, she searched for an excuse to decline but came up empty.

"Okay, so how's everything? What's new with you?" Lily asked, her tone suggesting she already knew the answer, as the three friends settled at their table.

"Good, everything's fine," Elena replied, deflecting. "How about you two?"

Lily simply stared at her, expecting more.

Unaware of what had happened between Rodrigo and Elena, Mary jumped in. "Things are great with me! Max and I are talking about getting married soon and starting a family right away. We both want kids, so we figured, why wait?"

"That's amazing, Mary. I'm really happy for you," Elena said, her voice flat.

Mary and Lily exchanged a look, recognizing the distance in her tone. "Not going well with Jake?" Lily probed.

"We're fine. We just moved in together."

"Uh-huh, and why don't you sound more thrilled about it?" Mary pressed.

Lily leaned in. "Yeah, what's up? Is there someone else?"

Elena's eyes narrowed. "He told you?" she asked, piecing it together.

"Yep," Lily confirmed, without elaboration.

Mary glanced between them. "Okay, clearly, I'm missing something. What's going on?"

Elena scanned the room for the waiter, already dreading the conversation ahead. She needed something stronger than water to make it through this. When he finally approached, she ordered a vodka soda, then turned to face her two friends with a resigned sigh. "Fine, Lily apparently knows, but only his side of the story. Rodrigo and I... we were seeing each other for a while."

"What?!" Mary gasped in shock.

Lily picked up where Elena had left off. "It wasn't just casual—it was more like they were practically dating, except for the distance. A couple of months ago, he told her he loved her. Instead of saying it back, she told him she loved Jake and ran off."

"Again, what?!"

"Lily, you don't understand how hard this has been for me."

Lily sighed deeply. "No, but I know how much it's hurt him. And I know you love him, too, or else this wouldn't be so painful. Why didn't you just tell him? You could have worked out everything else afterward."

Elena reached for her glass, her fingers brushing the rim, but paused. She stared into the vodka mixture, watching the ice clink softly against the glass as she swirled the liquid, unsure of how to begin.

After a few moments, Mary spoke up gently, "Because those words can be the hardest to say. When you're young and it's your first love it's tough because you've never experienced anything like it. You get scared the other person won't feel the same way, but that fear can make you push forward anyway. And if that first love ends, you walk away feeling broken. Those words become hard to say because you've been burned, and you know how much they can hurt. It's a risk, Elena. You and Alex had this amazing, effortless love, and then he left you all alone in California. I remember how deeply you were hurt after that. I know how badly my first love hurt me. I was terrified to say 'I love you' to Max. What if it didn't work out? What if I couldn't survive it again? I know you felt the same way."

"You got hurt, Elena, but I've never known you to let fear control you," Lily said, gently placing her hand over Elena's, which still clutched the glass like a lifeline.

Mary nodded thoughtfully. "They're the hardest words to say, but with the right person, they're the best words you can say. But is Jake the right person for you, or is it really Rodrigo?"

Elena finally looked up at her friends, "Jake wants the same things I want. He wants to get married and have a family like I do. Rodrigo doesn't, he's got a wanderlust soul and he's never going to settle down and I wouldn't want to force him to. He and I would end up hurting each other beyond repair. I think Jake's going to propose soon. That's what I want. He's who I love. Rodrigo and I just…

sometimes those words should be left unsaid."

Mary and Lily looked at one another, knowing their friend well enough to not push it further, but also knowing that she was completely in love with Rodrigo, but too afraid to say those words.

Lily told me you moved in with him. She's pretty sure he's going to propose soon. Guess you'll get everything you've always wanted—picket fence and all. I'm happy for...

"Hey, man, want another hit of this?" Chris asked, holding out the joint.

Rodrigo took it and inhaled deeply. He reread the message he had typed into his phone, trying to finish the sentence. He wanted to tell her he was happy for her, but he couldn't lie. So, after handing the joint back to Chris, he deleted the message.

We had a fight today. It's rare for us to fight, you know? Well, you wouldn't know that because we never talked about my relationship with him—obviously. It was a stupid fight, the kind all couples have, I'm sure. But what was I thinking about while we were fighting? You. I thought about you. How I wish it had been you I was fighting with, how it would have mattered more if it was you, how the stakes would have been higher with you. I fought with him and ended up bored. It finished with a well-thought-out, sweet compromise. I imagined if it were you and me fighting over something silly—like who should do the dishes or whatever—that we'd end up naked and satisfied, and the dishes would still be there, untouched. But we wouldn't care. I miss you...

She sat on the balcony of the beautiful apartment she now shared with Jake. They had been living together for a few months now. He was in bed—it was one in the morning, after all. She couldn't sleep. She had lain there for a while, but thoughts of Rodrigo kept her awake. Finally, she got up, grabbed her computer, and went to the balcony. Looking out over the stunning view of the San Francisco skyline, she thought of her desert skies and their stars. She typed yet another message to Rodrigo—one she knew she wouldn't send. She never sent any of them. She didn't even know why she bothered to write them anymore. All she knew was that she missed him.

She told me she loved me today. I told her I'd applied to NYU, and if I got in, I'd leave her. She left instead. Lily said I was coldhearted. I blamed you for that. Lily punched me in the arm. I blame you for that, too. I didn't even care that she left—maybe I am coldhearted. I haven't felt that fire since the night you left. You left. I don't know what we could have been, but you left. I get it, though—sort of. Maybe. He's safety. I'm... well... not. Maybe with you, I could have been...

He thought about how that sentence would end. Could have been different? Could have been steady? Reliable? Loving? Loved?

I went to the beach today—the one I took you to. No dolphins this time. I always see dolphins when I go, but not lately. Is it a sign, or just a coincidence?

"Smile, beautiful," Jake said, pointing his camera at her as she looked out over the water, holding her phone in her hand—once again, not sending the message.

"Don't you have enough pictures of me?" she asked, smiling anyway.

He snapped the picture. "Never."

I saw your mom today. I rarely go to town, and of course, the one time I do, I run into her at the store. You'd probably call it a sign. I didn't say hi. I couldn't bear hearing any good news about you. The news I know is coming soon. Lily keeps telling me to suck it up and talk to you. Maybe I'll actually send this one. Tell you he isn't good enough for you. Tell you to leave him and be with me. Then again...

Seeing her mom in the store shocked him. They looked so much alike that for a moment, he thought it was Elena. He froze, holding a California-grown avocado in his hand. Stupid California. When he realized it was her mom, he quickly turned and left the store, abandoning his groceries.

He couldn't risk running into her and being forced to talk. When he got home, he opened his laptop and typed yet another message. Of course, he didn't end up sending this one either.

I found an old playlist I once gave you. It made me wonder if you still have it. Can you bear to listen to it? I couldn't. If you do, does it bring happy memories or sad ones? It made me think of that old movie with the Russian mouse. But instead of wondering if we're looking at the same star, I wondered if we're listening to the same song at the same time, feeling the same thing. I can almost hear your voice in my head, telling me I overthink everything.

"Elena, did you hear me?" Emi asked, waving her hand in front of Elena's face.

Elena shook her head to clear her thoughts and looked up from her computer. "No, sorry, Em. I got kind of distracted."

"It's alright. You looked sad. You okay?"

'No,' she thought. "Yeah, I'm fine. What were you asking?"

"Just wanted to see if you could read over my methods section. I want to make sure it makes sense."

"Of course. Could you check mine, too?"

Emi nodded, and Elena deleted the message before swapping computers with her.

It's become clear to me that I'll never send any of these messages I keep typing. I keep writing, telling you everything I normally would, but can't say to you anymore. Words, words, words. You were always so good with words—well, after you got over that strange shy phase. Then came all the words. Never-ending words. I miss hearing your words in my head.

His phone rang as he deleted the message. "Hello?"

"Hey Rodrigo, whatcha doing?" Lily's voice came through the speaker.

"Thinking about the importance of words," he replied.

"Huh?"

"Never mind. What's up?"

"You talk to her yet?"

She made this call every few weeks, so he wasn't surprised by the question. "No, and you know that will be my answer every time."

"You should tell her."

"Tell her what?"

He could hear her annoyed sigh, "Tell her you love her."

"Been there, done that, failed miserably."

"They're looking at buying a house."

"Good for them."

"You're annoying. I love you both, but you're both so dumb."

"I'm hanging up now."

“Love you, dummy.”

“Love you, too,” he said as he hung up. He collapsed onto his bed, feeling defeated. He was going to lose her for good soon, and he was going to let it happen.

CHAPTER 18

August 2014

Elena stood at her locker in the science wing of the high school, methodically placing a few books and folders into her bag. She was so engrossed in her task that she didn't notice Rodrigo approaching. Typically, when she was distracted like this, he'd sneak up behind her and give her a playful scare. Today, however, he chose not to, and she silently appreciated the change.

"Hey, you're back. Were you sick? Because if you were, I'll walk the other way—I don't want to catch your cooties," he joked with a laugh that died away as he caught sight of her expression.

"Hey, Rodrigo. Don't worry—you won't catch any cooties. My cootie shots are up to date," she replied, managing a faint smile despite the overwhelming urge to cry.

His smile vanished instantly. "What happened?"

She hesitated. She wanted to confide in him, to let him shoulder her burden, if only for a moment. But at the same time, exposing her vulnerability made her feel uneasy. She hated appearing weak. Intellectually, she understood that grief wasn't weakness, but emotionally, she wanted everyone to still see her as strong. Realizing she had stayed silent for too long, Rodrigo gently grasped her arms, turned her to face him, and searched her eyes. "What happened?" he asked again, this time more softly.

'He knows me too well,' she thought. "Umm...my dad... he, umm... he passed away yesterday. I'm just here to grab some things so I don't fall behind," she said, her voice flat and numb.

Rodrigo's eyes widened in shock. He knew her dad had been ill for a long time and had recently been hospitalized, but she had never let on how serious it had gotten. He didn't say a word. Instead, he wrapped his arms around her, holding her close. They stood there, locked in the embrace, even as the bell signaling the start of first period rang.

Elena tried to pull away. "You should get to class. I'll be fine," she murmured, her voice barely audible.

"I know you'll be fine, but I'm not going to class. What do you need to do today?"

"I... I'm not even sure," she admitted, feeling disoriented and lost.

"Okay, that's fine. Did you get all your books and homework together already?" His voice was calm, free of the clichés people often say when someone dies. There was no 'I'm sorry for your loss,' no 'It was his time' or 'It was God's will,' and certainly none of the hollow reassurances like 'At least he's no longer suffering.' Instead, he offered her practical support and a comforting presence. For Elena, it was exactly what she needed. She didn't have to manage his feelings or soothe any discomfort he might feel about death. There was no need for her to play along with the standard rituals of responding with 'Yeah, he's in a better place,' or 'Thank you.' She didn't have to fake it. Death was awful—plain and simple. No sugarcoating, no matter how it happened or how long someone had been sick. For those left behind, death was a brutal reality. No

one really knows how to navigate it, but Rodrigo was handling it better than most.

"Yeah, I'm done here. I need to go home, grab some clothes for my mom and me, and then head back to Albuquerque." Her thoughts were slowly becoming clearer.

"All right, let's go. I'll drive," he said, shutting her locker and taking her bag. He placed his arm around her shoulders, guiding her towards the parking lot with quiet determination.

"You don't have a pass to leave campus," she said, trying to keep her focus on practicalities.

"Eh, the guy at the front gate buys weed from my brother sometimes—he'll let me through," he replied casually, retrieving her keys from the front pocket of her bag with practiced ease. She always kept them in the same spot, a habit that hadn't changed even now, as she moved through her day on autopilot. Together, they climbed into her car and left the school grounds without any trouble.

Elena wished Rodrigo were with her now, comforting her as he had before. The call had come in around four o'clock that morning. Calls made between midnight and six a.m. are never good, and this one was no different. Somehow, she must have sensed that something terrible was coming; she had left her phone on instead of putting it on silent, as she usually did before bed. For that, she was grateful. Had her phone been on silent, she would have missed the chance to say goodbye. Her mother had sounded both relieved and tearful when Elena picked up the call. Right away, she knew it was about her grandmother. Her grandmother had been sick for a very long time and wasn't improving. Though her grandmother could no longer speak, Elena had the chance to tell her she loved her one final time before she passed.

Now, as Elena drove through the dark expanse of the desert, she thought about Rodrigo and how he had comforted her after her father's death. She wanted nothing more than to call him again, to feel his presence and support. He had a way of making her feel better when life dealt her a cruel hand. Losing her grandmother—one of the few people she could confide in—was another crushing blow. Without her grandmother and without Rodrigo, she felt numb and adrift.

Jake had offered to accompany her to New Mexico, but he didn't provide the comfort she needed. He had never experienced loss, and everything he said felt hollow and predictable. When she told him about her grandmother's passing, his response was, "At least she lived a good, long life." He didn't understand; he hadn't lost anyone close to him. He still had all his grandparents, both parents, siblings, cousins, and friends. Elena, on the other hand, had lost her father, stepfather, cousin, and Eddie—all before she turned twenty-one. And then there were the losses her friends had suffered. The list of people she knew who had died was long, with most gone before the age of forty; her grandmother was the exception.

She longed for Rodrigo, but it didn't seem fair to ask him for comfort when she couldn't tell him she loved him. She had told him she was in love with Jake. If that was true, she should be letting Jake support her. But everything Jake said made her feel worse. His well-intentioned words only heightened her longing for Rodrigo and deepened the sense that Jake didn't really know her. Maybe she wasn't being fair to him. He was trying to get to know her, but she wouldn't let him in, afraid to open up.

'Damn,' she thought, this road trip isn't helping me feel better; it's giving me way too much time to think. Jake had even offered to pay for a flight to New Mexico. She didn't need to drive to save on a pet hotel—Jake would have kept the dogs and looked after them. Still, she chose to drive, bringing the dogs for comfort and relishing the freedom of having her own car. She decided to call someone to distract herself from thoughts of Rodrigo, Jake, and death. First, she tried Emi, but there was no answer—maybe she was asleep or hadn't heard the phone. Next on her list was Lily. Elena had already called earlier to share the news of her grandmother's passing and her overnight drive. Lily, who had known Elena and her family since they were five years old, was like family herself. She would pick up.

The phone rang three times before Lily picked up. "Hello?" she answered, her voice heavy with a yawn.

"Hey, it's Elena. Sorry to wake you up, but I needed someone to talk to while I drive."

"No problem. I'm glad you called instead of trying to drive straight through without someone to keep you awake. How are you holding up?" Lily's voice softened, sensing Elena's need.

"I miss her so much. She was one of my favorite people," Elena said, her words catching on the tears lodged in her throat.

"I know," Lily replied gently. "Is there anything I can do? Is there anyone you haven't told yet who needs to know?"

"I don't think so. I'm pretty sure my mom and aunts are taking care of all that," Elena said, trying to steady herself.

"What about…umm…" Lily paused, clearly unsure, "Did you tell…umm… Rodrigo?"

Elena let out a shaky breath. "I called you so I wouldn't have to think about him anymore. All I want to do is call him. He was really there for me when my dad died. He said and did all the right things. I miss that so much, but I can't do that to him now. It wouldn't be fair." Tears began to stream down her face, though her voice remained composed enough that Lily wouldn't hear her crying.

There was a long silence. Elena began to worry the call had dropped, as often happened during her drives through the desert. "Are you still there?" she finally asked.

"Yeah, I'm here," Lily responded, her voice measured. "I'm just trying to figure out how to say what I need to say."

"Just say it," Elena urged, bracing herself.

"Okay, but remember I don't know how to say this without it sounding harsh."

"Alright." Elena's curiosity was piqued.

"You're a fucking idiot."

Elena blinked in shock. Lily rarely spoke so bluntly. "What?"

"Do you really think Rodrigo wouldn't drop everything to be there for you?" Lily's tone was firm but tinged with quiet urgency.

"Not anymore," Elena whispered. "Not after I told him I loved Jake."

"See? You're a fucking idiot."

"Lily," Elena said, incredulous. "My grandmother just died. Do you have to be so mean?"

"Rodrigo loves you, and if he knew you needed him, nothing you said before would matter. He would come. You should call him."

"I can't. He doesn't want to hear from me," Elena said quietly, her voice subdued.

Lily practically growled in frustration. "Then do it just to prove me wrong! Call him, and if he doesn't come running to your side, then you can rub it in my face and be as mean as you want."

Elena sighed heavily. "I can't, Lily. I told him I couldn't love him the way he loved me. It would be too cruel to call him now, just because the man I chose can't comfort me the way I need."

"Doesn't that—"

Elena cut her off before she could finish. "And before you say it, yes, the reason he doesn't know how to comfort me is because of me and my walls. It's not his fault."

"I still think you should call Rodrigo."

"Noted," Elena said, her tone resigned. "But I can't. I may want to, but… I just can't. And don't even think about telling him anything about me, okay? We cut ties, and it's better that way."

Lily let out a small chuckle, which she quickly masked with a fake cough. "Don't worry. I haven't seen Rodrigo since that New Year's Eve party years ago. Sure, we talked a bit when everything happened, but you know him— eventually, he kind of slipped away. We're just social media acquaintances now. I won't say anything."

"Good. I'm going to go now, okay? You're starting to piss me off, and I can't afford to be angry while driving."

"Okay. Love your face."

"Love yours too." With that, Elena ended the call. Damn Lily. She hadn't helped take her mind off Rodrigo at all.

Instead, her thoughts circled back to how much he had been there for her when her father died.

"Okay, so we have clothes for you and your mom for the services, pajamas, and outfits for the next few days. Anything else?" Rodrigo asked, double-checking the suitcase lying open on Elena's bed.

"I think I packed everything—make-up, clothes, hair stuff, and my school supplies," Elena replied, though her voice sounded distant to her own ears.

Rodrigo paused, watching her closely as if weighing his next words carefully. "You okay being here?"

Elena felt the familiar sting of tears welling up, but she stubbornly held them back. She hadn't cried since her father passed away, afraid that if she started, she might never stop. She needed to stay strong for everyone else. "I'm fine."

"Liar."

"I don't have another choice," she whispered. "I have to be fine. I have to be strong for my mom."

Rodrigo glanced around her room, then stepped to the doorway, peering down the hall to confirm they were alone. "Your mom's not here right now. It's just me and you. Your dad only knew me well enough to joke about charging me a quarter every time I called you before you got a cell phone. He seemed funny, but we weren't close. You don't have to be strong for me."

"I'm fine," she repeated, her voice cracking slightly.

"Elena, I know you," Rodrigo said, his tone gentle but firm. "The next few days are going to be hard enough. You don't have to hold it all together for me. I know you'll be strong for everyone else, but with me, you can let it out. Just let it out." He sat down beside her on the bed, wrapping an arm around her shoulders in a comforting embrace.

Elena met Rodrigo's eyes for a moment. She was so tired of holding back her tears. Everyone looked to her for cues on how to react. She had just lost her father at sixteen. If the sixteen-year-old could keep it together, the adults would too. But if she broke down, they would feel they had permission to do the same. All eyes had been on Elena this

*past week, and she was exhausted. She didn't want to cry,
didn't want to let herself crumble, but in the safety of her
room, with Rodrigo's arm around her, she felt a small crack
forming in her resolve. "I... I miss him so much, and I hate
that he's gone. But I'm also relieved he's not in pain
anymore. I feel so guilty for that relief."*

*Finally, she admitted the thought people are often afraid to
voice when someone dies. No one wants to say that they're
relieved. No one talks about the relief of no longer fearing
to come home and find a lifeless body because their loved
one's health had deteriorated so badly. Or the end of
constant hospital visits, waiting, wondering, and worrying.
Elena wrapped her arms tightly around Rodrigo's neck,
letting her tears spill freely. "He was sick for so long,
Rodrigo. He was angry and tired all the time. At the end, it
felt like he wasn't even my dad anymore. I know it's
horrible, but I'm relieved. And then I feel like the worst
person alive for thinking that." She felt the words tumbling
out of her mouth, a flood she couldn't contain. "The last
thing I said to him... they told me he didn't have much time
left, and I could say goodbye. I told him it was okay to go.
That I'd be okay. And then... I said our thing. He used to
say, 'I love you,' and I'd answer, 'I love you, too.' He'd*

always ask, 'You know why?' and I'd say, 'Why?' Then he'd tell me, 'Because you're my favorite-ist girl in the whole world.' I said it to him, hoping he'd wake up, but also hoping he'd let go. What kind of person does that make me?"

Rodrigo held her tightly, letting her sob into his shoulder. He rubbed her back gently and spoke softly, "It doesn't make you a terrible person. It makes you human. It's okay to feel relief and sadness and guilt all at once."

"I miss my daddy," she whispered, before breaking into deep, heart-wrenching sobs. Rodrigo didn't let go. He cradled her in his arms as she drew her knees up, curling into the fetal position. He rocked her slowly, his hand tracing comforting circles on her back, his voice a steady presence assuring her it was okay, that he was there.

Eventually, her sobs subsided. Rodrigo studied her tired face. "When's the last time you got any real sleep?"

"I... I think maybe an hour or two last night," she murmured, sniffling.

"Then you need to rest," he said gently.

"I can't. I have to get back to Albuquerque."

"I think your mom would rather you get some rest than risk driving when you're this exhausted." Without hesitation, he scooped her up and laid her down on her bed. He tucked her under the quilt and picked up her phone from the nightstand. "I'll call your mom and let her know you're taking a nap."

Elena wanted to protest—there was too much to do—but her eyelids grew heavy. Exhaustion from crying overtook her. "Okay... just, call my mom. And... will you stay? I don't want to wake up alone."

Rodrigo hesitated only briefly, his eyes warm with understanding. "Of course."

Elena remembered falling asleep in Rodrigo's arms and how it was the most rested she'd felt in weeks. In the month surrounding her father's death, peace like that had been rare. But I can't call him, she reminded herself, gripping the steering wheel tighter as she continued driving.

"You need to call her," Lily demanded without any greeting, her voice cutting through the phone line.

"Huh? Call who? Who is this?" Rodrigo asked groggily, clearly just woken up by the ringing.

"This is Lily. Check your caller ID before you answer next time," she snapped.

"Lily? Why are you calling me at this hour?" Rodrigo's voice was still thick with sleep.

"Rodrigo!" Lily nearly shouted, either to get his full attention or out of pure frustration.

"Damn it, Lily! There's no need to scream in the middle of the night," he grumbled, still trying to shake off the remnants of sleep.

"Will you focus for a second? Are you awake enough to hear what I'm saying?" she pressed, her impatience evident.

"Fine. Just tell me what's going on. Who do I need to call?" he asked, still confused but slowly waking up.

"Elena," she said, her voice softer now.

Rodrigo closed his eyes and rubbed his face, already anticipating where this conversation was heading. "Lily, we've talked about this. Elena made it clear—she doesn't want me. Whatever we had is over. A late-night call isn't going to change that."

"Her grandma died," Lily said bluntly, knowing it was the only way to break through his defenses.

The words jolted Rodrigo awake. "Her grandma? The one in Albuquerque?" He knew Elena's connection to her other grandmother was complicated.

"Yeah."

"Damn. How's she holding up?" he asked, suddenly alert.

"She's on her way to Albuquerque now. I just talked to her."

"That's what she's doing, not how she's doing," Rodrigo replied, already getting out of bed and pulling on a shirt, even though he had no idea what he planned to do.

"You know Elena. She's strong. She won't show anyone how much she's hurting."

Rodrigo sighed deeply. "Yeah, that sounds like her."

"You should call her," Lily urged, a hint of hope creeping into her tone.

Rodrigo sat back down on the edge of his bed, feeling the weight of the conversation settle over him. "Lily, I can't call her."

"Why the hell not? She needs you!"

"If she needed me, she'd call," Rodrigo replied quietly, resignation heavy in his voice.

Lily's exasperation was clear in her voice as she said, "You know she always feels like she has to be strong for everyone else. She's never going to come out and say she needs help. You have to call her."

Rodrigo thought back to when Elena's dad passed away. She never asked him for help, not once. She only accepted it when he took charge. "If she needs me, she'll call," he said, though deep down he didn't really believe it.

"You know that isn't true, Rodrigo. She'll keep saying she's fine until she collapses. She'll always put her family's needs first and completely ignore herself," Lily pressed, her frustration growing.

"Lily, she chose Jake. He's the one who should be looking out for her now. If she really needs me, she'll reach out. She always gets in touch when things get too hard for her. She'll call when she's ready."

Lily let out a frustrated groan. "You and Elena are the two most stubborn people I have ever met!" she yelled before hanging up abruptly.

Rodrigo slowly set his phone back down on the nightstand. He stared at it for what felt like forever, silently willing it to ring, hoping that she would make the decision for him. But, of course, this wasn't a movie. His phone stayed silent. If he was going to reach out, it would have to be his choice.

He picked the phone back up, scrolled through his contacts, and stopped when he reached her name. He stared at it, memories and emotions swirling. He wanted to be there for her. She had been there for him before, even while dealing with her own pain.

It was just two weeks before Eddie's 20th birthday. Two weeks. Rodrigo stood outside the church, uncertain if he could go in. Eddie was gone now. Two weeks. Eddie's family and friends continued to file inside, ready to pay their respects and say their goodbyes. But Rodrigo didn't want to say goodbye. Two weeks. Eddie was more than a best friend; he was like a brother—closer than Rodrigo's actual brother. Nineteen years old. Gone because of cancer. No marriage, no children. Two weeks. He fell in love once, graduated high school, had friends who adored him, and a family who loved him. Two weeks. Just nineteen years old. 'I can't go in there,' Rodrigo thought. 'I can't say goodbye. It's too soon.'

"Hey," Elena said softly, sidling up beside him. Her black heels barely made a sound against the sidewalk. Rodrigo wondered how she managed that; heels almost always made noise.

"Hey," he replied, still staring at the church.

"Are you going in?" she asked.

He kept his eyes fixed ahead. "Haven't decided yet."

"Two weeks," she murmured, as if that said everything.

"Yeah, almost made it." He felt numb. For a moment, he wondered if this was how she had felt when her dad died.

"You know you don't have to go in," she said gently.

He turned to her, finally meeting her eyes. "What do you mean?"

"You can wait until everyone else is gone."

He considered it. Could he put it off? Would that make it easier? "I should just do it now. Get it over with."

She nodded and slipped her hand into his. "Okay. Let's go, then."

She left it up to him but made sure he knew she was there no matter what. If he had chosen to wait, she would have waited with him.

They walked into the church together, hand-in-hand. As they stepped inside, it hit him—Elena had a boyfriend.

"Where's your guy?" he asked, desperate for any distraction.

"He's here for me if I need him, which lets me be here for you." He knew her well enough to recognize the pain in her voice. She was grieving, too, but she would set that aside for him today.

They joined the line of mourners slowly moving toward the front, where Eddie's body lay in the casket. Rodrigo knew how much Elena hated viewings. He didn't want to force her to see Eddie this way. "You don't have to stay with me. I'll find you afterward."

She studied his face carefully, as if measuring his pain. She must have seen what he was trying to hide because she said, "I'm not leaving you."

Relief washed over him. He squeezed her hand, grateful for her strength and sacrifice. He remembered there hadn't been a viewing for her father, and he knew how much she hated this—the sight of preserved bodies, the false attempt to make death seem less terrible. It was fake and grotesque to her. Still, she walked with him to the front, her hand firmly in his, letting him face the hardest reality: Eddie was truly gone.

They approached Eddie together. "Seriously, Elena. I know you hate this."

She stopped and turned him to face her. "I'm here for you. You need this, so I'm here."

It was their turn. Rodrigo looked at Eddie. His friend looked peaceful, with a small grin on his face. But that wasn't Eddie. Eddie was curious, always questioning, never fully confident despite how others admired him. This wasn't the friend Rodrigo knew. Now he understood why Elena despised viewings. "It doesn't even look like him."

"I know," Elena whispered, her voice tight. He noticed her eyes were closed. But she was still by his side, supporting him.

"Two weeks," he said softly, giving her hand another squeeze as they turned and walked away from the casket.

'Call her,' he told himself. She had been there for him when Eddie died, even while she was carrying her own heavy grief. She forced herself to confront something she despised, for his sake. She pushed her limits for him, giving him strength even when she barely had any to spare.

They all stood together outside the church after Eddie's service—Lily, Mary, April, Rodrigo, and Elena. Elena's boyfriend, Alex—Rodrigo was pretty sure that was his name—stood a few paces away, just outside their small circle. He wasn't intruding, but his mere presence felt like interference. Rodrigo knew it was unfair to think that way; Alex seemed like a decent guy, and Elena had said he was helping her through her grief. But still, Rodrigo couldn't help but wish it was just their original group again, unencumbered.

Elena and Rodrigo stood very close, almost touching but no longer holding hands. Rodrigo let go to make it clear there was nothing more between them and to remind himself that he needed to stand on his own now. "Man, Eddie would've hated all that attention," Rodrigo said, attempting a laugh to break the somber mood.

The four women turned to him, tears glistening in their eyes. But his comment worked; after a moment, everyone let out soft giggles. "He really would have," Mary said, wiping away a stray tear. "Especially when everyone kept talking about how amazing he was. He never knew how to take a compliment."

They all smiled, each silently acknowledging the truth in the statement. A somber silence settled over the group for a few moments as they stood together, each lost in their own thoughts. It was April who finally broke it. "I'd better get going," she said softly, her voice tinged with finality. "I'll talk to you guys later." She hugged each of them tightly before walking away. Deep down, they all knew she wouldn't keep in touch after that day.

"Yeah, I should head out too. My mom's waiting for me," Lily added, stepping forward to give out hugs and kisses on the cheek. "Love you guys."

"Love you too," Elena replied sincerely. She then turned to Mary. "You headed home as well?"

Mary's expression grew sad, but she nodded. "My flight's early tomorrow morning. I need to pack and spend some time with my mom. I just had to go to school abroad." She had only just begun her semester in Paris when she had to return home for the funeral.

"I'm really glad you could come back to say goodbye," Elena said, pulling her into a tight embrace.

"Me too. Bye, you two."

When Mary had left, it was just Elena and Rodrigo. She glanced at him, concern evident in her eyes. "You going to be okay?" she asked, now that they were essentially alone.

Rodrigo held her gaze briefly before looking past her at her boyfriend, who lingered a few steps away, trying to seem unobtrusive. "I'm fine," he insisted. "You should go. Your guy looks like he's getting impatient."

Elena glanced over her shoulder and waved dismissively. "He's fine. He's been through this too. We actually have that unfortunate bond—losing loved ones."

"Seriously, I'm fine," Rodrigo repeated, but his voice wavered slightly.

She placed a comforting hand on his arm and squeezed gently. "Wait here for a minute." She walked over to her boyfriend, whispered something, and gave him a soft kiss. He nodded, smiled faintly, and then walked away. Elena returned to Rodrigo's side. "Alright, what do you need to do today?"

Rodrigo's eyes narrowed slightly, a flicker of anger sparking in his voice. "Did he seriously just leave you here?"

"No, I asked him to go," she said, her tone calm. "I told him you'd take me home later. So, what do you need to do today?"

Rodrigo exhaled, the anger ebbing away. "Honestly, I don't know. Nothing that matters, really."

"Okay, let's start with the basics," Elena said gently. "Have you eaten? Gotten any sleep?"

He shook his head stubbornly. "You don't have to take care of me. I'm fine."

She smiled knowingly. "Yeah, I remember saying that a lot when it was me a few years back. Good thing you didn't listen. Now it's my turn. Come on—I'll drive you home, *make you a sandwich, and then you're going straight to bed."*

He rolled his eyes but didn't protest as she took him by the arm and led him to his truck. "You know how to drive stick?" he asked, without a trace of innuendo for once.

She laughed softly. "I grew up in the country—of course I do."

When they reached his apartment, Elena kept her word. She made him eat a sandwich, then guided him to bed. Rodrigo climbed under the covers but knew sleep would evade him, as it had every night since Eddie's death. To his surprise, Elena kicked off her shoes and slid in under the blankets next to him. "You're staying?" he asked, his voice low.

"Obviously," she replied firmly.

'Call her,' he thought again, the words echoing in his mind. He lay in bed, staring at his phone, feeling its weight as the minutes ticked by until sleep finally forced the decision from him.

Meanwhile, Elena kept expecting him to call. She busied herself preparing a slideshow of her grandmother's life, sorting through old photos, listening to family stories, and discussing her grief with friends who reached out. Through it all, her phone never left her side. Jake called often. He tried to comfort her, but he was unskilled with death's sting, his attempts clumsy though sincere. Her family had chosen to hold a viewing, something Elena found hard to face. She stayed away until the casket was closed. When she finally stepped through the doors, she instinctively searched the room, hoping Lily had reached Rodrigo, and that he might appear by some miracle to support her. But he didn't. This wasn't a movie; reality rarely bent for hopes like that.

Rodrigo woke slowly, emerging from a rare, dreamless sleep. He immediately noticed the emptiness beside him—Elena's comforting warmth was gone. He opened his eyes and saw her phone next to his on the nightstand, reassuring him. Elena wouldn't just leave without a word. Rising from bed, he scanned the apartment and noticed the balcony door left slightly ajar.

"Elena?" he called softly, stepping outside. The cold rain poured down, instantly drenching him.

She stood there with her arms outstretched, her face tilted up into the sky. Water soaked her hair and clothes, but she made no move to shield herself from the chill. "It's raining," she murmured, as though the simple fact held some profound meaning.

"Yeah, I see that," Rodrigo replied, perplexed. "Why are you standing out here?"

"It's raining," she repeated, her voice laced with an unspoken weight he struggled to grasp.

"I know," he said, concern deepening. "You're going to freeze. Come back inside."

Finally, she turned to him, letting her arms drop to her sides. "It's raining, Rodrigo. It's January. Usually, it snows, or the wind howls, but rain is rare. And today, the day we bury him, it rains."

He studied her, trying to understand. "Are you saying it's a sign? Like God or Eddie is sending us a message? You know I don't believe in that stuff, and neither do you."

She shook her head, water dripping from her hair. "I'm not saying it's a sign from God, or the universe, or Zeus, or anyone else. I'm saying this rain is rare, and I'm letting it pour over me. I'm hoping it will wash away some of this pain."

He looked at her, unsure if the water streaking her face was just rain or tears. Her voice was steady, yet he thought he caught the faintest hitch in her words. She had spent the entire day looking out for him, even though she had lost a friend too. If standing in the rain helped her in some way, he would stay by her side and brave the cold. Without saying anything, he stepped closer, gently took her hand in his, and allowed the rain to pour over him too. He clung to the faint hope that maybe, just maybe, the rain could wash away some of his pain as well.

The next time he woke to the sound of rain, it was accompanied by rolling thunder. The monsoons stubbornly lingered over the desert. This time, he chose to face it head-on. Stepping outside into his front yard, he felt the rain pelting his skin, cold and unrelenting, and hoped for a similar comfort to that cold January night. He closed his eyes, tilting his head up toward the dark, stormy sky. But instead of relief, he felt only the chill seeping into his bones. The weight of everything remained. He was simply soaked and miserable. Why hadn't it worked? It had back then. But deep down, he knew why. "Elena," he whispered to the rain. It had never been about the rain. It was her. She had been his healing force.

He trudged back inside, water dripping from his hair and clothes. Picking up his phone, he stared at her contact photo and, with a deep breath, pressed the call button. His heart pounded as it began to ring—but he quickly hung up before it could connect.

I thought for sure you would have called, or shown up, or sent me a message, or even flowers—anything. I don't know why. I never told you what was happening. Maybe I expected you to be psychic, or maybe it's just

wishful thinking. I need to stop writing these messages I'll never send.

"I have to stop this," she muttered to herself, fingers hovering over the keyboard. First step: block him on social media. She hesitated, staring at the screen. "Ugh," she groaned aloud before snapping her laptop shut, leaving the message unsent and the block list untouched.

November 2014

Happy birthday.

The message was the simplest he had written since they stopped speaking. It had been months since her grandmother's passing. He had picked up the phone countless times, intending to call her. More often than he liked to admit, he wrestled with the urge. But he never followed through. He wouldn't send this message either.

December 2014

I think I've figured out our problem—or at least, my problem. We're like a binary star system. We orbit each other, and sometimes, we drift too close, and you steal

some of my mass. You've taken too much of me, leaving me smaller and dimmer, yet I remain stuck in orbit around you, despite the pain of losing myself. I can't break free from you.

She had captured too much of his heart, leaving him powerless to reclaim it. No matter how hard he tried, he couldn't push her out of his mind or move on. 'Just let go, dude. Let go or hit send.' He did neither.

January 2015

It's a new year. I haven't written to you in months. Does that mean I'm finally moving on? Have I accepted a life where you no longer exist in it? Maybe I'm just growing numb to the constant ache in my chest.

Her own secret resolution for the new year was to stop writing unsent messages to him. She saw two ways to achieve this: either stop composing them altogether or finally press send. She chuckled softly before erasing the words. Oh well, no one ever keeps their New Year's resolutions anyway.

February 2015

Every major holiday fills me with anxiety now. Lily keeps saying he could propose to you at any moment. She's convinced it's coming soon. Yesterday was Valentine's Day, and it appears you're not engaged yet. I can breathe easier—at least for now. But deep down, I know she's probably right. He won't wait forever. If I were in his place, I wouldn't either.

He stared at the last sentence, weighing its meaning. Did he really feel that way? Would he marry her if given the chance? He erased the message and tried to avoid lingering too long on that thought. Maybe a long run would help clear his mind.

March 2015

Today, I heard our song on the radio while riding in the car with him. When I teared up at a Three Dog Night track, he gave me a baffled look. He asked if I was okay, and I shut down. He let it go. You wouldn't have. You would've respected my need for space for a while, but eventually, you'd ask again—and I would have told you.

Why is talking to you so much easier, even when I know you'll never read this?

Naturally, she deleted the message. Then, to steady herself, she silently listed all the reasons why she and Rodrigo would never work, and all the reasons why Jake was perfect for her. It helped—sort of.

CHAPTER 19

April 2015

'What am I doing?' she thought, staring out the plane window as the Golden Gate Bridge grew smaller with each passing second, the aircraft veering eastward. This trip was impulsive. She had just spent $400 she didn't have on a one-way ticket to Albuquerque. She felt unhinged. No luggage, only a blue dress far too formal for a no-frills airline flight. There had been no time to go home and change. She needed to leave—not just the museum where it happened, but the entire state. She continued gazing outside, even as thick clouds obscured any remaining view.

A flight attendant approached. "Would you like something to drink?"

"Tequila," Elena replied.

"Would you like anything with that?" The attendant's expression carried a hint of judgment.

Elena met her gaze coolly and handed over her nearly maxed-out credit card. "Nope." The attendant took her payment and walked away, shaking her head slightly.

If she only knew what I was going through, she'd understand why I need this drink. When the mini bottle finally arrived, Elena wrapped her fingers around it and swallowed the liquor almost instantly, then ordered another. Her thoughts drifted to Jake. How was he coping? Her response had been to run and drink, despite the disapproving glances of strangers. Guilt churned within her. It wasn't as though Jake had done anything terrible. In fact, he had done something extraordinary and deeply romantic.

Reaching into her purse, she pulled out the box and opened it, oblivious to the flight attendant's return. "What a beautiful ring. Congratulations! When did you get engaged?"

Elena took the second mini bottle of tequila, downed it in one go, and then replied, "He asked tonight," her tone making it clear she wasn't in the mood for conversation. The attendant resumed her duties without further comment.

'Damn, nosy people,' Elena thought, noticing curious glances from nearby passengers. Poor Jake. He had been so thoughtful. She'd woken up late that morning to a bouquet of stargazer lilies—her favorite—sitting beside their king-sized bed, its fluffy bedding disheveled from their sleep. Next to the flowers lay a note, instructing her to dress up and head downstairs. She had sensed what was coming, feeling equal parts exhilarated and terrified. She chose the blue dress Jake adored, styled her hair, did her makeup, and touched up her chipped nail polish. When she stepped out of their apartment, a limo waited, its driver holding a sign with her name. She smiled as she climbed into the backseat, spotting her favorite champagne chilling nearby. "Where are we headed?" she asked the driver.

"Golden Gate Park," he replied without elaborating.

During the ride, she felt a mix of nerves and excitement building inside her. When they pulled up to the Academy of Sciences, the driver stepped around to open her door. "Here we are, ma'am."

"Thank you," she said, taking a steadying breath as she made her way up the museum's stairs. She had no ticket, but a part of her knew she wouldn't need one. Just inside, another person stood holding a sign with her name on it.

"I'm Elena," she introduced herself.

"Wonderful. This way, miss," he responded with a warm smile, guiding her into the planetarium.

The first thing she noticed was the intoxicating scent of lilies—her favorite. As her eyes adjusted to the dim light, she took in the stunning display above: a "sky" filled with countless stars, mirroring the desert skies she loved so much, with the Milky Way prominently shimmering. Jake was waiting at the front of the room, looking exceptionally handsome in a gray suit paired with a blue tie. 'Did he know I'd wear this dress?' she wondered, noting how perfectly his tie matched her outfit. She walked toward him, each step slow and deliberate as anxiety and anticipation swirled inside her. She knew what was coming. Did she want it? She loved him—she truly did. She could see a future with him. He wanted children, could support her financially, and made her laugh. He was driven, dependable. Yet, an image of Rodrigo kissing her in his truck, snow falling softly around them, suddenly invaded her mind.

She closed her eyes for a brief second to push the memory away. When she opened them, Jake was speaking. "I know how much you love the stars and how much you miss the skies back in New Mexico. So, I wanted to bring that sky here for you."

"It's incredible," she whispered, her eyes moving from the stars above back to him.

"You deserve incredible things. To me, you are incredible," he continued, his voice earnest. "You're so dedicated to your clients, and you care deeply about everyone around you. You make me laugh, and you've taught me more than I ever imagined. You're strong and independent, but you let me in—you let me care for you, even when I know you don't need anyone to. I love you." He dropped to one knee and opened a black velvet box, revealing a gleaming diamond ring. "Will you marry me?" he asked, his eyes soft and filled with hope.

Elena was speechless. Her thoughts were racing, too fast for her to process. He wants to marry me. He loves me. Her eyes flicked to the ring. That ring is huge. I'm definitely going to get mugged. She shifted her gaze back to Jake. Jake is such a good man. I should say yes. Should I? Her mind scrambled. What about Rodrigo? Rodrigo. What about him? They hadn't spoken in over a year. He hadn't called when her grandmother passed away. She had hoped, so badly, that he would reach out. Jake had tried to help her through the loss, but he didn't understand the depth of it the way Rodrigo did. Is that Jake's fault? No, it wasn't. Can I say yes? Do I even want to say yes? Her chest tightened, her heart pounding in sync with her racing thoughts. Her breathing quickened, and the scent of lilies—her favorite flower—became overwhelming, suffocating. It all felt too much. The panic attack was starting.

It struck her as strangely ironic—A psychologist who can't even manage her own panic attack? If she could have caught her breath, she would have laughed, but at that moment, she couldn't remember the first thing about how to calm herself. Breathe. Think. You know this.

"Elena?" Jake stood, his expression filled with concern.

She closed her eyes, focusing on her breath. You're safe.
You're not dying. Breathe in for five counts, nice and slow.
Hold it. Now breathe out slowly, counting to eight. Make
your exhale longer than your inhale. Slow your breathing.
Slow your heart rate. You're okay. You're safe. Her mind
repeated the mantra, but her training came back to her
slower than she would have liked. She focused on her
feet—how they felt in her shoes, the sensation of her toes
shifting, the pressure on the soles connecting her body to
the ground. Ground yourself. Breathe.

After a few minutes, her breathing began to even out. She
opened her eyes again, meeting Jake's concerned gaze.

"I'm so sorry," she said, her voice shaky. "That's never
happened to me before. It's just… this is such a big
decision, and it scared me for a minute."

Jake's brow furrowed, his worry palpable. "Are you okay
now?"

Elena looked up at the artificial New Mexico sky above
them, her mind still whirling. "I need to think about this
before I give you an answer. Everything you've done

today… it's incredible, and I love you. But I have to go. Please understand."

He nodded, his voice soft. "Do what you need to do. I'll see you back at home... when you're ready."

His understanding only made her feel worse, like a failure in a moment when she should have known what to do. But there was no time for that now. She turned, her heels clicking on the floor as she hurried out of the museum. She caught an expensive ride to the airport, then an even pricier flight to Albuquerque. As she sat waiting to board, she pulled out her phone and texted Rodrigo. **I need to see you tonight.** Without a second thought, she pressed send.

Rodrigo walked into his house, his body still buzzing from his run. He held his mail in one hand, his other hand wiping the sweat from his forehead. He stood in the doorway for a moment, savoring the rush of endorphins. Running always helped him clear his head. He focused on the rhythmic sound of his feet pounding against the dirt, the steady thrum of his heart in his chest, and the deepening rhythm of his breath.

He turned toward the small table near the door to drop the mail. Most of it was probably bills, but his attention was caught by the envelope on top—it was from NYU. His heart skipped a beat. This was it: he had either made the cut, or he hadn't. The thought of it made his stomach tighten, and for a moment, he hesitated. He was almost afraid to open it. He thought of Elena then, and how much he wished she was there to open it for him, to make this moment feel less heavy. But she wasn't there, and he needed to stop thinking about her. He reminded himself of that at least once a day, often more.

He stared at the envelope, noting that it wasn't very thick. 'Probably not a good sign,' he thought. "Now or never," he muttered to the empty house.

With a sudden burst of energy, he ripped open the envelope and unfolded the letter inside. He had to read it twice before he could believe what he was seeing. Congratulations, it said, and welcome to New York University's Environmental Engineering Master's program. Look for a welcome packet arriving shortly… He didn't care what the rest of the letter said right now. He was in. He couldn't believe it, but after reading it again, and then again, the truth began to sink in. Yep, still in. No matter how many times he reread it, it still didn't feel real. And he knew exactly why. Good things never felt real until she knew. Until Elena knew.

They hadn't spoken in a year. Not since the night she'd told him she couldn't love him. He moved numbly to his bedroom and grabbed his phone from its charger. 'I'll tell Chris,' he thought. But when he glanced at his phone, he saw a message from the one person he most wanted to talk to.

I need to see you tonight.

He stared at the words, reading them again and again. Just like the letter, he couldn't quite believe it. His heart started to race. After rereading it several times, he decided he had to respond. Despite everything, despite the distance, the silence, and the heartache, he realized something: he hadn't moved on. She was still there, lingering in the back of his mind, like a pink elephant. The more he tried to forget her, the more she remained with him, occupying his every thought. He still loved her. And he needed to see her. He needed to tell her his news. But there was something else. Why had she reached out to him? What did she need?

The sun was beginning to dip below the horizon as the plane started its final descent into Albuquerque. The orange and pink sky spread out before her, and for a moment, it reminded Elena of the time she and Rodrigo had watched the sunrise together at his house. The memory made her smile, but it was quickly followed by a heavy weight of dread settling in her chest. 'What am I doing?' she thought. 'This is bad. This is really bad.'

She repeated the words to herself like a mantra, over and over, as the wheels hit the runway and the small, familiar airport came into view. Her fingers trembled as she reached into her purse to put away the ring box, her mind still spinning.

She pulled out her phone and hesitated, wondering whether Rodrigo would even respond. Would he want to see her after everything that had happened? After what she had done to him? Her breath caught in her throat as she read his simple response:

Where?

Rodrigo pulled into a parking spot on the street across from the bar. He paused for a moment, staring at the building, before reaching for the door handle. He imagined her inside, sitting at the bar, a drink in hand, waiting for him. With a deep breath, he climbed out of the truck and walked toward the bar. The letter in the back pocket of his jeans felt like a ten-pound weight, despite its small size. He stopped mid-step. How was he going to tell her that he was leaving? Why had she been in town and in contact with him on the very same day he'd received his acceptance letter? Was it all a coincidence, or was this always how it was meant to be? The butterflies in his stomach flapped wildly, intensifying his nerves as he approached the bar. He hadn't felt this nervous about anything in a long time. 'I should just turn around and go home,' he thought, It would be so much easier that way.

He started to turn back toward his truck but muttered a frustrated "Fuck" under his breath. He thought about her, up in the bar, waiting for him, wanting to tell him something important. The thought of leaving without saying goodbye, of moving across the country without closure, made him stop in his tracks. He couldn't walk away now. With a determined sigh, he crossed the empty street and headed toward the downstairs entrance of the bar.

It was still early enough in the evening that Elena could sit at the bar. She didn't face the room but could hear a group of twenty-somethings laughing and enjoying a pool game at one of the tables. She brushed some invisible lint off the skirt of her blue dress and nervously checked her phone. He was ten minutes late—nothing unusual there. 'What if he doesn't show up?' she thought. What if this was all for nothing? She ordered two shots of tequila with limes.

"Nervous about something?" the bartender asked. She had brown hair in a pixie cut and an amazing sleeve tattoo on her arm. Elena especially liked the monkey surfing on a walrus.

"Am I that obvious?"

"The two shots gave it away."

"I'm meeting an old friend here. We haven't talked in a while, and I've got something pretty major to tell him."

"Old friend or old boyfriend?"

"Sort of both and neither at the same time," she replied with a nervous chuckle.

"Oh, I see," the bartender said, nodding like she understood the strange situation. "Well, these are on me. Everyone needs a little liquid courage now and then."

"Thanks," Elena said, taking the first shot. As she swallowed, her eyes caught the mirror behind the bar, and she saw him walk in. Her heart stalled for a moment, and she instinctively rubbed her thumb over the velvet box in her lap. 'Shit,' she thought, 'I can't do this.' But when she tried to turn away, she realized she couldn't. She couldn't run from this. She had to tell him.

He slid up next to her at the bar, almost silent. Without looking at him, she pushed the second shot of tequila his way. He took it without hesitation, both of them avoiding eye contact but stealing glances through the mirror behind the bar.

"You should leave while you still can," she said, her voice low, still not looking at him directly. "I have a feeling tonight is going to suck."

He noticed the velvet box in her lap as he glanced at her. A quiet laugh escaped him. "I know what you're going to say."

She finally looked at him, surprised. "You do?"

He nodded, pointing at the velvet box. "I know what you're going to say. But I'm not leaving."

She opened the box, revealing a large engagement ring. "I haven't said yes yet."

"Why not?"

She took a deep breath, but the words wouldn't come. She gestured to the bartender for two more shots. The bartender, having been within earshot, had already poured them before Elena could even ask. With a wink at both Elena and Rodrigo, she set the shots down in front of them. "You looked like you might need these," she said with a knowing smile, tucking the receipt into her pocket as she walked away.

Elena raised her shot glass towards him, still not meeting his eyes. He mirrored her movement and raised his glass as well. "What are we toasting to?" he asked.

"We're toasting to courage," she replied, clinking her glass against his and downing her shot in one motion.

He followed suit, then asked again, "So why haven't you said yes yet?"

For the first time since he'd walked into the bar, she met his gaze. The weight of the moment settled between them. She took a deep breath and closed her eyes for a moment before speaking. "I love you. I should have told you last year after you told me you loved me, but... I figured what would it have mattered? I still live a thousand miles away from you, and you still have a girlfriend. I still have a boyfriend. We want different things in life. So, I thought... what would it matter if I told you? It would just hurt us both in the end."

He stared at her, disbelief written across his face. She continued, her voice trembling slightly. "In that moment, I overthought everything. I looked at all the possible outcomes of me saying it back, and none of them ended well for us. I thought the best thing to do was ignore my feelings, go home, and keep my distance. I'm sorry... I feel like I'm babbling now."

"Sorry? You're sorry?" His voice was rising, frustration building in his chest. He stood up from his stool, drawing the attention of several other patrons. "I don't know how you did it, but I can't just turn off how I feel. And since when do you know what's best for everyone? You've said it yourself—just because you're a therapist doesn't mean you've got your own life figured out. You're too close to it. You can't be objective when it's your own life on the line. If you really thought it would hurt us both, why the hell are you telling me now?" His words grew louder as his anger took over.

Elena swallowed hard, feeling the weight of his words. "I can't help it! This is who I am! I overthink everything, and I find it so hard to follow my heart. When he asked me to marry him, all I could think about was finding you and telling you that I love you. I couldn't marry him without knowing if you still loved me... or if I'd ruined everything between us."

She stood up as well, but her voice remained quieter as she noticed the curious stares from the other bar patrons.

He closed his eyes, shaking his head. "Figures. Of course, you'd tell me all this today." He pulled the acceptance letter from his back pocket and handed it to her, the gesture rougher than he meant it to be.

"You were accepted?" she asked, her voice barely a whisper.

"Yep," he replied. "Got the letter this afternoon."

"So, I guess it's pretty clear what we should do now."

"We should walk away," he said, taking a step closer to her.

"We should walk away," she agreed, her own step bringing them even closer. Now, there was no space left between them, and he could feel the heat of her breath against his neck.

He looked up and noticed several patrons still watching them. Without thinking, he grabbed the velvet box and his acceptance letter, stuffing both into his pocket. He called the bartender over, she looked so familiar but he couldn't quite place why. "Can I pay our tab?" he asked.

"Already taken care of," she replied casually.

He turned to Elena, taking her hand. "Let's go somewhere more private to talk about this." They started toward the exit.

"Did you drive?" he asked as they crossed the street to his truck.

"No, I literally got off the plane and took a cab straight here."

"Good," he said, "We can take my truck then."

He opened her door for her and helped her in. As he walked around to his side of the truck, a million thoughts raced through his mind. She loves him. It wasn't just in his head. She thinks he's still with Ana. She loves him. She might be getting engaged—she isn't engaged yet. She loves him. He got into NYU. He hasn't accepted yet. She loves him. They still live a thousand miles apart—and even more if he moves to New York. She loves him. She loves him. She loves him.

He put the truck in gear and pointed it towards the airport viewing area. They sat in silence, neither of them knowing how to say what they needed to say. He turned on the radio, hoping to break the tension, flicking from station to station. Elena grew increasingly irritated with his aimless searching, so she grabbed the auxiliary cord, plugged it into her phone, and quickly found a song. It was a band he didn't recognize—some kind of folksy emo alternative. As the song played, he realized it was the perfect choice, capturing the mood in the truck: something about driving at night, with cherry lipstick.

He pulled into the empty viewing area, relieved to see they were the only ones there. He parked the truck, and they both continued to listen to the music, each lost in thought, unsure of how to begin the conversation.

"So, you think we should walk away?" she asked, breaking the silence at last.

"So do you," he shot back defensively.

"I don't know what we should do," she said slowly, "I know what I want to do... but I can already picture how it might turn out."

"Oh, so now you can predict the future?" he asked, anger flaring in his chest. "You realize that your 'prediction' is why you waited until you were engaged to tell me how you really feel about me." He couldn't bring himself to say the words "you love me." He was afraid he had imagined it all.

"What if we pretend that night never happened? What if we pretend that the night you told me you loved me is still ahead of us, and we can have a do-over?" she asked, her voice hopeful.

"You want to pretend the last year didn't happen?" he asked, his voice heavy with doubt.

"Just for tonight... please?" She looked at him, waiting for an answer. She wasn't sure if it would help them figure things out, but she couldn't think of anything else to try. All she could focus on was the idea of redoing that night. Why not give it a shot?

He didn't look at her for a long moment. He'd wished a hundred times over the past year that he could go back to that night. He didn't see how it would help now. He prepared to tell her that it wouldn't change anything, but when he saw the hopeful look in her eyes, he couldn't bring himself to turn her down.

"I love you," he said simply, the words heavy with emotion.

Her smile was a mix of joy and pain. "I love you too," she replied softly.

In that moment, words were no longer needed. They reached for each other, their lips meeting in a kiss. It had been so long since they'd kissed, but it felt just as natural and familiar as before. This kiss wasn't playful or rough— it wasn't wild. It was deep, filled with longing. She ran her hands up his arms, tracing his face before slipping her fingers through his hair. He kissed her neck, his hand sliding up her thigh, slipping beneath her blue dress. He quickly removed her panties and tossed them onto the floor of the truck. She pulled off his shirt, pressing a kiss to his chest, right over his thumping heart.

"I love you," she whispered again, looking into his eyes as he gently laid her down on the seat of the truck.

"I love you," he said immediately, holding her gaze.

This was love-making in its purest form. After he entered her, they found a slow, steady rhythm, savoring the deep connection of body, heart, and soul as they came together. When they finished, he lay on top of her for a moment, their bodies still intertwined. She could feel his heartbeat, and as strange as it seemed, she could almost swear his heart was beating in time with hers. Her eyes welled up with tears, but she didn't cry. She wasn't sure if this was the beginning of something beautiful or the painful end of it. 'Crying would be overthinking,' she told herself. She refused to let doubts ruin this moment, so instead, she reached up and softly stroked his hair.

They lay there for a long time, holding each other in the quiet, listening to the music from her phone. Every song seemed to speak of love and pain. He marveled at the coincidence, but then thought about her methodical nature and realized she had probably created the playlist herself. Some of the songs were familiar, ones he had heard when they spent time together or from her social media posts. Others were new to him, but all of them perfectly captured the mood in the truck—hope, love, pain, loss, and uncertainty. He desperately wanted to know what she was thinking, but at the same time, he didn't want to ruin the fragile peace they had, terrified that by the end of the night, everything between them would be over.

The silence was broken by the buzzing of a cellphone vibrating on the floorboard. He fumbled around, trying to find the source of the sound and accidentally brushed against the engagement ring box. He moved past it, finally locating the phone. It was hers—her phone had likely fallen off the seat during their lovemaking. If not for the long auxiliary cord, they would have been lying in complete silence. He didn't need to guess who was calling. The picture on the screen confirmed it.

"It's your fiancé," he said, his voice flat, sitting up and handing her the phone. As she took it, he began gathering his clothes, getting dressed. The phone continued to buzz. "Are you going to answer it?"

"He's called three times in the last hour. I kind of left in a hurry. He doesn't even know I flew out of state," she said, feeling guilty. She had just cheated on Jake, and in a sense, answering the phone now would feel like she was cheating on Rodrigo too.

"I guess that's your answer then," he said, trying his best to sound neutral, though the hurt in his voice was unmistakable.

She slid her finger across the screen to answer. "Hey, sorry I missed your calls." She avoided looking at Rodrigo as she spoke, her voice a little shaky. "This is a big decision, and I want to take the time to think about it, like I said, but don't worry about me, okay? I'll see you soon." She paused, listening intently. Rodrigo tried not to listen, but he couldn't help hearing Jake tell her he loved her.

"Me too," she said quickly, her voice almost too soft. "I'll see you soon." She ended the call and glanced down at the phone in her lap. When she hung up, the music resumed. He almost laughed because the song that started playing was about diamonds, old barstools, and things that didn't quite go together. It was such a fitting, ironic tune, and they both knew it.

"So, you love him too," he said, his tone flat. It wasn't a question—it was a statement of painful fact.

"I don't want to fight with you," she replied quietly.

"I don't want to fight either," he said, the words coming out heavy. "But not long ago, we both agreed that we should walk away... and then we didn't."

"I wanted to come here tonight and tell you how much I love you, how much you mean to me," she said, her voice breaking. "I wanted to tell you how terrible my life has been this past year without you. You know I lost my grandmother this year. It reminded me of losing my dad, Eddie, and... losing you. I wanted to talk to you more than anything, but after the last time we saw each other, I didn't think you would want anything to do with me." Elena was crying now, her tears mixing with the pain in her voice. "I needed you, but I didn't reach out, and I regret that every day. I regret so many things about this last year. I wanted to come here and tell you that I've changed, that this time I wouldn't mess things up for us."

Rodrigo wanted to hold her, to stop her tears, but he couldn't shake Jake's voice from his mind, telling Elena that he loved her. "I knew about your grandmother. Lily told me. She said I should call you, that you needed me, but I thought if you really needed me, nothing would stop you from reaching out. It never stopped you before. I kept waiting, but nothing. You let him take care of you instead!" His voice cracked, betraying the hurt he was trying to suppress. "Now, answer me: do… you… love him?" He spoke each word slowly, painfully, making sure it was clear. He looked her in the eyes, the anger rising, because he already knew the answer.

"Fine," she said, her voice trembling. "The truth is, yes, I do love him, and I love you too, but it's different." The words stung, but they were honest. She felt a deep ache, knowing he'd been aware of her grandmother's death, yet had done nothing. She could hear the pain in his voice, and it tore her apart. She wanted to hold him, to ease his pain, but she felt paralyzed. She couldn't stop focusing on the things he hadn't done—how he hadn't been there for her during the tough moments this past year.

"How can you love us both?" He asked, the question heavy with disbelief. He knew he should stop pushing her, stop questioning her. He should take her in his arms, kiss the tears away, tell her that he loved her, that he would do anything to be with her. He should reassure her that none of this mattered, that they would find a way. But instead, he kept sabotaging himself.

"I thought you would understand. You love Ana too, don't you?" She said, her voice barely a whisper.

"No," he replied firmly. "Ana was a distraction, a temporary escape. But it's always been you. Only you. I ended things with Ana when I applied to school. Well, she ended it before I had the chance to. If I wasn't willing to do long-distance with you, I wasn't going to do it with her."

"If you won't do long distance, then what are you saying? Are you willing to give up school and move to San Francisco?" She felt a flicker of hope. Maybe, just maybe, she hadn't ruined everything between them. She reached out for his hand across the seat of the truck, believing that, despite everything, there was a chance. Maybe, maybe this could work.

"Are you going to break up with your fiancé?" he asked, his voice filled with a mixture of hope and desperation. He let himself imagine a life with her—a life that could still be possible.

He hadn't answered her question directly. She could feel it—he wanted her to make the sacrifices, to break up with Jake and move to New York, to start over. But what was Rodrigo willing to give up? She felt a surge of anger, pushing aside the hurt and the hope. "See, this has always been our problem! Neither of us will give up on our dreams or each other. We hold on to both so tight, but it's getting us nowhere. If we don't compromise, this will never work."

As her anger grew, so did his. "So, what's the compromise? We both give up what we want and move to Kansas? I know you. You're not giving up your life in San Francisco."

"And you're not giving up school in New York. Plus, I still want to get married and have a family. Have you changed your mind about marriage and kids?"

He had changed. He wanted to marry her, build a life together, raise a family, take them on adventures around the world, and come home to a house in the suburbs, near good schools. "No, I haven't," he replied softly, the words feeling hollow in the dark truck. It felt like everything was falling apart. They kept saying things that hurt each other, offering hope only to take it away. He couldn't take it anymore. He loved her, and she loved him, but love seemed like it wasn't enough. Love wasn't enough to make them take the risks they needed to take. Love wasn't enough to give them a future. Love wasn't enough to erase their pain. For him… for her… love had become a weight they couldn't bear. He started the truck.

"Where are we going?" she asked, slipping back into her panties. As she redressed, a deep sense of dread settled in her chest, as though her world was about to end.

"I'm taking you to the airport."

"What? Why? We aren't done talking!" She felt a surge of panic. Her heart was racing—she had to fix this. She could fix this. Her mind took control, seeing the inevitable outcome. She wiped the tears from her face, fastened her seatbelt, and began to close off her heart.

He was numb. He imagined he would always be numb after this night. "Yes, we are. We are going to make the easier choices. You're going back to California, marrying the lawyer who wants kids and a suburban life. You'll work in community mental health, start your own practice. I'm going to move to New York, get my master's, travel the world trying to save it, never settling in one place for too long. Those are the easier choices. The ones we're comfortable with. They're safe. You and me, we're…"

"Complicated." This was it. The end. Love like this was too painful. Love like this was a killer.

"Always have been. We never would have worked. You were right not to tell me you loved me a year ago. You shouldn't have come back now," he said, his voice laced with anger as he pulled up to the airport drop-off area. Anger felt like an improvement over the numbness.

"You're my best friend," she said, not looking at him, afraid he'd see the tears in her eyes, even though he could hear them in her voice. Her heart had shattered once more, desperately trying to salvage any part of their relationship. Maybe their love wouldn't lead to their destruction.

"And you're mine. I never said the easier choice wouldn't hurt," he said, venom lacing his words. He knew he had to cut ties. He knew he wouldn't survive a 'just friends' relationship with her. It was all or nothing. Nothing was too painful, and all was too hard to choose.

"So, we're walking away?"

He handed her the engagement ring from Jake. "We were always going to. That's one of the few things we have in common."

"We love one another, but we're too stubborn to compromise on certain dreams."

"And that's all we've got," he lied.

"I guess so," she lied. She took the ring box from him, opened it, and slid the ring onto her left-hand ring finger. She glanced at him, hating herself a little for giving Rodrigo up so easily. 'I'm an idiot,' she thought. She also hated him a little for giving her up too. She unplugged her phone, abruptly stopping the music. The silence between them was thick with everything they weren't saying to each other. She reached for the door handle and started to climb out of the truck. As her foot touched the ground, she felt his hand grip hers. She turned back, waiting for the words that could change everything. He grabbed her left hand, not wanting to let her go. He started to speak, "I want you…"

"Yeah?"

"…to have a good life." He still couldn't bring himself to ask her to stay. The engagement ring on her hand felt like a knife in his heart. He knew he was choosing the easy path, and as she slammed the door, he understood she was doing the same.

He drove toward the exit. "You're a fucking idiot," he muttered to himself. "Turn this truck around and go get her!" But he kept driving. The silence in the truck was oppressive, especially since Elena had taken the music with her when she took her phone. Still, there was one song that kept playing in his head. One of her songs, something he'd heard countless times before, maybe even earlier that night. He couldn't remember all the lyrics, but certain lines kept echoing in his mind. Lyrics about driving away, having regrets, and spending your life alone, waiting for the stars to align. Her music always seemed to fit the scene just right. He kept berating himself, telling himself to turn around. He passed the road that would lead him back to the terminal. Instead, he left the airport behind and headed south.

The song was still playing in his head. 'This needs to stop,' he thought. He turned on the radio, but all he got was a string of commercials—nothing that could distract him. He remembered the CD in the visor of his truck, though he couldn't for the life of him remember what it was. "Doesn't matter, anything to get this song out of my head," he muttered. He grabbed the homemade CD and put it in the player. Immediately, he regretted his decision. It was a CD Elena had made for him. The first song that came on was the one he was trying to escape.

"Son of a bitch!" he yelled, rolling down the window, ejecting the CD, and tossing it out onto the freeway. "I can't fucking escape it!" He thought she would see this as a sign that he should turn around. "And now I'm thinking like her." He swerved into the next lane, preparing to take the exit and head back to the airport.

"Fuck!" he yelled, his fist slamming into the steering wheel. He jerked the truck back into the left lane and pressed the gas harder. Turning the radio on, he tuned it to a metal station, cranking up the volume as loud as it would go, trying to drown out the image of Elena, her music echoing in his mind, and the weight of his regret.

He reached his mother's house, but the noise and speed hadn't succeeded in drowning anything out. He parked the truck and walked inside. The familiar scent of fresh tortillas and cookies filled the air—home, always home. Yet, the comfort of it all did little to change his mood. His mother appeared from the kitchen, drying her hands on her white apron. "Mi amor, what are you doing home? I didn't expect you tonight," she said. When she saw the pain in his eyes, she moved quickly to hug him.

He stopped her before she could reach him by slipping his hand into his pocket. He pulled out the small object and took her hand, turning it palm up. He placed the object gently in her hand and closed her fingers around it. "Turns out I didn't need this after all. Maybe someone else in the family will want it. " Without another word, he turned and walked back out of the house. His mother stood in the doorway, staring down at her mother's engagement ring now resting in her palm.

Elena stormed into the airport, furious with herself and with Rodrigo for their cowardice. "This is so stupid," she muttered aloud, causing the security guard to glance at her with some concern.

"Sorry," she said quickly, her face flushing. 'Great, now I look like a crazy person,' she thought to herself. I am a crazy person. I'm letting the love of my life drive away. What am I doing? She turned on her heel and sprinted back toward the door. "Rodrigo! Wait!" She glanced frantically around the drop-off area, but of course, she was too late. He was already gone.

CHAPTER 20

June 2016

It was the night before the wedding. He had been worried that he wouldn't be able to sleep, but as soon as his head hit the pillow, he drifted off. Of course, he dreamt of her. He could see her clearly in his mind: as beautiful in her white gown, with her hair and makeup done professionally, surrounded by flowers, as she had been wrapped in an old blanket, watching the sun rise in his living room. She was walking slowly up the aisle toward Jake, who stood at the end in a tux, smiling as his bride approached. Rodrigo watched this from the back of the room, sitting in the chair furthest from the aisle. He tried to remain hidden, but it was as though Elena could feel his presence. She turned her head slightly, almost as if sensing him, before looking back at her groom. She continued down the aisle, and when she reached Jake, she placed her hand in his, and they faced the officiant.

Rodrigo remained still in the back row, watching the happy couple. A few times, Elena seemed to start to look his way, as though she wanted to, but each time she was distracted by the officiant or her groom. Then came the moment when the officiant asked if anyone objected to the marriage. Rodrigo felt a fierce urge to stand, to run to the couple, and steal the bride away. But instead, he stayed seated, watching them exchange vows, rings, and a kiss, officially becoming husband and wife for eternity. The newlyweds walked back down the aisle, and Elena's eyes finally swept over Rodrigo. Her gaze passed over him without recognition—as though he was just another face in the crowd. As though he meant nothing to her.

Rodrigo shot up in bed, cold sweat dripping down his back. For a moment, he couldn't breathe. So much for getting a good night's sleep. It had been over a year since the night he dropped her off at the airport, and they hadn't spoken since. She had removed him as a friend on every social media platform they shared. His only updates about her life came from Lily, though he suspected their mutual friend wasn't telling him everything. But he would see Elena in a few hours. He sat up in bed, watching infomercials until morning, almost buying a blender. He hoped his dream wasn't a premonition, and that his own blender could chop frozen fruit as easily as the one on TV.

Elena paced around the hotel room. Tomorrow was a big day, and she should be asleep. Instead, her mind kept wondering if Rodrigo would magically appear. It would take magic, after all. According to Lily, he hadn't left New York since he moved, not even for Christmas. Lily was always good for gossip, but if she knew anything more about Rodrigo, she wasn't sharing it. Elena had even tried to look him up on social media, but either he had blocked her or shut down his account entirely. He didn't exist there anymore. Would he even know what tomorrow was? It had been a year since they last saw each other. They had walked away from one another. Why would he be there? He wouldn't.

A knock at the door startled Elena, interrupting her pacing. She glanced through the peephole. It was Lily.

"Open up, I know you're still awake."

Elena rolled her eyes at the closed door but unlocked it and let Lily in.

"Tomorrow's an important day. You need to get some sleep," Lily said, grabbing Elena by the shoulders and gently guiding her toward the bed.

"I was just about to turn off the light when you came knocking," Elena complained.

"Yeah, right."

"Would I lie to you?"

"You would, but I've known you long enough to spot your tells," Lily replied, watching Elena climb into bed.

"You wouldn't be able to see any tells if I actually put effort into the lie."

"Sure, I wouldn't."

"Shouldn't you be getting some sleep too?" Elena asked.

"I'm on my way to bed now, but I knew you'd be nervous, so I wanted to check on you first."

"Thanks," Elena said, feeling loved but still restless.

"See you in the morning!" Lily said as she skipped out of the room.

"Can't wait," Elena muttered, her voice barely audible as the door clicked shut.

She turned on the television, hoping to find a lighthearted show that would calm her nerves and help her fall asleep. Instead, the only thing she found was infomercials. She watched one about a blender, mesmerized by its amazing ability to blend kale with frozen fruit, until she finally drifted off to sleep and dreams overtook her.

She stood in the airport, waiting to board her flight. Jake stood next to her, holding the hand of their four-year-old daughter. The little girl had green eyes and curly brown hair, just like her mother. Elena could already tell she would be taller than her one day, a trait she inherited from her dad. Elena rocked her infant son in her arms, trying to keep him asleep. His eyes were blue like his father's, but he had Elena's brown hair. Jake was busy pointing out the big planes and explaining how they flew to their daughter. Elena, however, was lost in thought, people-watching as she held their son. The family was on their way to visit Grandma for Christmas, and she was looking forward to seeing her mother. She loved her little family, but there was still a lingering feeling that something was missing.

As she continued to watch the hustle and bustle of the terminal, she observed the usual scenes. Frazzled parents wrestling with children to get them to the right gate. Teenagers barely following their parents, too absorbed in their phones to notice the world around them. College students, duffle bags full of dirty laundry, on their way home for the holidays. Young couples traveling to meet the parents for the first time. Retirees escaping to the Bahamas or Europe for the winter. And scattered among the crowds, lone travelers, some for business, others the lucky few heading to their families.

A tall, muscular man, about her age, with long dark brown hair, dark skin, and dark eyes, walked past Elena's gate on his way to the nearby coffee shop. He stood in line, counting his money, which from her vantage point, appeared to be foreign bills. None of it was the familiar green of American currency. Intrigued, Elena stood up and walked toward the man, knowing exactly who he was despite the beard. She reached into her purse, pulled out some cash, and handed it to the barista.

"Merry Christmas," she said, as the man began to protest.

"Elena?" Rodrigo asked, disbelief in his voice.

"Yep," she replied softly, a little shy.

"You have a son," he said, his tone cold.

"A daughter too," she said, nodding toward Jake and then waving at the two of them as they noticed her.

"Exactly what you wanted," Rodrigo replied, still distant.

"You too, it seems," she said, gesturing to the foreign bills in his hand. "You grew a beard." She almost reached up to touch it but stopped herself when she saw the coldness in his eyes. It was the look of an acquaintance you run into but who would rather not have seen you. The look of someone who would rather avoid the encounter and the forced pleasantries that came with it.

"It's a pain in the ass to try and shave in the jungle," he said.

"The jungle?" she asked, curiosity sparking in her voice.

"Yeah, I travel a lot for work. Guess the easy choice was the right one for both of us," he replied, his words almost like a distant echo.

"Yeah, I guess so," she agreed. But as she said it, she felt that familiar tug deep inside her—a missing piece she couldn't quite reach, though it felt so close.

"Thanks for the caffeine. It was good seeing you," Rodrigo said as he grabbed his coffee. His tone didn't convey the warmth of someone who was happy to see her. In fact, it felt as though he'd rather never have seen her again. He grabbed his duffle bag, which was covered in a light layer of dust, slung it over his shoulder, and walked toward a gate further down the terminal.

"You too," Elena said, but the words came too late. As she watched him walk away, her baby began to cry. She rocked him gently, tried to feed him, and checked his diaper. Everything seemed fine, but no matter what she did, she couldn't stop him from crying.

Elena woke up to the news playing softly on the television and the sun peeking through a slit in the curtains. Big day today, she thought to herself, her mind still foggy from sleep.

The morning passed in a blur. There were so many things to do that Elena hardly had a chance to sit down, let alone process what the day really meant. The women were all gathered in her hotel room—doing hair and makeup, adjusting the bouquets, ensuring the dresses still fit, and making sure every blemish was expertly covered. Elena sipped a glass of champagne, hoping it would calm her nerves, which were still just under the surface despite her constant busyness. After several hours of preparations, it was finally time to head to the church.

Rodrigo couldn't bring himself to go to the church. The thought of it stirred too many painful memories of Eddie, and he'd avoided churches ever since the funeral. 'I couldn't sit through the wedding anyway,' he thought as he pulled up to the hall where the reception was being held. 'It'll be easier to face her here, without the feeling of judgment from God.' He tried to convince himself that he was avoiding God, but since he wasn't a man of faith, he wasn't sure why he bothered with the excuse. The truth was, he was avoiding the church because he wasn't ready to see Elena yet. He wasn't ready to know how she would react to his presence today. He parked his rental car in the lot and took a deep breath before heading inside.

The hall was beautifully decorated in dark blue, white, and gray. Flowers and twinkling lights filled every corner. People were already dancing, while others were still eating.

Many had gathered around the bar, laughing and toasting the night away. Rodrigo recognized several people there—if not by name, then by face. A few waved at him, but his focus remained solely on Elena. He scanned the room, searching for the familiar sparkle of her green eyes. But he didn't see her anywhere. Had she already snuck off with Jake? As he continued searching, Lily slid up next to him.

"Who're you looking for?" she asked, a playful lilt in her voice. She knew exactly who he was searching for.

"Where is she?" he asked, his voice low with panic. The thought of seeing her happy, laughing, or dancing with Jake terrified him—he couldn't bear the idea of her being with him in such an intimate way

"Did you bring it?" Lily asked, leaning in with a conspiratorial whisper.

He quickly patted his pockets to confirm it was still there, then pulled it out to hand to her. "Yeah, I brought it, but I still don't get why you wanted it."

She gave him a sly smile. "I'll explain later."

He narrowed his eyes, feeling the tension building inside him. "Where is she?"

"Dude, relax. I saw her just a minute ago. She was sitting at a table." Lily scanned the room, her finger pointing to where Elena still sat. She wore a black dress with delicate straps that showcased her stunning cleavage. The skirt fell to the floor, but the high slit revealed her leg up to her thigh. Her black stiletto heels had a soft pinkish-gold shine to them. Her hair was curled, cascading over her left shoulder. She looked as beautiful as ever.

"Thanks," he muttered, already turning to rush off.

"Hey, aren't you going to tell me how pretty I look?" Lily teased.

He smiled, leaning in to plant a quick kiss on her cheek. "You look beautiful."

"Thanks," she said, giving him a gentle push toward Elena.

Rodrigo crossed the room toward her, his mind racing. What would he say to her? How should he start this conversation? Should he tell her everything that had happened to him over the past year? Should he just grab her hand and run away with her? Or maybe... "How you doin'?" He chuckled to himself. That might at least make her laugh. He was nearly across the room when the fast pop song faded out, replaced by a slow ballad. He knew exactly what to do now.

"Dance with me," he said, extending his hand toward her.

"Did you just order me to dance…" She couldn't finish the sentence, the indignation fading as her eyes met his. Realization hit her like a wave—it was Rodrigo. She fell silent, her words suddenly lost. Without saying anything else, she placed her hand in his and let him guide her to the dance floor.

He led her to a secluded corner of the floor, far from the other dancers. As they moved, he glanced around at the other couples. There were the older couples, the ones who had been together for decades, their movements familiar and effortless. Then there were the younger couples, the ones filled with hope, hoping their love would last. He noticed friends dancing together just for fun, and the people sitting along the edges of the floor. Some looked longingly

at the couples, wishing they had someone to dance with.
Out of the corner of his eye, he saw Lily, who effortlessly
pulled a man away from a group of men taking shots by the
bar. It seemed like it took no convincing at all for Lily to
get her new husband to slow dance with her. She truly
looked radiant in her white dress.

Elena watched Rodrigo as he observed the room, his
attention flicking from one couple to the next. He was
dressed in a dark blue suit, a blueish-gray shirt, and a dark
blue tie with tiny light blue dots. His pocket square, light
blue like his tie, added a subtle elegance to his look. His
black shoes gleamed under the lights, completing the look.
He looked incredible—handsome, composed, and distant.
Elena had no words. Lily had lied. Lily had definitely
invited him and knew he was coming. She was going to be
in serious trouble when she came back from her
honeymoon. Elena thought she should have gotten Lily a
better wedding present. How could she possibly begin to
tell him everything that had happened to her over the past
year?

Finally, Rodrigo turned his gaze back to her, smiling softly
but saying nothing. Then, in a graceful move, he released

her right hand and took her left, guiding her into a spin before returning to their original dance position. As his hand brushed her left ring finger, he noticed the absence of a ring but chose not to comment, despite the strong urge to ask. Elena couldn't help but laugh a little, remembering the first time they had danced together.

"Do you remember the first time we did this?" she asked, her nerves momentarily forgotten.

It had been six months since he first asked her to borrow a pencil in math class, and in that time, they had become close friends. At first, their friendship grew slowly due to her shyness, but after he had come up with a clever comeback to her first sarcastic remark, she started to feel more at ease around him. He made her laugh often with his quiet jokes during math class. Humor was the key that helped her open up, and from the moment he made her laugh, their bond deepened. He and Eddie had even started sitting with her and her friends—Lily, Mary, and their new friend April—at lunch every day. Eventually, the Valentine's Day dance came around, their very first school dance. Elena secretly hoped that Eddie would ask her to the dance, but being in middle school, she knew very few people went as couples.

Elena, Mary, Lily, and April went as a group to the dance in the cafeteria. The lights were dimmed, and multicolored strobe lights from the DJ flashed throughout the room, setting the mood. When the girls arrived, about half of the school was already there. Some students were on the dance floor in small circles with friends, a few were dancing with their boyfriends or girlfriends, and others sat at tables around the room, chatting.

"Hey, there's Eddie and Rodrigo, and they've got a table we could steal," April said, pointing to a booth where two handsome but still awkward boys sat across from each other.

"Perfect," Lily replied, and they made their way over.

The four girls slid into the booth, squeezing the boys between them so that there were three on each side. "Thanks for the table, guys," Elena said with a smile.

"Who are you again?" Rodrigo asked, raising an eyebrow at her.

"The person helping you pass math. You owe me for all my hard work, so I'm collecting by stealing your table, but still letting you sit here," she teased, giving his arm a light push.

He glanced across the table at Eddie and then smiled sarcastically. "What a deal. They get a good table, and I still have to do my own math homework."

"Stop sucking at math, then," Eddie replied, grinning.

"Hey, aren't you supposed to take my side? Does our friendship mean nothing to you?" Rodrigo said, pretending to be hurt.

"I'm just using you for your mom's cooking," Eddie shrugged.

Rodrigo looked at him for a beat before saying, "Well, she is a great cook, so I can't blame you."

The two boys continued teasing each other while the girls laughed at their antics and danced to the fast songs they liked. Occasionally, one or two of them would get up to grab snacks, dance with other friends, or go to the bathroom. At one point, Rodrigo and Elena were left alone at the table.

"Why do you always make me do my own math homework?" he asked, suddenly serious.

Elena blushed, taking a moment to think before answering. "Because I actually like school and learning. Maybe one day you will, too. But not if I do your homework all the time. Besides, I'm not going to do all the work for nothing. Tutoring you is fun for me, but it makes you suffer a little, and I think that's funny. If I did all the work for you, or let you copy me, it wouldn't be as fun."

"You're kind of wicked, you know that?" he said with a raised eyebrow.

She laughed. "That's probably why we're friends. You like when I'm wicked because I don't look like I would be."

"True," he said with a laugh.

The DJ that night mostly played fast dance songs, but as Rodrigo and Elena sat there laughing, the pace shifted. A familiar slow song began to play, and Elena's eyes lit up. "I love this song." She closed her eyes and swayed slightly in her seat, a small smile on her lips.

"Then let's dance to it," Rodrigo said, standing up without waiting for her response.

Elena opened her eyes to see him on the dance floor, his hand extended toward her. "Don't make me slow dance alone. People will laugh at me, and I'll have to change schools—and probably my name." He grinned, his hand still outstretched.

Her heart pounded as she stood and walked over. This would be her first slow dance. She placed her arms around his neck while he rested his hands on her waist. They moved gently in time with the music. Deep down, she had always hoped her first slow dance would be with Eddie, but she found herself glad it was with Rodrigo. With Eddie, her nerves might have overwhelmed her, leaving her paralyzed or overthinking every step. But with Rodrigo, she felt both nervous and comfortable—an oddly reassuring mix. He smiled at her as they swayed, their steps forming a small circle. When the song ended, he spun her around, then dipped her unexpectedly.

"Woah!" she laughed, surprised. "I didn't see that coming."

"My mom made me practice a little," he admitted, a hint of blush rising against his darker complexion.

"I do remember that. You know Eddie was jealous of me that night."

"Why?" she asked.

"Because I asked you to dance, and he didn't."

"Liar."

"No, really. He always thought you were cute."

"Why didn't he ever tell me?" she asked, more curious than surprised. She had a feeling she already knew.

"I think he saw something that I didn't. He noticed things I missed."

"What did he see that you didn't?" she pressed, but he avoided the question.

"Do you remember the last time we danced together?" he

asked instead.

Senior Prom. The final major event before all the farewells, speeches, and tossing of graduation caps. Rodrigo had come alone, as had most of his friends. He and Ellie had broken up for good a month earlier, and he decided he'd enjoy prom more with friends than with a random date. Eddie, however, brought his girlfriend, Claire. By then, he was already aware of his illness but kept it hidden until the day before graduation. Prom remained a happy, carefree evening despite the shadows looming over him. When Rodrigo walked into the ballroom at the convention center, the first thing he did was look for Elena and their friends. She stood out immediately, stunning in a turquoise strapless dress, the only girl wearing that color in a sea of black, white, and red decorations chosen by the dance committee.

He snuck up behind her as she animatedly recounted a funny story to the rest of the table. "Hey, baby," he said, using a voice deeper than usual.

"Call me 'baby' again, and I'll rip your nutsack off and feed it to my dogs," she responded without even turning around.

"Damn, you're terrifying," he said, moving around the table to stand where she could see him.

She flashed him a smile. "You know I don't take crap from anyone, especially when they're using a voice faker than cheap Halloween props."

"I should've known trying to scare you would backfire and end with me having nightmares instead. At least you didn't give me your murder stare," he joked, trying to mask his genuine relief.

She raised her eyebrows and laughed. "The night is still young, my friend." With that, she joined her friends on the dance floor, leaving Rodrigo chuckling and shaking his head at the table. 'That woman is seriously scary,' he thought to himself.

The evening pressed on. Elena danced joyfully with her group, occasionally breaking away to dance with guys who asked for a slow song. Rodrigo spent most of the night chatting and laughing with other people. Eventually, he found himself sitting at a table, watching the dance floor. His eyes naturally landed on Elena as she laughed and twirled with Lily, Mary, and April.

"Are you planning to dance with her?" Eddie's voice came out of nowhere, startling him.

Rodrigo looked up, startled, as Eddie slid into the seat next to him and took a sip of punch. "Dance with who?"

"Um, the girl you've been staring at for the past five minutes while I've been trying to get your attention."

Rodrigo shook his head quickly. "I'm just watching people dance. No one in particular."

Eddie went silent for a moment as the music changed to another song. Rodrigo glanced over and noticed a serious, almost solemn look on his friend's face—an expression rarely seen. Eddie sighed heavily. "Listen, man. From what I've heard, you don't usually regret the things you do. You learn from them, even if they go sideways. It's the things you don't do that you end up regretting. Don't let yourself look back and wish you'd done something."

Rodrigo stared at him, the words sinking in.

"Just go... go dance, man." Eddie stood up, walked toward Claire, who greeted him with an outstretched hand and a

bright smile. Together, they began to dance.

Moments later, Elena walked back to the table, taking a sip from her water bottle. She smiled at Rodrigo. "Having fun?"

"Yeah." He paused, his eyes following Eddie and Claire before settling on her. "You and I should dance. One more time before graduation and before you head off to become some big-shot psychologist and forget us all."

"You do know I'm going to college here in the city, right?"

"You and I both know you won't stay here forever."

She shrugged. "Maybe. Who knows what the future holds?"

He stood and extended his hand. "You're right. The whole world could end tomorrow, so we might as well dance."

She laughed softly. "Good point. And I do love this song." She placed her hand in his, feeling a slight flutter as he led her back to the dance floor. The fast-paced song was nearing its end, so he spun her playfully and dipped her low, making her laugh. "More practice with your mom?"

"All me now, baby," he teased, his smile wide.

She pinched his arm. "What did I tell you about calling me 'baby'?"

"You secretly love it... Also, ouch." The music transitioned to a slow and familiar tune.

Her smile softened. "I love this song." Wrapping her arms around his neck, she felt his hands move gently to her waist. They began to sway slowly, mirroring the movements of their seventh-grade dance. Back then, they could have fit another person between them. Now, they danced closely, and she rested her head on his shoulder, their movements syncing effortlessly. Rodrigo glanced around, taking in the sight of the other seniors swaying nearby. He caught Eddie's gaze; his friend smiled.

"Promise me you won't disappear after graduation," she murmured, her voice muffled against his shoulder.

"Never. You're stuck with me forever."

She smiled against his shoulder, a soft laugh escaping. "Damn."

"You sure you can handle my brand of crazy forever?"

Lifting her head, she looked at him, a playful glint in her eyes. "Obviously."

"I think he knew," Rodrigo said softly. They continued to dance slowly, swaying together even as the music's tempo shifted around them. Rodrigo chuckled lightly. "We're not even following the music anymore. Want to take a walk outside?"

Elena nodded and moved towards the door with him. "So, what did Eddie know back then?" she asked, curious.

"I think he realized that you and I might end up together. He was a good friend, and I think he chose to step back."

"How can you be sure he stepped back?" she pressed.

"I'm not completely sure," Rodrigo admitted. "But I think he saw how easily we got along, even back in middle school. When we first started hanging out, he used to tell me how he thought you were cute. After that dance, though, he stopped bringing it up, even though I'd catch him looking at you sometimes. I once told him in high school that you had a thing for him, and he just shrugged. He said he wasn't going to get in the way of what you and I had. I told him we were just friends at the time, but… maybe he saw more than I did."

"He stepped back because he saw what we couldn't," Elena murmured, finishing his thought. She couldn't be sure if what Rodrigo was saying was true, but it didn't matter now. It was part of their past.

Rodrigo hesitated for a moment before asking, "Do you want to go somewhere?"

"Last time we did that, it didn't exactly go well," she replied, her voice tinged with anxiety.

"Maybe this time will be different," he said, taking her hand and leading her through the reception hall.

She paused abruptly. "Wait. I'm the Maid of Honor. I can't just leave."

"Yes, you can," came a voice from behind them. Lily walked over, a determined look on her face. "I'm tired of being the go-between for you two. You're both stubborn idiots who need to talk to each other instead of using me as a messenger."

"Lily, it's your wedding day," Elena protested. "This can wait."

Lily rolled her eyes and began nudging them toward the door. "It is my wedding day, which means I get whatever I want. And right now, I want you two to leave. If I see you back here tonight, I'll be seriously pissed. Go."

Rodrigo squeezed Elena's hand and led her toward his rental car. "I think she means it," he said with a grin.

Elena laughed. "She was the calmest bride I've ever seen. I guess she saved all her fire for kicking us out of her wedding."

"Where do you want to go?" he asked, even though he already knew the answer.

"Come on, Rodrigo, you know."

"Of course," he replied, steering the SUV toward the airport viewing area.

The drive was quiet. Once they parked in their familiar spot, both felt the weight of their last conversation. Neither wanted to repeat past mistakes. They sat in silence for a moment, both unsure of how to start. Elena thought about everything that had happened over the past year and knew she needed to open up—but where to begin?

"So," Rodrigo said with a nervous smile, "how's life?"

She laughed, shaking her head. "You always know exactly what to say."

He thought back to their last encounter. "Not always. But this line felt right."

"I don't even know where to start," she confessed, feeling overwhelmed. "I need some air. Can we sit outside?" He nodded, and they climbed out of the SUV. He helped her up onto the hood, then joined her.

"I feel the same way," he said quietly. "I have a lot to tell you too, but it's hard to know where to begin. But maybe you can start with that." He pointed to her left hand, her ring finger bare.

She glanced down at her hand, following his gaze. "Oh, so you noticed that, huh?" she said, attempting to sound casual.

Rodrigo gently took her hand in his, his thumb tracing the spot where her ring had once been. "Kind of hard not to. The last time I held this hand, there was a pretty significant engagement ring here."

A wave of anxiety tightened in her chest, sending butterflies fluttering from her stomach to her throat. She knew this was her moment to be honest. No more hiding. She took a deep breath to steady herself, then began from the beginning.

CHAPTER 21

Back to April 2015

Elena called Jake just before her plane left New Mexico, asking if he could pick her up at the airport. Her heart still ached from everything that happened with Rodrigo, but they had made their choice, and she was determined to move forward. Jake deserved her smile, and she was ready to give it. She did love him—at least, she kept telling herself that.

When she arrived, Jake was waiting for her by the baggage claim, his face lighting up the moment he spotted her. Fortunately, she didn't have any luggage, allowing her recent trip to remain a secret a bit longer. She paused, taking a moment to watch him. He is so kind. How could I have done this to him? Should I confess? Do I have the courage?

"Hey, beautiful. I'd ask you out, but it looks like you're already taken," Jake said, his eyes sparkling as he teased her.

"Yes, I am. And you should know my fiancé is a strong, protective man—so be careful with your flirting," Elena replied with a lighthearted giggle. Jake pulled her into his arms, lifting her off the ground and spinning them both around before kissing her deeply.

"I don't know why you left," he said softly, his eyes filled with relief and love, "but if it led you back to me with a 'yes,' then I don't need to know the rest. I'm just happy you're here—and wearing this." He gently took her hand, caressing the engagement ring. Together, they walked toward the parking lot, hand in hand.

But inside, Elena felt a wave of guilt and self-loathing. She had walked away from Jake, fallen into Rodrigo's arms, shared her deepest feelings, and then returned as a liar. Jake deserves to know the truth. But he had just told her he didn't need answers. Confessing now would only serve to ease her conscience at his expense. 'I'll bear this secret if it means protecting his happiness,' she thought.

As they drove home, Jake talked excitedly about their wedding plans. He was brimming with joy and hope for their future. Elena tried to keep up, nodding and responding at all the right moments, but her mind kept drifting back to Rodrigo. 'I just need time to grieve, that's all,' she thought. 'Then I'll be happy with Jake again.'

When they got home, Jake showed his romantic side yet again by surprising Elena with another bottle of her favorite champagne. They toasted to a life full of happiness and danced slowly in the living room, their bodies pressed closely together. Elena tried to immerse herself in the moment, to let Jake's joy become her own. But no matter how hard she tried, her thoughts kept pulling her away.

"I love you, my future wife," he whispered into her ear, his lips brushing against her neck as he kissed her softly.

"I love you, too," Elena replied, forcing the words past the lump in her throat. She willed herself to hold back tears. 'This is the life you chose. This is the man you love, and you can find happiness with him,' she told herself. Taking a deep breath, she pushed away the ache in her chest, pasted on a smile, and leaned in, hoping to convince herself as much as him. She ran her hands through Jake's short blond hair and kissed him deeply, trying desperately to erase the memory of the last man who had touched her lips.

As Jake began to slowly unzip her dress, she focused on unbuttoning his shirt. Standing before him in her underwear and heels, a wave of shame washed over her. It hadn't even been six hours since she had lain with Rodrigo. Her heart pounded; she couldn't go through with this.

"I'm sorry, Jake," she said, backing away slightly. "I think I had too much champagne on an empty stomach. I feel lightheaded and need to lie down."

Jake's face softened immediately. "Why didn't you tell me you hadn't eaten? Sit down, okay? I'll grab some water, crackers, and your pajamas. We can celebrate another time."

His kindness cut her deeply. How could she have hurt someone who loved her so completely? She hated herself for every lie she had told him, and for the feelings she still harbored for another man.

August 2015

Elena had been determined to stay away from Albuquerque for a few more months, at least until Thanksgiving. She wanted to keep her distance from the memories of her time with Rodrigo. But life had other plans. Her dad's mother passed away, and she found herself heading back to New Mexico for the funeral. Another funeral. Another painful reminder of Rodrigo. This time, however, the service was less emotionally taxing. Her dad's side of the family was smaller, and there were fewer relationships and feelings she needed to juggle.

With a few hours left before her flight, Elena found herself at a local coffee shop, trying to distract herself. Her friends were all at work, so she turned to job hunting. She sipped her coffee, scrolling through job listings in the Bay Area when a shadow suddenly fell over her and her laptop. She glanced up, and her heart skipped a beat. She hadn't seen the man standing in front of her since he walked out of her life nearly four years ago.

"Hi, Elena," he said, and for the first time, she noticed a hint of shyness in his voice.

"Hey, Alex," she replied, forcing calmness into her tone, even as anxiety twisted in her stomach. He looked almost exactly the same as he had years ago, aside from his hair being slightly longer—a style she'd never been fond of. In the years since their last encounter, she'd barely thought about him. Rodrigo and Jake had consumed most of her heart and mind. But now, seeing Alex stirred up a mix of sadness and nerves. Running into an ex was never easy, no matter how much time had passed.

"Mind if I sit?" he asked, gesturing at the empty chair across from her.

She hesitated, searching for an excuse to refuse but couldn't come up with one. Her curiosity was too strong. "Um… sure, I guess."

"I saw you sitting here," he said, settling down across from her, "and I figured it would be even more awkward to ignore you than to come over and say hi."

"I'm not so sure about that," she replied with a small laugh. "I didn't even notice you, so it wouldn't have been awkward for me." She paused, unsure what to say next, her mind racing with unasked questions. Finally, she settled on a simple one. "So… how's life?"

He laughed nervously. "That's your opening line?"

"You have something better?" she shot back, a smirk playing on her lips.

He paused before laughing again. "Nope."

"Didn't think so."

"Okay, well... life. It's been a mix—some good, some bad. I got married, have two sons now."

She let out a light laugh. "I can only imagine the trouble those two must cause."

"They definitely keep me on my toes," he said, a hint of warmth softening his expression.

"You still teaching?"

"Yeah, I'm actually here to catch up on some homework. Working on my master's degree."

"Good for you." The words felt hollow to her, and the conversation, despite their efforts, remained stiff and awkward. She found herself wishing it would wrap up quickly.

"And you? Are you finally a doctor?"

"Graduated in June. I'm in town for a funeral—my dad's mom. I had some time before my flight, so I came here to work on job applications."

"I'm sorry about your grandmother. I know how close you two were. I lost mine just a couple of months ago."

"I'm sorry for your loss," she said softly, aware of how deeply he'd cared for his grandmother.

"Yeah, but I like to think she's in a better place."

She nodded, resisting the urge to engage in the cliché platitudes that often felt empty.

He gestured toward her hand. "I see you're engaged. Congratulations."

Her eyes dropped to the ring, a band that should symbolize a bright future but instead felt like a weight pulling her down. It often served as a painful reminder of Rodrigo. "Yeah, it happened in April. He's a lawyer. He takes good care of me."

He studied her face, his expression shifting to something more familiar, almost too knowing. "I knew you for over five years. You're not happy."

She rolled her eyes, bristling. "It's complicated."

He didn't say anything, just looked at her expectantly, his silence encouraging her to continue. He always had known how to wait her out. "There was another man. We loved each other. But I lived here, and he lived there. We couldn't—or wouldn't—make it work."

She saw the flicker of understanding in his eyes, as if he thought she meant him. She pressed on. "You met him, actually, at my friend's funeral. Rodrigo?"

"Yeah, I remember him. You two were close for a long time."

"Not anymore," she said, the bitterness catching her by surprise. "We made the 'easier' choices. I got engaged to someone uncomplicated, someone who'd never hurt me. Rodrigo moved to New York to follow his dreams. That's the end of it."

Alex stared at her, his coffee cup turning slowly in his hands. His leg bounced slightly under the table—a familiar sign of his nerves. She waited, feeling the tension stretch out between them. Finally, after what felt like forever, he spoke. "We used to know everything about each other, right?"

"Pretty much."

"And we could say anything?"

"Once. But things change."

He hesitated, eyes searching her face for permission.

She almost turned him away, but curiosity got the better of her. "Just spit it out," she said, her voice a touch too sharp.

"The easier choice is a lie."

She looked at him, waiting for him to elaborate.

He sighed, his voice softened. "I didn't want to move to California. I was afraid to tell you that, so I let you go, and I walked away. It was easier than trying long-distance. It was easier than opening up about my fears. It was the easier choice." He paused, looking down. "Shortly after we broke up, I met my wife. Don't get me wrong—I'm happy. I love my wife, my kids, and the school I work at. I love being close to the rest of my family. But the thing about taking the easier choice is, you're left with this endless wondering. You always ask yourself, 'What if?' What if I'd been braver, stronger? What if I'd taken those risks? And you'll always end up questioning who you really are."

She studied him, intrigued yet pained. "What do you mean, you'll question who you really are?"

"I mean," he said, choosing his words carefully, "I thought I was brave, that I was someone who wanted adventure. But when I took the easier path, I started doubting myself. The man I thought I was—the man I wanted to be—I don't know if I am him anymore. And I never will because I made the easier choice."

She looked at him a moment longer, feeling a sadness for him that she understood all too well. She had questioned her own strength and bravery ever since she and Rodrigo had walked away from each other. She took a sip of her chai latte, hoping it would steady her enough to swallow her tears.

Alex's voice broke through her thoughts. "I know you, even after all these years of not talking. You're brave and strong, and you don't back down when things get hard. You don't take the easier choice."

She sighed, giving a faint smile tinged with regret. "Alex, maybe you don't know me as well as you think. I already made the easier choice."

He glanced down at his wrist, his watch partly covering a tattoo—a tattoo he'd once gotten for her. She thought about the irony of tattoos, their permanency. Because of one impulsive decision, she would forever be part of his life, imprinted on his skin. His duck tattoo. He used to call her Duckie; she had been his Duckie. His wrist would forever remind him of that. She wondered if it brought him happy memories of their time together or if it was just a reminder of lost opportunities. Not just lost moments with her, but missed adventures, dreams, and the chance to be the man he'd always imagined himself to be.

"I have to get going," he said, standing up, "but remember—you haven't made the easier choice until you say, 'I do.'" He placed a hand gently on her shoulder before turning to leave.

"Alex?" she called, stopping him after just a couple of steps.

"Yeah?"

She hesitated, but curiosity won out. "What does my duck tattoo make you think of?"

He returned to her table, his expression serious. "You really want to know?"

"Probably not," she admitted with a sad smile, "but I can't help it. I need to know."

He took a moment, licking his lips as he searched for the right words. "That's the thing about tattoos. There's pain when you get them; there's even more pain if you have them removed. Mostly, it reminds me to be careful with my decisions, that I have a family depending on me now." He looked away briefly, and then, almost as an afterthought, he added, "And on rare, painful occasions, it reminds me of you and what might have been—if I'd chosen the harder path."

With that, he walked away, disappearing out of her life one last time.

January 2016

The months dragged on for Elena. Alex's words echoed in her mind like a haunting refrain: "You haven't made the easier choice until you say 'I do.'" But she kept trying to convince herself that he was wrong, even though deep down, she knew she had made the easier choice. She had chosen Jake. So, as she grieved the loss of Rodrigo, she was also trying to be happy, newly engaged, and in love. It felt like a balancing act, one that left her exhausted.

Everyone around her was thrilled, constantly asking about wedding plans. When was the big day? Had she picked out a dress? Where would it be? Indoors or outside? Band or DJ? Who were her bridesmaids? What were her colors? The questions were endless, and each one felt like a weight pressing down on her.

One Saturday afternoon, Elena was lying on the couch, absorbed in a book. She had just started a new chapter when Jake walked in from having lunch with his brother.

"Hey, beautiful," he greeted her, leaning down to kiss her on the top of her head.

"How was lunch?" Elena replied, her attention still half on her book.

"It was good. He told me he and Linda are going to start trying to have a baby. He's really excited about it."

Elena nodded absently. "Aww… that's cute."

Jake paused, observing her, then asked, "Did you get a chance to look at that email I sent with some possible wedding venues?"

She felt a pang of guilt. She hadn't forgotten to look; she'd just been avoiding it. "Oh, I'm sorry, honey. I got caught up in this book and totally forgot. Let me check them now." She slid a bookmark into her book, set it aside, and moved to her laptop on the desk. She opened her email, though her heart wasn't in it.

Jake's eyes followed her with a growing concern. She was so wrapped up in autopilot mode lately that she missed the subtle worry etched on his face. "Elena?" he asked, his voice softer than usual.

"Hmm?" she murmured, distracted as she scrolled through her inbox.

He hesitated, then asked, "Am I… am I missing a piece of you?"

Elena's head jerked up, surprised. "Huh? What do you mean?" Her stomach tightened with nerves, sensing a shift in the air.

Jake took a deep breath and tried again. "Let me put it a different way. Do you feel like you know me, completely? Like, 100%?" He sat down on the couch and motioned for her to join him.

Curious and a little apprehensive, she left her desk and sat beside him. They turned slightly so they could face each other. "Well… I mean, can you ever truly know anyone 100%? But yeah, I feel like I know you as well as I possibly can." Her heart pounded as she wondered where he was going with this.

"Okay, would you say that you have all of my heart?" he asked, his gaze steady.

"Yes, absolutely," she replied, trying to sound confident. "That's one of the most amazing things about you—you give your heart so completely."

He took a slow breath. "Well, I don't feel that I have your heart completely, Elena. And I've always been okay with that, mostly because I know you've always been guarded and slow to trust. I've loved watching you slowly let your walls down and let me in."

She felt a pang of guilt. "I'm sorry you've felt that way," she murmured, looking down.

Jake shook his head gently. "No, really, it's okay. I accepted not having all of your heart because you seemed fine with not giving all of it. It became our normal—a kind of balance in the imbalance, you know?"

"Okay…" She still couldn't quite see where he was going with this.

He continued, his tone softer. "But something changed after

I proposed, and you came back from…wherever you went. You didn't seem comfortable with that balance anymore. And the longer I saw you struggle with it, the more uncomfortable I started to feel, too."

Elena felt a tightening in her chest. "I… I don't know what to say," she replied, trying hard not to think about what this conversation might lead to.

"I'm a lawyer, so I do better with logic than with emotions," he said with a small, rueful smile. "That's your area of expertise. But I need to ask, Elena—am I missing a piece of you?"

What was he trying to get at? She wished he'd just come out and say it instead of using all these metaphors. "Well…you know I was in love before, and it ended badly. Maybe that's where the missing piece is?"

Jake shook his head slowly. "I don't think that's it. You had healed from that long before I came into your life. I think the piece I'm missing has to do with where you went after I proposed. I know I told you before that I didn't need to know the details, but I think now, for us to move forward, I do. I think before we get married, I need to understand why it feels like I still don't have all of you."

Elena looked away, fighting a wave of anxiety. "Jake… please don't ask me about that night." She could feel her heart pounding, dreading the idea of telling him the truth. If he knew, it would crush him. It would ruin them.

"Please, I need to understand this," he said, his voice filled with sadness and a glimmer of hope. It was as though he knew whatever she had to say would hurt, but he truly believed it could help them get back to where they were before. "I have some guesses about where you went and why, but they're just that—guesses. Please, help me stop guessing?"

She swallowed hard. "I don't know how to talk to you about that night," she said, feeling the weight of her words.

"Start with where you went," he urged gently.

"I went to New Mexico," she replied, unable to look him in the eyes. Instead, she focused on her hands and the engagement ring that now felt heavy on her finger.

He nodded slowly. "I kind of guessed that. What did you do

while you were there?"

She hesitated, her heart racing. It was time to end the lies. This is going to hurt, she thought. "I…I needed to talk to the only person who could help me decide if marrying you was the right choice for me."

"Okay, who was that?" His tone was calm, as though he already knew.

She didn't answer, just kept her eyes on her hands. But she was sure that Jake had figured it out. She remembered once hearing that a lawyer never asks a question he doesn't already know the answer to.

"You saw Rodrigo, didn't you?" he asked, his voice steady, without a trace of accusation.

"He was my best friend. I needed to talk to him before I could give you an answer," she admitted quietly.

"What happened between the two of you?" Jake asked, still calm. "You didn't speak to him for a year before that night, and you haven't talked to him since. You said he was your best friend—why did that night change everything?"

Her throat tightened as she felt tears forming. "I say he was my best friend because that night, we ended our friendship."

"Why?" he asked gently.

She took a deep breath. This was the conversation she had dreaded for so long. The one she hoped to avoid, yet knew was inevitable. She took another deep breath, preparing herself. "We ended the friendship because I want to marry my best friend. I want to marry the man I go to when things are tough, the one who makes my day better just by being there. I want to marry the man I have to share good news with, or it feels like it didn't really happen until he knows. I want to marry the one who drives me a little crazy, the one I can banter and bicker with. The one who makes me want to be a better person, who changes in the best ways just because I'm part of his life. I want to marry the man who can take care of me without making me feel like I can't be independent. The one who challenges me but also makes me feel safe. I want to love the man who loves me, even at my worst." She finally looked up at him, realizing the weight of her words. Realizing what they would mean to Jake—and realizing, fully, that she meant every single one.

"You and I rarely fight, I take care of everything you need, and neither of us has really changed since we started dating. We've been settled into a safe, secure routine for so long now. Elena, everything you just said—it doesn't describe me." He spoke calmly, but she could sense the sadness and frustration behind his carefully controlled voice.

"You're a good man, Jake. You're kind and loyal. You love so deeply and fully. You're honest and giving, and we both want similar things in life. You would never hurt me. You are everything anyone could want." Tears welled in Elena's eyes as she spoke. She held his gaze, hoping he understood that he was, in so many ways, the perfect partner—just not the right one for her.

"But?" he prompted, his voice barely a whisper.

She hesitated, then took a deep breath. "You were right, Jake. You're missing parts of me, pieces I didn't realize I'd given away. I think… I've been giving little bits of my heart to Rodrigo since we were kids. I thought I could give you everything I had left, but when you proposed… I realized that, deep down, I'd already given him all the pieces I had. I wanted to pretend there was enough left for you, hoping my feelings for him would fade, but…" She stopped, her voice choked by tears.

Jake took a deep breath, steadying himself. "Okay. I'll pack a bag and stay at a hotel while I look for a place." He rose from the couch.

"No, that's not fair. I'm the one who let things fall apart. I'll stay with Emi until I find a place, and I'll pack the rest of my things while you're at work next week. You deserve to keep this place, Jake." She stood and went to the bedroom, hastily throwing clothes into a suitcase as Jake sat motionless on the couch. When she came back, Jake stood up and turned to face her. His face was calm, but she could see the deep hurt in his eyes. Elena reached for his hand, placing the engagement ring in his open palm. "I'm so sorry." She gripped the handle of her suitcase and turned toward the door.

"Wait," he called, his voice strained.

She stopped, bracing herself. She owed him that much. "Yes?"

"I hate that I feel I need to say this because it confirms exactly what you think of me—that I'm too kind, too giving, that I take care of others even when they don't want me to. But I love you, and I want you to be happy, no matter what. So here it is: If you love Rodrigo, you need to find a way to be with him. You'll never be able to move on if you don't."

She gave him a sad smile. "You're probably right about that. But it's too late for me and Rodrigo. You know as well as I do that love alone isn't enough. We'll never be together." She leaned in, gently kissed his cheek, and walked out the door. Elena drove to Emi's apartment, tears streaming down her face. She had no home, no fiancé, and no Rodrigo. She knocked, suitcase in hand. "Can I crash on your couch for a while?"

"Of course, love. What happened?" Emi asked, leading her inside.

Elena told Emi everything she had kept bottled up for the past year and a half, her voice breaking as she relived each moment. Emi, uncharacteristically quiet, sat beside her, gently rubbing her back and holding her hand.

After a long silence, Emi finally spoke. "I can't believe you kept all that in for so long. What are you going to do now?"

"I'm going to find a place to live and focus on work," Elena said, her voice gaining strength.

"No, I mean about Rodrigo. Are you going to tell him you're not engaged anymore?"

"It wouldn't make a difference. I'm not moving to New York, and he's not coming here. I may love Rodrigo for the rest of my life, but we've never been able to make it work. I need to focus on my career now."

"That's ridiculous," Emi said, frowning. "Maybe he'll show up at your friend's wedding."

"I doubt it. He and Lily were never that close."

May 2016

"So, I moved out and got my own place. I had to leave the city to afford rent, but at least I don't feel guilty anymore," Elena said, her gaze fixed somewhere beyond Rodrigo. She avoided looking at him, afraid of what she might see in his expression. Would he feel disappointed that she'd chosen the harder path? Or worse—would he seem happy, like he'd been waiting for this? She didn't want to see any of it, especially not hope.

Rodrigo didn't respond right away. Instead, he chuckled softly, almost to himself. If he hadn't shown up at the wedding, he might never have found out that she'd broken things off with Jake. Thanks to Lily's insistence, he was here, facing Elena, instead of letting both of them slip further into their own stubborn ways, missing this chance altogether. "It's funny—you told your friend that Lily and I were never that close."

"Why do you say that?" Elena asked, surprised.

"Well, because she's actually the reason I'm here today. Sure, I wanted to congratulate her and see her happy, but… honestly, I hadn't planned on coming. She convinced me to." He paused, letting that sink in, his eyes searching hers.

CHAPTER 22

May 2015 again

It had been a month since Rodrigo had chosen the easier path, dropping Elena off at the airport and walking away from her, supposedly for good. He'd accepted his place in the environmental engineering program at NYU and was already planning to leave early to find an apartment. He was leaving in just two days, and Lily was furious.

They were meeting for a drink to say goodbye, and as soon as she saw him, she punched him hard in the arm. "I've been practicing that punch for weeks," she said, watching him wince as he rubbed his sore arm. "I wanted to make sure you'd leave with a bruise."

"What the hell, Lily!? Why would you give me a bruise on purpose? I haven't done anything to you!"

"You're an idiot," she replied simply.

He gave her a look as they made their way to the bar. Since it was a Wednesday night, they managed to find seats at the counter—his preferred spot, especially tonight, because he had a feeling he'd need easy access to the booze. Of course, Lily had picked the same bar where he'd last seen Elena, adding to the irony. Once they were settled, he asked, "Okay, why am I an idiot this time?"

"If you don't already know, then you're an even bigger idiot than I thought."

"Is this about Elena?"

"Of course, it's about Elena! Why are you moving across the country—and in the wrong direction? Why aren't you two together?"

He sighed. "I never should have told you what happened last month."

"But you did, so now I get to ask all the questions I want."

When he'd returned his grandmother's engagement ring to his mother, he'd felt shattered. Normally, he would have talked to Elena about something this painful, but she was out of reach now, and this time felt like it was for good. So, he'd called Lily instead. He'd told her everything, surprising himself; he usually kept things close, but losing Elena had left him needing someone who understood. Chris was never an option for this. "I'm moving across the country because I applied to NYU right after she told me she loved the lawyer," he explained. "We're not together because we both chose to walk away."

Lily rolled her eyes. "Those are just the surface reasons. I want the real reasons."

Just then, the bartender came over—a young woman with a pixie haircut and tattooed arms. "Hey, I remember you," she said. "You were here with your girl about a month ago. Seemed intense."

Rodrigo recognized her. She'd always seemed to be working whenever he'd stopped by. She'd overheard him venting about Elena before New Year's and had even witnessed the fight between him and Elena last month. "Yeah," he replied, "Can I get a Jack and Coke?"

"Sure, but only if you tell me what happened with your girl."

Lily looked intrigued. "I'll have a vodka cranberry and a

water, and here's what happened—he and the girl decided to be stupid and not be together."

"What?!" The bartender raised her eyebrows as she prepared their drinks.

"I know, right? Stupid," Lily said. "They decided to make the 'easier choice,' as he keeps saying, but I still can't figure out why."

Rodrigo stayed silent, taking a long sip from his drink. He didn't need to add anything, as Lily and the bartender—whose name he learned was Jade—continued dissecting his love life as if he weren't even there.

"So, what are they going to do?" Jade asked, genuinely curious. "Just never see each other again? I mean, I saw them together, and I've heard this guy talk about her enough to know they're completely in love."

Lily looked at Rodrigo, then back at Jade. "Wait, you've heard him talk about Elena before last month?"

"Yeah, he was here months ago, sorting out his feelings for her just before New Year's. She's been here too, talking about him with a friend. Honestly, one of the reasons I still work at this bar is because they keep coming in, and now I'm invested in the story." Jade laughed, only half-joking.

Rodrigo was surprised that this stranger remembered both him and Elena from their past visits. He thought to himself that they really should have picked a new bar by now. Then again, maybe it didn't matter anymore; they weren't likely to run into each other again.

"Well," Lily continued, shaking her head, "she went and got herself engaged to a lawyer, and this genius"—she jabbed her thumb at Rodrigo—"is now moving 3,000 miles away from her to New York."

Rodrigo finally cut in. "I'm right here, you know."

Lily pressed her hand over his mouth. "Shh. No one's talking to you."

Since he apparently wasn't allowed to have any input on his own life, Rodrigo drained his drink and signaled for another.

"A lawyer, huh?" Jade asked, raising an eyebrow.

"Yeah," Lily responded, "he's handsome, rich, and takes really good care of her. The proposal was pretty sweet, too. He rented out the planetarium in San Francisco, filled it with her favorite flowers, and told her he wanted to give her the New Mexico sky that she missed so much." Lily's voice was a mix of admiration and frustration as she recounted the story.

"You realize that I don't really want to hear about this, right?" Rodrigo muttered, visibly uncomfortable.

"He was even okay with letting her run away before she gave him her answer. Didn't even ask where she was or who she went to see. Which, honestly, is probably a blessing. Because she was with this idiot," Lily added, pointing at Rodrigo.

Jade, who had been silently listening, finally spoke up, her voice dripping with sarcasm, "And what did you offer her, exactly?"

Rodrigo shot her a look—a glare so fierce it could rival Elena's, but it did little to intimidate Jade. "Nothing," he replied coldly.

Lily leaned in, her voice thick with accusation, "Elena asked him if he'd changed his mind, if he wanted to marry her, have kids. And he lied. Told her no, even though he had his grandmother's engagement ring in his pocket the whole time." She was seething, and her voice wavered with anger.

Jade, sensing the tension, poured another drink for Rodrigo. "What made you change your mind?" she asked, her voice calm but full of understanding, a stark contrast to Lily's irritation. Rodrigo appreciated her approach—it was a welcome change.

He exhaled deeply, swirling the liquid in his glass before answering. "She loved him, too," he began, his voice quiet and strained. "He called her, worried, because he had no idea where she was. When she finally answered, he said, 'I love you.' And she said, 'Me too.'" He paused, his throat tightening as he relived the moment. "It broke me. I knew, even though she loves me, she loves him, too. Not only that, but he can give her a life I can't. A life without the struggle. I don't have money, and school isn't going to change that anytime soon. She's better off with him." His words hung in the air, and both women sat in silence, sensing the raw vulnerability in his confession.

Finally, Lily broke the silence, her voice thick with disbelief, "You're a damn idiot if you think any of that's true."

Rodrigo blinked, stunned by Lily's reaction. How could it not be true? Lily herself had just described Jake's proposal in such perfect detail. He couldn't compete with that. He had planned to propose in his truck, in a parking lot. He said it aloud to the two women, feeling embarrassed by the simplicity of his own idea.

"It might have been in your truck," Jade said gently, offering a soft but knowing smile, "but it still would have meant something."

Lily nodded, adding with quiet conviction, "Yeah. It would have been in your truck at the airport viewing area—the place that's sacred to the two of you. It was where you shared your first kiss, where you slept together. It would've been under the real New Mexico sky, not some fake one. She would have said yes. But she just wanted to know that you wanted the same things in life."

Rodrigo shook his head, his eyes clouded with defeat. "It wouldn't have been enough. I'm not enough," he muttered, the weight of his self-doubt pressing heavily on him. "If I had been strong enough, brave enough to make the harder choice, I would've. But I'm not that man. She deserves someone like that." His voice trailed off, and he stood up, feeling the full force of his decision crash down on him. He left enough money to cover both his and Lily's tab, not wanting to linger any longer. "Lily, I'm sorry," he said, his voice softening. "I've got to go. I'll call you when I get to New York." He leaned down and kissed the top of her head, the simple gesture holding a weight of finality.

Lily stood up as well, pulling him into a hug. "I love you, even if you're a dumbass," she whispered into his ear, the affection in her voice unmistakable despite her teasing words.

Rodrigo kissed her cheek, his heart heavy with the realization that things had changed forever. Without another word, he turned and walked out of the bar, leaving behind the only person that had held any comfort for him in recent weeks.

November 2015

Her birthday came and went, and for the second year, he didn't say anything to her. He felt horrible about it, but there was nothing he could do. He was 3,000 miles away, and they still weren't talking. They probably never would again.

Besides, he needed to focus on school. He was racking up large amounts of debt to get this education, and he couldn't afford to waste it pining for an engaged—or maybe even married—woman. He was working on being social, and he'd made a few friends in his classes. He'd even started trying to date, though the dating part of his life was proving disastrous.

The first woman he dated once he arrived in New York was someone he met at a bookstore near his apartment. She was cute and shy, and they both reached for the same travel book. It had been a book that Elena once recommended to him, and when he saw it, he knew he would buy it. Unfortunately, the other woman wanted it too, and it was the last one in stock. She agreed to let him take her to dinner in exchange for letting him have the book. At dinner, she talked about her seven cats the entire time. She said she liked having seven because seven was her lucky number, and that cats had saved her life once. He never really understood how the cats had saved her life, and he never found out because they didn't have a second date. She left the restaurant after learning he preferred dogs.

He met another woman at the farmers' market and took her to a raw vegan restaurant, per her request. He'd asked her out because he wanted someone completely different from Elena. This woman wore patchouli and made her own organic soap. She was vegan and lived in an artist's commune. She didn't have any education beyond high school, and she didn't like the fact that he was getting a master's degree. She believed education catered to the privileged few, and as a man of color, she thought he shouldn't be encouraging the oppression of his race by paying for higher education. Rodrigo also discovered that she was on strike from showering until all people were treated equally, no matter their race, religion, sexual orientation, gender, or their existence on Earth. The restaurant allowed her patchouli-covered body odor to become apparent. This did not lead to a second date either.

Another woman he met in a weekend seminar course seemed interesting. He liked the comments she made about genetically modified foods, so he asked her out for coffee afterward. They talked for a while and seemed to hit it off. Her laugh reminded him of Elena. But on the second date, she began talking about future dates. Did he want to go to her cousin's wedding in three months? Did he ever think about traveling to China, because she had found a good deal on flights? Did he plan to live in his studio much longer because her lease would be up soon? Rodrigo lied to her and said he had a wife and liked to pick up women on the side to keep his life interesting. She declined the offer of a third date, much to his relief.

Then, there were the few women he went out with just for physical comfort. The woman from Chile, for example, was the worst kisser he had ever met. She sucked his top lip so far back into her mouth that he could swear he felt her uvula. Then, she switched to the bottom lip. His lips were so swollen that the next night, a full twenty-four hours later, one of the girls in his study group commented on how big his lips looked. His study group was getting a kick out of his dating horror stories.

There were a few other women he kissed, but he could never bring himself to do more. He was lonely and had "man needs," as Elena would say, but every time he started to get more intimate with a woman, the thought of Elena would cause him to feel depressed and lose interest.

His dating life wasn't all crazies. There were some quality women too. One woman, a med student, he met in the student union building. She was ambitious and beautiful, like Elena. Unfortunately, she was also perceptive, like Elena. At dinner, as they were getting to know each other better, she stopped him mid-sentence. "You're in love with someone, aren't you?" she asked.

"What do you mean?" He was shocked. Was he that obvious?

The med student looked at him. "Every time you talk about yourself and tell a story to make your point, you mention a 'friend' of yours. From the context, I can tell that it's the same person in every story, and that this person is a woman. And when you talk about her, you smile, but your eyes still look sad."

Rodrigo shook his head. "You could tell all that?"

"My major in undergrad was psychology. Seems like maybe you should talk to someone about this woman before you continue to date. I don't think you'll find anyone until you get over her."

The med student was right, of course. She saw right through him. But talk to a therapist? He worried it would remind him of Elena too much.

December 2015

It was something that Rodrigo never thought he would find in his messages on social media. He had blocked Elena—mostly to protect himself from the urge to check up on her. It wasn't so much that he was worried she'd look him up; it was more about him being unable to see her profile, to keep himself from falling into that trap. But there, right in his inbox, was her face. The lips he once kissed were now pressed against another man's cheek—a man named Jake. Why was Jake sending him a message? Why even have a social media account, for that matter? Rodrigo cursed social media, cursing his inability to quit it completely.

Jake's message was simple. **I'll be in New York this**

weekend. Can we meet for a drink? I'm worried about Elena.

Rodrigo considered saying no right away. He had no desire to meet Jake, let alone share a drink with him. Then an image of punching Jake flashed through his mind, and a small smile flickered across his lips. It would be satisfying—though unfair. Jake had no idea what part he'd played in Rodrigo's heartache. In fact, Jake was the one who'd been cheated on. Elena either hadn't told Jake what had happened, or he was just an incredibly forgiving man.

Rodrigo read the message again. The last sentence stuck out to him this time. Why was Jake worried about Elena? Immediately, his mind went to Eddie. What if she was sick? There was a lot of cancer in her family. What if it was her mom? She could be gravely ill. How would Elena handle that, knowing how fiercely independent she was? Could he ignore this message and never know what was happening with Elena? He didn't want to make that mistake. So, he decided to call Lily to find out more.

"Hey Rodrigo!" Lily greeted him, her voice full of excitement.

"What's wrong with Elena?" he asked, skipping the pleasantries. He was too worried to bother with small talk.

"Well, she's stubborn, she overthinks everything, and she talks herself out of—"

Rodrigo's heavy sigh cut through Lily's words, halting her mid-sentence. "Lily, I mean, is she sick? Is someone in her family ill?"

"Not that I know of. It's been a few weeks since I've talked to her, though. I think she was getting tired of me always telling her she's too stubborn. Speaking of stubborn, why don't you give her a call?"

"Okay, Lily. I'll talk to you later," he said, abruptly hanging up before she could say goodbye. He was fed up with being called stubborn too.

Rodrigo didn't know what to do. He briefly considered calling Elena, but immediately shut that idea down. He couldn't talk to her—not after everything. Could he talk to her fiancé? Probably not. But would he do it anyway? Probably. His curiosity about the man, coupled with his worries for Elena, were too overwhelming. His message to

Jake was simple: **When and where?**

Jake had chosen an upscale restaurant in a neighborhood that Rodrigo had never ventured into before, simply because he couldn't afford anything the area had to offer. He hadn't thought to research the place before showing up, either, and ended up wearing blue jeans, a faded grey t-shirt, and black work boots, scuffed beyond recognition.

The restaurant was small, with no more than ten tables, all neatly set with clean, white linen tablecloths. Most of the men seated were dressed in sharp suits and ties, while the women wore stylish suits or elegant dresses. Rodrigo scanned the room, trying to spot Jake, but didn't see him anywhere. As he stood there, the hostess gave him a long, rude look, her gaze slowly traveling from his head to his boots.

"I'm sorry, sir," she said, her tone dripping with disdain, "but we have a dress code here. No jeans."

Feeling completely out of place, Rodrigo turned to leave without saying a word. But just as he was about to walk away, a voice called out behind him.

"It's my fault, Farrah. I forgot to mention the dress code to my friend here," Jake said, his hand resting casually on Rodrigo's shoulder as if they were old pals. "Maybe we can get a table in the back?"

"Oh, Mr. Shaw," Farrah said, suddenly smiling at Jake with a warmth Rodrigo hadn't thought her capable of. "Of course. My apologies to your friend. You know Mr. Elliot insists on keeping up appearances for his clientele, but I'm sure he'll make an exception for you. Right this way." She didn't acknowledge Rodrigo directly but led them both to a secluded table in the back of the restaurant. Better to hide the guy in jeans, it seemed, and protect their image.

"Can I get you and your friend something to drink, Mr. Shaw?" the server asked, her smile still lingering.

"Tequila," Rodrigo said flatly, before Jake could answer for him.

Jake returned her smile. "My usual Scotch?"

"Of course," she said with a nod, then turned away. Rodrigo's mind wandered. Should I call him Mr. Shaw too? He hadn't even realized Jake's last name until now. Elena

Shaw? The name didn't sit well with him. He shook his head, trying to clear his thoughts. 'Doesn't matter,' he told himself.

"I'm sorry I didn't tell you about the dress code," Jake said, his voice tinged with genuine regret. "I actually forgot about it. I'm usually here for work, so I'm always in a suit."

Rodrigo felt a flash of anger rising in his chest. He wanted to snap at Jake, wanted to make him uncomfortable, embarrass him in front of his classy friends. But he couldn't. Jake seemed sincere in his apology, and Rodrigo's frustration faltered.

"It's fine," Rodrigo muttered, trying to push the bitterness down.

"No, it was rude of me," Jake insisted, leaning back in his chair. "They're a client of the firm, and I come here all the time. I didn't even think twice about it. Elena complains all the time that I take her to places she doesn't feel comfortable in. She's always having to dress up to meet their dress codes. She told me once, 'I grew up in a single-wide trailer in the middle of the desert, in my small town's ghetto. I don't do well in classy-ass restaurants.' She still goes with me, though, but she tends to curse a lot more while we're eating."

Rodrigo couldn't help himself, he laughed. It was his Elena. He could even imagine her telling Jake some story about her day throwing every curse word she knew in the mix to make the people around her feel as uncomfortable as she did. "Well, I grew up down the hill from her, more in the main part of town, so I won't curse like she does." 'For now,' he thought to himself.

"If the urge strikes you, don't hold back. I'll tip enough that it won't matter." Jake paused as the server brought their drinks. "To new friends," he said raising his glass to Rodrigo. Rodrigo did the same and downed his shot. It was high quality and went down smoothly. "Would you like another drink? They have some excellent sipping tequilas." Jake asked him.

"Umm… sure, whatever you recommend," Rodrigo didn't even know there was such a thing as a sipping tequila.

Jake ordered the drink and took another sip of his scotch. "So, how are you liking New York so far?"

Rodrigo felt so unsure of himself in front of this man. Partly it was the money, but it was also that he was with Elena. There was also a part of him that felt guilty for his hand in Elena cheating on him. He felt as though he needed to review everything, he said so he didn't let it spill that Elena was with him the night of their engagement. "What I've seen of it so far is great. School keeps me busy though, so I haven't explored as much as I want."

"Yeah, Elena said that about San Francisco. You can be in a city like this for years and never feel like you've explored it enough."

The server brought Rodrigo's new drink. He took a tentative sip. It was delicious. It was getting harder to hate the man sitting in front of him. Dislike, yes, but maybe not hate. He had to steer the conversation to why they were there sooner rather than later, otherwise he may actually start to like the guy. "Look Jake, we could sit here and make small talk for hours, but I've got papers to write and study groups to go to, and I'm sure you have something lawyerly to get to, so why don't we cut to the chase. You said you were worried about Elena?"

"Straightforward. I like it. Okay. Since Elena and I got engaged, she hasn't seemed happy. I proposed and she ran away. I've never asked where she went or who she saw, but I've had my suspicions. When we first started dating, she talked about you all the time. Then all talk of her best friend Rodrigo stopped. I assumed it was because opposite sex friendships tend to fall to the wayside when people get more serious with their significant others but that was just an assumption."

'Shit,' Rodrigo thought to himself, 'he's going to ask about that night.' "Go on," was all he could think of to say.

"I don't have opposite sex friendships, not close ones anyway. Not like you and Elena, so I never really understood how you two could be best friends and be platonic. But I trust Elena, so I left it alone. When I've mentioned you lately though, she completely shuts down."

Rodrigo took another sip of his drink so he wouldn't say something he'd regret.

Jake continued, "It's felt as though she has been grieving since the night we got engaged. Then, last week, while I was looking for her address book to begin making a list of wedding guests, I found a stack of letters. They were all addressed to you."

And Rodrigo's opinion of Jake went back to the level of hate, "You went through her things?"

"No," Jake sighed, his voice tinged with frustration. "I didn't read the letters, although I really wanted to. Instead, I put them back where I found them, and I tried asking Elena about you again. She wouldn't talk to me, which is why I'm here."

Rodrigo remained silent for a moment, feeling the weight of Jake's words. "I don't know what to tell you. We were friends, and then we drifted apart," he said, keeping his response brief in hopes of ending the conversation.

Jake shook his head slowly, his expression troubled. "I feel like there's something I'm missing. Something important about her."

Rodrigo shifted in his seat, trying to keep things light. "She's slow to trust. That's probably all it is. She's marrying you, man. All those missing pieces will fall into place eventually."

Jake seemed unconvinced. "I'm not so sure. I think I know what happened. I think that after I proposed, she went to New Mexico. I think she went to see you. I think she needed you to answer a question before she could answer mine."

Rodrigo's stomach tightened. He wasn't sure how to respond to that, but Jake looked so sad, he had to say something, "You know she loves you, right?"

Finally, Jake spoke again. "I'm not asking you to confirm or deny anything. I just—" He sighed, running a hand through his hair. "I didn't know what else to do."

Rodrigo paused before responding. He needed to say something reassuring, something Elena might have said herself. "Elena doesn't make decisions lightly. She overthinks everything. She plans ahead, always considering all the possibilities. She's ambitious and kind, once you get past her sarcasm. She'll call you on your shit when you need it, and she'll put aside her own pain to take care of you when that's what you need. She loves with everything she has. She's the most loyal friend I've ever had. And she's chosen to spend her life with you. She obviously did that for a reason, man. A well-thought-out reason. She'll talk to you about whatever she's going through, but in her own time. She always does. Bottling things up forever? That's just not her style. You just need to give her time, okay?"

Jake looked at him for a long moment, his gaze unreadable. Rodrigo wasn't sure how to interpret it, but he felt a pang of worry. Had he inadvertently confirmed Jake's suspicions about him and Elena? Had he made things worse?

After a few seconds, the silence felt heavy. Finally, Rodrigo cleared his throat. "Umm… How much do I owe you for the drinks?"

"I've got it covered. Thanks, Rodrigo."

Rodrigo smiled, not wanting to argue, especially since he probably couldn't afford his share of the bill anyway. "Thanks. And tell Elena I said hello." He had a strong feeling Jake wouldn't bring up this conversation with her, and that suited him just fine.

Rodrigo stood up, feeling the tension in his chest ease just a little. He knew that neither he nor Elena were happy with the easy path. He walked out of the bar, the night air cool on his face, his mind already focused on what came next.

Later that evening, he began researching how to transfer to UC Berkeley. He was tired of making the easier choice. Even if Elena still chose Jake, at least he could say that he'd done everything in his power to make things right.

March 2016

"Why did I get a 'Regretfully cannot attend' response from you about my wedding?" Lily's voice came through the phone without any greeting, straight to the point.

Rodrigo sighed before responding. "Lily, I can't go to your wedding and watch her there with him."

"Who says she's going to be there?" Lily replied, her voice defensive.

Rodrigo shook his head, knowing her well enough. "Come on, Lily, I know she's at least going to be in your wedding party, if not your maid of honor."

"Who says I'm having a wedding party?" she shot back,

trying to sound casual.

Rodrigo chuckled, sensing her attempt to deflect. "You're going to have a beautiful wedding, full of flowers, twinkling lights, and bridesmaids. And one of them will be Elena. I don't want to see her there with Jake. I'm not going."

"Fine, so she is my maid of honor, and yes, she has a plus one. But I love you, and I want you at my wedding."

"I love you too, Lil. But I can't see her."

There was a long pause on the other end of the line. "You need to be there," Lily said, her tone softer now.

Rodrigo was quiet for a beat. "Why? So we can fight and I can punch that Jake guy in the face for ruining my life?"

"No," she said, frustration creeping into her voice. "You need to go so you can talk to Elena. It's important."

Rodrigo's voice hardened. "Give me one good, convincing reason why I should."

Lily hesitated, then spoke slowly. "Because I asked you to

be there. It's important to me. We haven't seen each other in forever. I'll look pretty in my dress, and it's an open bar."

Rodrigo softened. "I'm sure you'll look gorgeous in your dress. Where are you registered?"

There was a long pause. "I'm registered at 'GO TO MY FUCKING WEDDING!'" she yelled, her voice full of frustration.

Rodrigo quickly pulled the phone away from his ear until the yelling stopped. "I'll think about it," he muttered.

"Grrr," Lily growled into the phone. "Stop being a chicken shit and come to my wedding and talk to her!" With that, she hung up on him.

Rodrigo stared at the phone for a moment. Lily had never been so angry that she hung up on him. She was always the one he'd hang up on—not out of anger, but because he was tired of her pestering him to talk to Elena. If she hung up on him, though, it must mean she was serious.

"Maybe I should go... let her know I'm moving to the Bay

since my transfer went through," Rodrigo thought aloud, his mind already considering his options.

With a resigned sigh, he opened his computer—the one thing still unpacked—and began searching for cheap flights.

CHAPTER 23

May 2016

"So, you're saying we'll both be single, living in the same place, at the same time?" she asked, unable to keep the hopeful tone from creeping into her voice.

"Yeah, that's the plan, but there's something else I need to tell you before we go any further," he replied. He finally understood why Lily had asked him to bring the item in his pocket. She was clever. He wasn't sure if this was the right time or the right thing to do, but he couldn't stop now.

She felt a sinking sensation in her chest. She had been foolish to hope, but she couldn't help herself. What was he about to say? A thousand thoughts ran through her mind. What if he... She inhaled sharply, No, no. Focus. Don't overthink it. Listen to what he has to say first, then react. "Okay," she said, her voice laced with caution.

He saw the worry in her eyes. "No, no, it's not bad. Well, at least, I don't think it's bad. Maybe you'll think it is," he stammered, his nervousness causing him to ramble. He took a deep breath before continuing. "You remember the night you told me you were engaged?"

"How could I forget? It was the last night I saw you," she said, wondering why he was bringing that painful night up now when they were finally on the brink of something good.

"As soon as you asked to meet me, I went to see my mom. I got something from her that I planned to give you that night. I had a feeling he'd proposed, and I wasn't ready to let you go without a fight. Obviously…" He trailed off.

"You gave up that fight pretty quickly," she said, finishing the thought for him.

He lowered his head, a wave of shame washing over him, but he pushed through it. "When you asked if I'd changed my mind about marriage and kids, and I said I hadn't... that was a lie."

Her heart began to race, but she stayed silent, wanting to hear him out.

"Well, I sort of lied," he continued. "I don't want to be

married or have kids with anyone... except you. I wanted to tell you this sooner, but when you answered your phone and talked to him, I felt hurt and jealous. I stupidly let that get in my way."

He looked at her, his eyes full of longing. She felt as though she couldn't breathe.

"I had this thing in my glove compartment," he started, his voice a little shaky. "After I dropped you off at the airport and convinced myself not to turn around and go back for you, I gave this back to my mom and told her that someone else in the family might be able to use it. Luckily, she ignored me." He pulled his grandmother's engagement ring out of his pocket and held it in his hand, his fingers brushing over the smooth surface. He stared at it for a long moment, afraid to look at Elena. He worried that she would be looking at him as if he were crazy. Honestly, he felt a little crazy, but he didn't regret doing this.

He still hadn't looked at her, and Elena wasn't entirely sure if she was reading the situation right. But for once, she didn't feel the need to overthink it. She just felt something deep in her chest. She took his hand in hers as she slid off the hood of the SUV and onto solid ground. Trying to pull him with her, she found that he didn't move when she tugged on his hand, and he still hadn't looked at her.

"Come dance with me," she said softly, pulling on his hand again.

He finally looked at her, his expression caught between disbelief and uncertainty. "I tell you that I've wanted to marry you for the past year, and you ask me to dance? There isn't even any music."

She grabbed his other hand—the one with the ring in it—and pulled him toward her as he finally relented, sliding off the hood of the SUV with a resigned sigh. "Just shut up, and dance with me," she said again, a mischievous smile tugging at her lips.

He looked at her in disbelief, wondering if she understood the gravity of what he was saying. He hadn't exactly been clear, but he was almost certain she knew. "Elena? Don't you get that...?

She places her left hand over his mouth, and he realizes, in that moment, that she has slipped the ring onto her finger.

He hadn't even felt her take it from him.

Smiling, she whispers, "Shut up and dance with me." He chuckles, letting her pull him close.

They sway together, dancing slowly to a song only they can hear. As he pulls her in, his lips meet hers for the first time in over a year. They break the kiss when she starts to laugh. "Are we crazy?" she asks, eyes twinkling.

"Everyone will think we are. But they have no idea what we've been through these last few years," he replies, his voice steady. "When we tell people, they'll look at us like we're nuts. But we'll just smile back, let them judge, and know in our hearts that this is what's right."

She looks at him, eyes softening. "You realize there's a lot we'll need to figure out, right? We have to learn how to actually be in a real relationship with each other."

He nods, smiling. "I know. And maybe, in the end, we won't be able to make it work. But I'm not afraid to give it a shot anymore."

She gazes at him, her mind calm, free from worry. "I'm not

afraid to try, either. I love you," she says, her voice steady, with no trace of hesitation.

"I love you too," he murmurs, pulling her closer for another kiss.

They dance to the silent music only they can hear, wrapped tightly in each other's arms. After a while, Rodrigo glances at her. "Should we head back?"

She grins, shaking her head with a mischievous sparkle in her eyes. "No, we don't want to take the spotlight from Lily and Mark. We'll catch up with them later. Besides, she might actually make good on her threat to murder us if she sees us again tonight."

He chuckles softly, pressing a gentle kiss to her forehead. "Okay."

Suddenly, Elena gasps, her eyes wide with realization. "Oh, no!"

Rodrigo's heart skips a beat. "What happened?" He braces himself, fearing this might be the moment where everything falls apart again.

"I brought my friend Emi as my plus one since I had already RSVP'd for a plus one. I left her all by herself at the reception!"

"You should probably call her, ya jerk," he teases, laughing lightly.

She nods quickly, pulling her phone from inside the rental car. "I'm blaming all of this on you," she says, shaking her head with a playful smile.

"There you are!" a very loud voice bursts from the phone's speaker. "I've been looking for you for almost two hours!" Emi's voice is excited, but there's a touch of annoyance beneath her words.

"Sorry, Em, I got distracted," Elena laughs, rolling her eyes.

"Eh, it's okay," Emi says, her voice shifting. "I got distracted too. I met a very cute bartender," she continues, describing the bartender with a pixie cut and sleeve tattoos. "I figured if anyone had seen you, it would be the bartender. So I showed her your picture. She recognized you—though, not from tonight. Turns out, she's the bartender at that bar downtown, the one we went to that one time we were both in town. She remembered us talking about Rodrigo. She seemed to know a lot about the two of you. She even asked about you, said the last time she saw you, you were with him, and things were… heated. That must've been that last night you saw him." Emi pauses for a moment. "Crazy, huh? That she knows so much about you two. Where did you go, by the way?"

Emi finally stops long enough to notice that Elena has been trying to get her attention for a while. Elena chuckles, the corners of her mouth lifting into a mischievous grin. "Let's just say I've got a lot to tell you over brunch tomorrow."

"Mmm, I love brunch," Emi replies, sounding pleased. "Okay, I'll see you in the morning. But don't come to my room tonight—I'm definitely going to have company," she adds with a laugh.

"Deal," Elena says, smiling. "See ya later." She hangs up, a satisfied smile spreading across her face as she turns to Rodrigo. "Let's go."

"My room?" he asks, raising an eyebrow.

"Please," she responds, her voice low with a playful undertone.

The next morning, happily exhausted, Elena and Rodrigo meet up with Emi at a local restaurant for brunch. As they stand outside waiting for a table, Emi immediately begins firing off questions.

"Is this who distracted you last night?" she asks, her eyes widening with curiosity. "He must be good in bed if you're bringing him to brunch."

Elena sighs, her cheeks flushing. "Emi, I'm so sorry for abandoning you last night."

Emi continues without missing a beat. "I should've brought my distraction with me. She's amazing. You're going to love her. I think this could be something incredible. Long distance won't be easy, but who knows? She's a bartender, so it's pretty easy for her to relocate…"

"Emi…" Elena starts, trying to get a word in.

"She's gorgeous and funny and—" Recognition suddenly

hits Emi. Her eyes widen, and she exclaims, "OMG!"
She straightens up, her voice rising. "You're Rodrigo! How
is this even happening? How are you here? Wait—what is
that on your finger?"

"Emi, you're so loud," Elena mutters, looking around. She
notices that most of the other people waiting for a table are
staring at them.

Emi looks around, flashing a grin. Most of the people
quickly turn away, clearly trying to avoid the attention.

Elena sighs and turns back to her friend. "Emilia, this is
Rodrigo, my fiancé." The words feel strange but right as
they leave her mouth. She smiles at Rodrigo, who returns
the smile and gently kisses her cheek.

"Really?" Emi asks, still looking at them in shock.

"Nice to meet you, Emi," Rodrigo says, extending his hand.
Emi takes it, still staring at them in disbelief.

"How do you go from single to engaged in one night?" Emi
asks, voicing the big question.

Elena and Rodrigo exchange a smile, knowing they'll have

to explain this many more times.

May 2017

Elena began, "This man makes me a better person..."

Rodrigo continued, "And she makes me a better man..."

"He has always been there for me," Elena said, her voice softening. "When things were shitty, he always knew exactly how to make me feel better..."

Rodrigo added, "And the good things weren't truly real until she was a part of them..."

"He has been my person for longer than I can even remember," Elena said, her eyes glistening.

Rodrigo's smile was tender. "She was my person the moment I laid eyes on her..."

Elena chuckled. "We've put each other through hell to get here..."

"And we tried to live without each other," Rodrigo said with a wry grin.

"Without him in my life, I wasn't whole," Elena continued, her voice barely a whisper.

Rodrigo nodded. "Without her in my life, I wasn't me."

"I had slowly given him pieces of myself since we were twelve," Elena said, her gaze drifting as memories flooded her. "Until I realized that I had given him so much of myself, I couldn't imagine being complete without him..."

Rodrigo squeezed her hand gently. "She had every piece of me, and I gladly gave her all of it, without even realizing it until now..."

"And today," Elena said, her voice breaking slightly with emotion, "I marry my best friend..." She placed a simple silver band onto Rodrigo's finger.

"And today," Rodrigo echoed, his voice thick with emotion, "I marry my best friend..." He added an identical band to Elena's finger, along with his grandmother's engagement ring, the gesture adding a layer of sentimentality to the moment. Jade, who was officiating their wedding, looked at them and smiled. She had been with them through their journey, even if from behind the bar at times. It felt right for her to be a part of this moment. "Do you, Rodrigo Marquez, take Elena Crawford to be your wife?" she asked, her voice filled with warmth.

Rodrigo never took his eyes off his bride. "Obviously," he said, his voice unwavering.

Jade turned to Elena, her smile wide. "Do you, Elena Crawford, take Rodrigo Marquez to be your husband?"

Elena nodded, her gaze never straying from Rodrigo's face. "Obviously," she replied, the word heavy with the depth of her feelings.

"By the power vested in me by the state of California," Jade said, her voice rising with excitement, "I now pronounce you husband and wife! You may now seal this deal with a kiss!" She announced enthusiastically.

Rodrigo didn't hesitate. With a grin, he grabbed Elena and dipped her in a passionate kiss, their guests erupting into applause. They broke the kiss and smiled at one another, hand in hand, walking down the aisle. Lily, Rodrigo's best man, followed behind them, practically bouncing with joy for her friends. Emi, Elena's maid of honor, beamed at Jade before sharing a quick kiss with her girlfriend, before falling in step behind Lily and the newlyweds.

Epilogue

Elena sat on the large beach blanket they had brought down from their suite, the soft sand beneath her warm. She carefully applied sunscreen to her pale, but visibly pregnant belly, enjoying the gentle breeze coming off the ocean. Rodrigo had taken their two other children—a lively five-year-old girl and an energetic four-year-old boy—down closer to the water's edge.

They were excitedly hunting for seashells, their giggles carrying on the wind as they searched.

They were in Costa Rica to celebrate the finalization of the adoption of their two children, a moment they'd all dreamed of for years. It was the first time they could travel together as a family, free to embrace this new chapter in their lives without the weight of uncertainty hanging over them.

Rodrigo looked back over his shoulder and smiled at Elena, his eyes squinting in the sun. He raised a hand to shield his gaze, but his smile remained wide, a reflection of the peace they had fought so hard to achieve. The children's laughter echoed as he turned back to them, clearly soaking in the joy of this perfect moment in their new life.

About The Author

Kaye Scott lives in the Bay Area with her giant dog. Although this is her first published work, she had been writing since she was a kid thanks to her second grade teacher encouraging her students to write often and turning their little stories into "books". She enjoys spending time at the beach or creating more worlds in DnD. She hopes to keep writing while managing her day job.

www.ingramcontent.com/pod-product-compliance
Lightning Source LLC
Chambersburg PA
CBHW070302310726
48976CB00005B/1534